More Florida Stories

UNIVERSITY PRESS OF FLORIDA
Gainesville
Tallahassee
Tampa
Boca Raton
Pensacola
Orlando
Miami
Jacksonville

MORE

Florida
Stories

EDITED BY KEVIN M. McCARTHY

Copyright 1996 by the Board of Regents of the State of Florida
Printed in the United States of America on acid-free paper
All rights reserved
Illustrations by Larry Leshan

01 00 99 98 97 96 c 6 5 4 3 2 1
01 00 99 98 97 96 p 6 5 4 3 2 1

LIBRARY OF CONGRESS CATALOGING-IN-PUBLICATION DATA
More Florida stories / edited by Kevin M. McCarthy
p. cm.
Includes bibliographical references (p.).
ISBN 0-8130-1468-9 (acid-free paper).—ISBN 0-8130-1485-9 (pbk.: acid-free paper).
1. Short stories, American—Florida. 2. Florida—Social life and customs—Fiction.
I. McCarthy, Kevin.
PS558.F6M67 1996
813'.010832759—dc20 96-14366

The University Press of Florida is the scholarly publishing agency for the State
University System of Florida, comprised of Florida A & M University, Florida
Atlantic University, Florida International University, Florida State University,
University of Central Florida, University of Florida, University of North Florida,
University of South Florida, and University of West Florida.

University Press of Florida
15 Northwest 15th Street
Gainesville, FL 32611

Contents

Introduction

WHEN NINETEENTH-CENTURY French science-fiction writer Jules Verne needed a site to launch his fictional rocket ship to the moon in 1865, he could not decide between Texas and Florida. The former offered a vastness, a cockiness, a bravura that spelled success for any venture. On the other hand, Florida offered an unsettled land, an isolated landscape in which cities would not be harmed if a spaceship crashed. Texans marveled that "a wretched little strip of country like Florida" would dare to compete with their great state and predicted that the force of the cannon shot would destroy the Sunshine State. In the end—presaging what would occur at Cape Canaveral to the east of Orlando—Verne chose Florida for his novel, scientists launched their rocket to the moon, and Florida was not destroyed. Since that time, authors who have variously visited Florida, lived here for all their lives, or never even come near the state have been choosing this peninsula for their settings.

The question of what constitutes a Florida author—whether it be short- or long-term residence in the state, kinship with its mores, or fascination with its history and culture—has long vexed academics trying to pigeonhole writers. Should we call someone who lives here year-round but writes about distant places a Florida author? What about someone who came for a brief time but wrote a significant work about the state? Or should we include only those writers who have lived here a long time and have written extensively about the state? I once put together a collection of "Florida writers" and came up with over two thousand names and five thousand works of literature written in and about the state, and all of the works had been published since 1950. What is it about this place that inspires so many people to put down the suntan oil and take up the word processor? What does this land offer that others do not?

Careful readers of the following stories will quickly see how a rich history, culture, and diversity of peoples have inspired writers to set their stories in a land so big it has two time zones and stretches eight hundred miles, from Key West to Pensacola. As in *Florida Stories* (1989), the main criteria for inclusion in this collection have been the quality of the writing, a significant Florida setting, and a story well told. The Florida antecedents of the writer were not relevant, although the majority of the authors did, in fact, live here most of their lives.

But is there a Florida fiction? And, if so, how does it differ from California or New York or Arizona fiction? One can legitimately ask whether Florida fiction is an artificial category or whether it is a sub-genre of American literature in general and southern literature in particular. The characters of that Florida fiction can probably be found elsewhere. This state surely does not have a monopoly on villains (the civil rights violator, the crooked businessman, the corrupt land developer, the bribable politician) or heroes (the environmentalist, the attorney defending the hopeless, the courageous newspaper editor).

What distinguishes these works from fiction set elsewhere (excluding certain characters and animals mostly unique to Florida, such as the alligator poacher and the manatee) is the setting: the particular Florida habitat that shapes and dominates the story. It could be the swamplike labyrinth in the state's northern (Woolson's "The South Devil") or southern region (Douglas's "A Flight of Ibis" and Powell's "Bonaparte's"). It could be the deadly hurricanes (Lyons's "A Blade of Grass"), or the rivers that crisscross the state (Dorr's "A Slow, Soft River"), or the ocean off its east coast (Munroe's "Cap'n I's Closest Call"). Or the setting could be near an old Spanish graveyard near Pensacola (Buntline's "The Fast Duel") or in a church during a revival (Cox's "That Golden Crane"). Racist towns play a part in these stories, as they have in our history, whether unincorporated settlements (Stowe's "Old Cudjo and the Angel"), small towns (Kennedy's "Color Added"), or army camps (Blassingame's "Man's Courage"). Finally, that habitat could include tales of attacks by animals (Hall's "Panther!" and Rudloe's "Master of My Lake") or tales about Native Americans (Thompson's "Cape Florida Lighthouse").

Readers of these stories may be surprised to learn how unsettled Florida was until the middle of the twentieth century. Several of these stories hearken back to a time when the state looked much different than it does today. A hundred years ago Floridians endured frontier conditions, especially in the land below Orlando. Today the Miami–Palm Beach and Fort Myers–Tampa areas, each a megalopolis and growing rapidly, attract thousands of visitors and new residents each year, but these communities barely existed at the beginning of the century.

What is it about Florida that has inspired writers for almost five hundred years to set their stories here? Could it be the exotic nature of the frontier, which allowed only resourceful, creative settlers to wrest a living from the land? The people, the rich and famous, the villains and heroes, who have lived here or merely passed through? The weather, from Category 5 hurricanes to deadly tornadoes, from tidal waves generated by underwater cataclysms to swamp fires that destroy everything in their path? Or the state's history, long dominated by an absentee Spanish king, or the fact that it was admitted to the Union in 1845, long after other East Coast states, and then seceded sixteen years later?

How Florida has captivated writers is most clearly articulated in the experiences of two women: Harriet Beecher Stowe and Marjorie Kinnan Rawlings. When Stowe, the author of the immensely successful *Uncle Tom's Cabin* (1851), arrived in Mandarin, near Jacksonville, in 1867 to nurse her sickly husband back to health, she worried that Confederate sympathizers would treat her badly, especially because many believed that her book did much to solidify antislavery feeling in the North. While living here, she wrote many descriptions of the animals, the climate, and of people she came to know well, all of which were collected in one of the first travel books about the state, *Palmetto-leaves* (1873). She described Florida in terms of art: "If we painted her, we should not represent her as a neat, trim damsel, with starched linen cuffs and collar; she would be a brunette, dark but comely, with gorgeous tissues, a general disarray and dazzle, and with a sort of jolly untidiness, free, easy, and joyous." Stowe's glowing reports of the Sunshine State did much to start the steady influx of visitors and settlers that continues unabated.

Some sixty years later Marjorie Kinnan Rawlings arrived in Cross Creek, intent on writing romance novels set in distant places, and perhaps even continuing with her poetry column, "Songs of a Housewife," about the glories of dusting and cooking. Instead, she too came under the spell of the place—the wildness of the Ocala National Forest, the serenity of the St. Johns River, the loneliness of the Florida scrub. She concluded her

Cross Creek with a question about who really owns the land: "It seems to me that the earth may be borrowed but not bought. It may be used, but not owned. It gives itself in response to love and tending, offers its seasonal flowering and fruiting. But we are tenants and not possessors, lovers and not masters. Cross Creek belongs to the wind and the rain, to the sun and the seasons, to the cosmic secrecy of seed, and beyond all, to time." Her novels and short stories did much to enshrine the Florida Cracker in the pantheon of American literature.

After the occasional airing of one of the films based on the works of Rawlings, whether *The Yearling*, or *Gal Young'un*, or *Cross Creek*, thousands of visitors descend on her home at Cross Creek, intent on discovering what it was like to live in the isolation of central Florida. Similar literary pilgrimages can be made to Travis McGee's houseboat at Bahia Mar in Fort Lauderdale, to Zora Neale Hurston's grave-site in Fort Pierce, to Ernest Hemingway's writing loft in Key West, and to James Weldon Johnson's house in Jacksonville. In each case litterateurs can experience the exhilarating, pervasive influence of place on a great writer.

Most of the stories in this collection have long been out of print. A few (Hall's, Powell's) are chapters in novels. Others (Dorr's, Stowe's, and Woolson's) have been included in short-story collections. A brief introduction to each story gives relevant details about the author's life, the importance of the story in the author's published works, and an explanation of details in the story that might be overlooked.

This anthology mirrors the fascinating story of the territory first encountered by European settlers, the last to be civilized on the eastern coast of the United States. This is a land that promised early adventurers a lost Fountain of Youth; later, seafront property that fueled get-rich-quick schemes; and, even later, a launching pad for trips to the moon. All of the stories explore what it means to be a Floridian: how the land and water affect us deeply. In the Florida of the late twentieth century—a place and time where numerous disparate cultures (Spanish, Seminole, Confederate, Yankee, rich, poor) have collided—writers continue to find endless sources for their stories, poems, and plays.

Wyatt Blassingame

Wyatt Blassingame (1909–85) was born in Demopolis, Alabama, and died in Bradenton, Florida, near the island where he had spent much of his adult life. After working as a newspaper reporter and writing instructor for several years, he devoted himself full-time to writing in the early 1950s and for the next thirty years produced some fifty-three juvenile books and five adult books, as well as over 650 short stories and articles for national magazines. He once wrote, "The one good thing about writing for a living is you can live wherever you wish. For forty-six years I have lived (most of the time) on Anna Maria, an island joined to the Florida mainland by a bridge. It is a fine place for fishing, swimming, and walking on the beach." That island, which was several islands away from the home of another very prolific Florida author, John D. MacDonald (1916–86), enabled him to do research for books he did on raccoons, crows, and egrets.

Blassingame's Florida books include *Live from the Devil* (1959), *The Golden Geyser* (1961), *The First Book of Florida* (1963), *Ponce de Leon* (1965), *Osceola* (1967), *Jake Gaither: Winning Coach* (1969), *Wonders of Alligators and Crocodiles* (1973), *The Everglades: From Yesterday to Tomorow* (1974), and *Wonders of Egrets, Bitterns, and Herons* (1982).

The short story presented here, which appeared in *Harper's* in April 1956, won the Benjamin Franklin Award for the best magazine story of the year and later appeared in *O. Henry Prize Stories for 1957*. It takes place in north Florida after the Korean War, in a camp that may have been based on Camp Blanding, east of Starke. The story makes clear how prevalent segregation was in Florida towns and how the integration of the armed forces by President Truman, which brought together formerly separated men and women of different races, failed to eliminate deeply held feelings of racism.

Blassingame saw his share of segregation; he had attended schools in several small Alabama towns, graduated from the University of Alabama

in 1930, worked as a police reporter on the *Montgomery Advertiser* for a
year, and then returned to the University of Alabama for two years of
graduate work. This story—notable for its sensitivity, drama, and ten-
sion as it describes the elemental emotions of two men pitted against
each other under trying circumstances—is one of his best.

Man's Courage

Wyatt Blassingame

THE FACT THAT Lieutenant Henderson was a Negro did not alone cause the trouble. At least part of it went deeper, springing from one of those curious, instantaneous, apparently chemical dislikes that two men sometimes feel and for which there is no logical reason, the men simply recoiling from one another like reversed magnets.

But certainly it would be wrong to say that Henderson's color, and the fact that Lee Stewart, the private, was from Mississippi, did not affect the matter. At least it dramatized it, gave it a foundation in the obvious that we could all see and understand, just as we could sense without understanding the other deeper feeling between them. And surely Stewart himself did not understand, could not until it was all over, that the problem went beyond color, that there existed a deeply personal relationship, even if founded on sudden and instinctive dislike, between him and a Negro.

Until that final and climactic night all his references to Henderson as a coward and a misfit in our regiment were predicated on the simple fact of color; his hatred was based on this even after the more personal reasons—the repeated KP, being stopped on the sidewalk and forced to salute, the matter of the car and the liquor—were obvious to all of us.

It was so obvious that when word went around Lee Stewart was going to kill Henderson, none of us doubted it. It was just a matter of time and method. And soon we (the enlisted men; Henderson was probably the only officer to know what was happening before it was all over) knew that too.

"Because only a fool would get himself in trouble over a nigger," Stewart said. This was at Mac's Bar. There was a group around him as always, paratroopers wearing their half boots and managing to look both rakish and competent in that way no other outfit can simulate, not even the Marines. It was one of these, a corporal in the same platoon, who had asked him. "And I'm no fool," Stewart added.

Belle, the girl who tended bar, said, "You're sure about to get yourself in trouble."

"Not me, Sugar." He reached across the bar to pat her arm. "We're going on maneuvers next week. You think you can get along without me for a while?"

So we knew then it would be during maneuvers in the Florida swamps: a fouled parachute, a rifle that went off by accident. There were always opportunities for that sort of thing. There were even rumors that it had happened in our regiment before. We were a tough outfit that took pride in its toughness, no man more than Lee Stewart. There weren't many left who had been with the regiment when it was the first to jump over Normandy, but they were enough to carry on the legend and the pride. And there were more who had helped stop that first, now almost-forgotten, breakthrough in Korea and who later jumped so near the China border we could see the Yalu as we came down and then had to walk back, looking, we thought, like Washington's army the winter at Valley Forge while we did it.

There had always been considerable fraternization between officers and men, as there is in most fighting outfits, and our respect for officers was not so much in the bar or leaf on the collar as in the man. Weak officers, as well as weak men, had been weeded out.

And most of us, not only those who instinctively resented Henderson because of his color, believed he was a weak officer. He was West Point, only too much so. He had one of these quiet, restrained, sensitive faces you see sometimes on members of his race, but over it was a kind of mask as though he had put it on with his academy uniform, or even before that, when he got the appointment: the long and constant awareness of being a responsibility to his race, an officer, and a gentleman.

We had heard he was coming before he reached camp: a Negro officer, the first Negro officer most of us had served under. Then we saw him, small, precise, his cap as squarely on his head as if it had been placed there with the aid of engineering instruments.

"My God," one soldier said. "Do you think that when he jumps he comes all the way down at attention?"

"Why not?" Lee Stewart said. "He's probably too scared to bend."

꒳ ꒳

It was a week later they had their first personal contact. Stewart was working on a jeep outside one of the hangars. Inside someone was tuning up the engine of a C54 and the sound of it filled the eardrums like wax. Stewart, his head and shoulders under the jeep's hood, did not see Henderson, did not know he was present until the dark hand, the salmon-colored palm came over his shoulder and took the wrench from his own hand.

Then, their heads close together, Henderson said, "You can break things that way, Soldier," and working carefully he got loose the plug at which Stewart had been yanking. He stepped back and put the wrench on the fender, and as the two men stood looking at one another it slid off and fell to the ground between them.

Neither moved. Perhaps Stewart (who as a child had never known or even seen a Negro who was not some white man's servant) had for an instant forgotten the bar on the other's collar. Anyway—and to all of us working on the hangar apron this was perfectly apparent—he expected the Negro to stoop and pick up the wrench.

On the lieutenant's face there was no expression at all. They just stood there, looking at one another with the wrench on the ground between them. After a moment Henderson took a clean handkerchief from his pocket, wiped his hands, and turned away.

At the same instant, inside the hangar, the C54's engine was silent. In the sudden quiet Lee Stewart's voice was saying, "Well I'll be god-damned . . ." speaking not so much in anger as baffled amazement.

Henderson stopped. He looked back at Stewart, the handkerchief still in his hands, his face withdrawn, expressionless.

"What is it, Soldier?"

Stewart merely stared at him. Henderson put the handkerchief in his pocket, turned, and walked away.

It was that same afternoon Stewart drew KP. He blamed it loudly, openly, on Henderson, damning not the man so much as the incredible stupidity of some unknown "they" who would assign a Negro, and there-fore a coward, a misfit, to a paratroop outfit that considered itself, even in peacetime, a strictly combat unit.

"To us," Stewart said, his voice dazed, aghast. "Of all the outfits in the army they assign a nigger officer to us."

Then he drew KP again. He began to get work details far more often than they would have come to him in the normal cycle of things. And soon we all knew that Henderson was aware of Stewart not only as the leader of that group which will always instantly and violently resent a Negro officer, but as an individual. Perhaps it was the white officers that reported to him, perhaps it was some of the scattering of Negro enlisted men in the regiment, but soon it was apparent he knew of Stewart and was retaliating, deliberately, precisely, riding hard the uncrossable advantage of rank.

～ ～

He began to ask for Stewart as a driver and we would see them on the camp streets, even on the highway into town: the white man, the servant, on the front seat, the officer behind him, neither speaking until Henderson would say, not even leaning forward,

"Turn right at the next corner. Stop here."

He said it this time in front of Mac's Bar and Stewart stopped the car. He sat there, holding the wheel, beginning to breathe a little hard now, knowing that Belle was inside and probably looking out through the dirty, lettered glass of the window.

Henderson's hand came over the back of the seat, appearing at Stewart's right shoulder with a five-dollar bill between his index and third finger.

"Would you go inside and get me a bottle of bourbon?"

Stewart looked at him then, as much with unbelief as with anger.

"What? What is it you want?"

"A bottle of bourbon," Henderson said. And then, "When we get back to the post I won't have a chance to go by the Officer's Club. And this is north Florida. They won't want me coming in the bar. Or is there a back entrance a Negro can use?"

"No," Stewart said. He took the money and got out of the car. He went slowly, his head bent forward a little in thought, through the hot gold sunlight of late afternoon and into the dimness of the bar.

Belle was already moving to meet him. He named a brand of whiskey, "A bottle. To take out."

And she said, "You drinking with him now, Lee?"

This was when he told her he was going to kill Lieutenant Henderson, saying it softly as though he had thought about it a long time and now it was as good as done. Then he went outside and gave the lieutenant the bottle and drove him back to the post.

᧬   ᧬

The night before maneuvers the regiment had orders to be back on the post at midnight. Some of us made quite a party of it at Mac's Bar. Then it was quarter of twelve and we were crowding through the door, leaving, when we looked back and saw Stewart sitting at the far end of the bar.

"Lee, you resigned from the Army?" a soldier said.

"You don't think I'm leaving without telling Belle goodby?" Stewart said.

So that was the last we saw of him, for a while anyway: a big man with a broad, hard face and red hair sitting there at the far end of the bar with Belle across from him trying hard to blush or look indignant.

We moved out the next morning and he did not go with us. But he was in camp when we returned and it was then he told us what had happened, telling it with the same baffled, awed amazement with which he had always regarded the idea of a Negro officer in our outfit. Only now there was something new in his voice: not just the knowledge that here was something he did not understand but, and for the first time, an attempt, a straining to understand.

He had left Belle's shortly after two. From there it was a half-mile walk to the camp, where he must climb a fence and reach his barracks without being seen, a thing he had done often enough before. But now as he stepped into the road a man said, "Stewart." It was Lieutenant Henderson.

This was a back road with no traffic. On both sides the pines closed in, solid and dark, with a piece of bent moon above those to Stewart's left. In the dim, almost nonexistent light Henderson's face was featureless; but Stewart could see the uniform, the square-set cap, the gun the lieutenant wore.

"Yes?" Stewart said.

"I'm glad I met you," Henderson said. He spoke as always in a brisk, precise manner with no accent of any kind. "I don't have a car. I have to walk back to the post."

Stewart said nothing. He was thinking hard, trying to figure the angle but with nothing to work on yet.

Then Henderson said, "I understand there is talk around the regiment that someone is going to kill me."

And still Stewart did not answer, just leaning a little forward now, beginning to breathe more quickly, until Henderson's hand moved, not hurriedly but quick, and even as Stewart started to leap he saw the gun was held out toward him, butt first.

"So I'm going to need a bodyguard," Henderson said.

"What?" Stewart said.

"Take it," Henderson said. And when Stewart did not move, "It's loaded. Take it."

Later Stewart said, "I thought it was going to be some kind of a duel."

So he took the gun and when it was in his hand Henderson said, "I don't want anyone to shoot me in the back, so you will follow me at three paces." Then in the same clipped voice, he said, "You can consider that an order," and turned and started along the empty, moon-touched road.

"Wait!" Stewart said. But the officer did not stop, did not look back. And Stewart said again, "Wait—"

Then he began to curse, running until he caught Henderson by the arm and swung him around, still cursing. And Henderson said, "I ordered you to stay three steps back of me," and went on again.

"So I followed him," Stewart said later, "holding his gun and waiting for him to stop, or start to run, or whatever he was going to do." No traffic passed them. On the left the pines stopped and there was open prairie, dark under the moon, on the right the wall of pines. Then the pines closed in again. The road curved through them as through a tunnel. There was no sound except that of their shoes on the road and somewhere, sourceless, and persistent, the call of a whippoorwill.

♪   ♪

Then they were around the curve and there was a light ahead. This was the junction with the main highway; the light was at the camp-gate. The lieutenant went on until he was within a hundred yards of the gate and the MPs who stood there were visible under the light. Then Henderson stopped and turned.

"All right," he said. "You had your chance. Why didn't you shoot me?"

"I couldn't," Stewart said. He was to repeat it later, sitting in the barracks, his big hands with the red hair on the back of the fingers locked and twisting. "I couldn't shoot a—a man—not any man—in the back. Not with his own gun when he gave me the gun and turned his back on me."

And then, to Henderson, crying it almost, "You knew that! You *knew* it!"

"No," Henderson said. "I hoped. But the girl would have said anything you wanted. And a nigger's body—a white jury . . ."

"Then why—?" And answering himself, saying, "So that's it. So you had to prove to me you weren't yellow even if you are a nigger."

"To the regiment," Henderson said. "Don't you even believe, can't you believe, that I am proud of it too?" And when Stewart did not answer, "I tried every other way to stop you talking. And it had to be stopped. You understand that."

"Yes," Stewart said.

"All right," Henderson said. He took the gun now. He said, "You were due back on the post by midnight. You will report to the MPs for being past hours."

"Yes, Sir," Stewart said.

And later, in the barracks, telling it slowly in an effort not only to make us understand but to understand himself, "Because he really didn't know I wasn't going to shoot him, couldn't shoot him that way. I reckon a nigger wouldn't know." And then, with a kind of defiance in his face, "So I thought he had the Sir coming to him."

Ned Buntline

Edward Zane Carroll Judson, who used the alias "Ned Buntline" to write many highly dramatic stories about nineteenth-century Florida, specialized in the dime novel, so called because of its inexpensive cost. Judson (1823–86) had an adventurous life that formed the basis of much of what he wrote about; he ran away to sea as a youngster, became an apprentice in the United States Navy, fought in the Second Seminole War in Florida (1835–42), and was involved in many dangerous forays along the territory's seacoast and into the Everglades.

After he left the Navy in 1843, Judson went to Cincinnati, where he helped establish and edit the *Western Literary Journal and Monthly Magazine*, for which he wrote several embellished articles about Florida's Seminole War. He later moved to Nashville, where he established *Ned Buntline's Own*. That project ended in 1845 when he killed his mistress's husband in a duel; his knowledge of dueling, used in the following story, is therefore firsthand. A mob actually lynched him but mistakenly cut the rope before completing the execution; the jury, perhaps feeling that he had already cheated death, refused to indict him, and he went free. After a dishonorable term of duty in the Civil War, he wrote a series of dime novels about William Frederick Cody, on whom he supposedly bestowed the name "Buffalo Bill." Judson died in New York in 1886 after several careers, four marriages, and a place in the development of American fiction, even if only of the subgenre of "potboilers."

The hoax detailed in this story is similar to a later one involving baseball great Casey Stengel when he played for the Brooklyn Dodgers in 1915. When the Dodgers were having spring training in Daytona that year, under the direction of manager Wilbert Robinson, a former major-league catcher, another player went up in an airplane with the intention of dropping a baseball for Robinson to catch. However, instead of dropping a baseball, which could have caused serious harm if mishandled by the catcher below, the player substituted a grapefruit but did not tell the unsuspecting Robinson. The dropped grapefruit fell very quickly, hitting Robinson's outstretched mitt and splitting open on his chest. Robinson fell to the ground, splattered all over with grapefruit juice, at which point he cried out, "Jesus, I'm killed! I'm dead! My chest's split open! I'm covered with blood!" When he found his teammates roaring with laughter at the hoax, he swore at all of them and particularly blamed Casey Stengel, one of the players he suspected of such pranks.

The following story appeared at the beginning of the Civil War in 1861, in the April 20 edition of a newspaper, *The Family Friend,* of Monticello, Florida. The West Indian Squadron alluded to in the second paragraph of the story was the fleet that Union commodore David Porter commanded while ridding the Caribbean and Gulf of Mexico of pirates. Among the difficult words here are *spoony,* describing a silly, foolish person, and *reefer,* a midshipman.

The Fast Duel: A Sketch from Life

Ned Buntline

MAYBE YOU have read the "Fastest Funeral on Record," and other fast stories written by fast men, but I'll bet a sixpence to a kid of mush, that you never heard of the fast duel.

It occurred ten or twelve years ago—yea, thirteen of them—when I was a young man aboard the sloop of war Boston, in the West Indian Squadron.

We had just got in from a cruise up amongst the Windward Islands, and had not had much fun for some time, for 'twas in the hurricane season, and we had seen heavy weather enough to satisfy any old Blowhard that ever smelt salt water.

The very day we came to anchor at Pensacola, however, we had a godsend in the shape of a fresh caught midshipman, who, coming from the back woods of Alabama, had never seen anything higher than a flat boat, and was as green as a prairie colt in harness, and pretty near as wild. His name was Ezra Blizzard, and the Commodore ordered him aboard of us, as we had a couple of vacancies, one of our men being shot in a duel and the other having done worse by falling in love with an heiress ashore, marrying her and resigning.

Mr. Blizzard therefore was as I said before a perfect godsend. He was soon initiated into the duties of keeping his own watch and watch for some of the rest of us occasionally; taught how to pay over his mess money; persuaded out of a dash of wine for his "footing," and made the victim of a few harmless tricks; such as having his hammock cut down by the head, when he was asleep in it, being baptised by a sailor, by getting a bucket of salt water poured over him when he was with his mouth open; finding a dead rat or two occasionally in his pocket, or salt instead of sugar in his coffee, etc., all of which he bore so mildly that we began to consider him a regular spoony, and not calculated to become a credit to his mess in particular or the service in general.

To settle the point and determine his quantum of spunk, it was voted that he must be made to fight a duel, and a plot was made up between three of us, that it should be a harmless one, just to try his spunk.

Accordingly Hogan B., one of the best shots in the squadron, by the way, insulted him in due form, and much to our astonishment, was knocked down for his pains—. He arose as wrathy as a mad bull, and would have pitched into his opponent on the spot, had we not interfered and insisted upon the quarrel being settled according to the "code of honor." Hogan therefore challenged Blizzard, at the same time insisting with us that the fight should be real, and not fun with cork balls as at first proposed. But we overruled him, inasmuch as the insult he had given was uncalled for; and the youngster accepted the writer's volunteered service to act as his second.

"Must I fight him with pistols?" he asked; "I could wollup the life out of him in my own way."

"Gentlemen only use pistols—you struck him, and of course must give him gentlemanly satisfaction. I hope you are a good shot—he is," I replied.

"I never shot off a pistol in my life, but I'm some with a rifle."

"Rifles are not allowed in the code; pistols are the only weapons, and Hogan has a first-rate pair, has killed two reefers already!"

I could see that Blizzard didn't like this news, but he tried to look calm, and asked when he would have to fight.

I told him we would have it out that afternoon, as it was bad to let the blood cool over such affairs. And accordingly, in an hour afterwards we managed to get ashore with the case of pistols wrapped up out of sight in an old pea jacket.

We immediately went out to the old Spanish graveyard, back of the town. To heighten the effect and as luck would have it, we found a freshly dug grave, which was probably to be tenanted on the morrow. Blizzard looked at it and wanted to know what that was for. We told him that the death of one or the other party only could atone for a blow, and that the grave had been prepared for the one that fell.—The youngster turned a shade paler as he heard this, but still he gave no stronger signs of backing out.

Reaching a little orange grove near the newly dug grave, we halted, picked out and measured the ground. Myself and the other second now opened the pistol case and commenced preparing the pistols. Hogan coolly lighted a cigar, looking as ferocious as a meat-axe at his opponent, who nervously watched our movements.

"Blast the luck," I exclaimed, pretending to try the lock of one of the pistols.—"The main spring of the pistol is broken—what shall we do?"

"Fight with the other—toss up which shall have the first shot," growled Hogan in a fierce tone.

"Yes," said his second, "that's fair."

"No it ain't. Supposed he gets the first shot, he'll kill me without me getting a shot at him," said Blizzard.

"Yes, sure as winking," I added, "but then if you get the first shot you are safe. Trust to luck, my boy, you'll stand as good a chance as he."

Very reluctantly, B[lizzard] consented, declaring that he never had any luck; but to his delight and our surprise, won the first fire.

He was now more nervous than ever, and, as I handed him the pistol, loaded very heavily with powder only, his hand shook so that he could hardly handle it.

"If I should miss him, he'll kill me sure," he muttered to me.

"Yes," said I, "but you mustn't miss him. Take good aim. I'll give the word very slow, bore him right through the heart, for you're dead if he gets a shot at you."

They were placed—the distance only ten paces, and Hogan stood with his arms folded, full breast to the toe, scowling at him as if he wanted to blast him.

"Are you ready, Mr. Blizzard?" I asked.

"Yes—but I—I don't like to shoot at him so, as he is standing there without a chance."

"Come—be quick—no trifling—it's my turn next," said Hogan in a bitter tone.

Blizzard's hand trembled worse than ever, but his eye flashed and he answered—"I'm ready now—I'll see if it's your turn next."

As I gave the word very slow, he raised the pistol, not as I had shown him, but with both hands, taking sight as he would with a rifle, and fired. Having held it too close to his nose, the recoil of the heavy loaded weapon nearly knocked him down, drawing the claret from his nose. But to his utter horror and astonishment, the first sight that met his bewildered eyes was Hogan standing there with his arms folded, a most diabolical smile on his face, and evidently untouched.

"Oh Lord!" he exclaimed, "how could I have missed him. I was sure I had killed him."

"You grazed his ear—that was pretty close!" I said by way of a comforter.

"Bear a hand and load the pistol—I'm hungry—want to punish him and go to supper!" cried Hogan, sharply.

Poor Blizzard. He looked as though he would sink into the earth—he was pale as a ghost, but he had stopped trembling. He was evidently trying to nerve himself to meet his fate like a man.

"Is there anything I can do for you after you have gone, my friend?" I asked coolly.

"Yes," he replied, hoarsely, "write to my father and tell him that Ezra Blizzard died like a man—just as he told me—and cut off a lock of my hair (here his voice trembled) and send it to Mary Neal in the same letter; poor gal, she'll break her heart for this. That's all—good-by, Buntline!"

"Good-bye, Blizzard, I am sorry for you, but it can't be helped," I replied, putting my handkerchief up to my face as if to hide my tears, but really to conceal the laugh that was trying to break adrift in spite of my efforts to look serious.

"Give the word slow!" said Hogan fiercely.

"The devil is in his eye—he'll kill him for sure!" I muttered just loud enough for Blizzard to hear me. I could see the poor fellow begin to tremble.

"Are you ready?"

"No," said Hogan, "wait a moment till I finish this cigar."

Blizzard's tremor increased every moment—suspense was too severe. I added to his agony by again remarking in an undertone that I never saw Hogan so deliberate and murderous.

At last Hogan said he was ready—and again said, "give the word slow, now!"

"By heavens, I can't stand this, it's murder!" I cried, as if dreadfully agitated.—"Run, Blizzard, run!"

My earnest cry, added to what he had already endured, decided poor Blizzard, and off he started like a wounded buck.

"Stop, stop till you are killed!" yelled his second.

"Go it Blizzard!" I shouted, at the same moment seizing a half-rotten orange from the ground and hurling it with all the force I could after him.

The orange struck him plum upon that portion of his body named by philosophers as the seat of honor, bursting and deluging him with its juice at the very instant that Hogan fired his pistol.

Poor Blizzard heard the shot, felt the orange, and tumbled forward flat on his face, close beside the new-made grave.

"Are you killed!" I cried rushing up and kneeling by his side.

"Oh Lord—oh Lord!" he groaned—"dead—shot in the back, too. Oh Lord—tumble me into the grave—I don't care, only I'm shot in the back."

"Maybe—I can stop the blood!"

"No, don't try, I don't want to live. I'm shot in the back!" he groaned. "Don't let Mary or father hear of it—bury me as soon as I am cold!"

"Don't the wound hurt you?"

"No, no, nothing hurts me but being shot in the back. What did you tell me to run for? It was all your fault. I was ready to die like a man."

I could hold in no longer! I burst into a yell of laughter, and lifted up my principal to his feet. Hogan and his second came up and the cat was let out of the bag—everything explained.

About the maddest person that I think I ever saw in my life was that same Ezra Blizzard just at that time. He was utterly wolfish. He wanted to fight all of us on the spot one after the other, and nothing but our assurance that we were satisfied that he was true to the very backbone would satisfy him.

He afterwards became a smart and popular officer, and in real service by my side in the swamps of Florida, proved himself a trump card, and, though wounded on two occasions, he was never "shot in the back," except in that "Fast Duel."

James Trammell Cox

Writers have normally tended to shy away from describing the South's distinctive religious life, either from a fear of offending zealots or because of its complexity. Though southern writer Flannery O'Connor once called the South "Christ-haunted," and Florida writers Harry Crews (*The Gospel Singer*) and John D. MacDonald (*One More Sunday*) have written novels about the profound effect that religion in the South has on its followers, most such writers avoid writing about the region's religions. But not James Cox (1920–62), who was also a southerner, born in Virginia. Cox graduated from the University of North Carolina and taught at Clemson College, at the University of Iowa (where he earned a Ph.D. in creative writing and was managing editor of the *Western Review*), and at Florida State University.

He set the following story in Florida's capital. This choice is significant because, while we normally think of Tallahassee as the legislative hub of the state, it was also where Spanish explorers may have celebrated the first Christmas in the New World, in 1539, and where Franciscans set up missions in the seventeenth century. The story deals with four religious conventions prevalent throughout the South: the importance of the Bible, direct access to the Holy Spirit, traditional morals, and informal worship. The protagonist, Junior Lester, represents a religious phenomenon in Florida and elsewhere that the country's old, sparsely settled towns and isolated farms necessitated: the itinerant preacher. Junior's car has replaced his forefather's ponies, but his peripatetic ways follow a long tradition of traveling from town to town for services. Junior is similar to famous evangelicals like Dwight Moody, Billy Sunday, and Billy Graham; the fact that he is young does not matter to his congregation because he has great charisma. The revival he leads often crosses denominational lines and is an integral part of southern religion, as is the preacher's emphasis on individualism and conversion.

This story, whose author died before publication, won the O'Henry Award and was named one of the best American short stories of 1963. It first appeared in the spring 1961 issue of *MSS* magazine and then in a collection of O'Henry Award–winning stories edited by Richard Poirer and published in 1963. Here Cox depicts with great skill the Cracker dialect of the three main characters, especially the middle-aged lovers who wait for the permission of the woman's eleven-year-old preacher son to marry.

That Golden Crane

James Trammell Cox

"WHERE'S JUNIOR?" asked Mr. Gillespie as he stood beside the car. He had changed the tire, and now he was ready to go. It was hot. Down the long flat stretch of road toward Tallahassee, heat waves writhed above the asphalt like flames. From the car Mama Lester's reply was "Praise the Lord."

Removing his glasses to wipe the perspiration off them, Mr. Gillespie stared myopically at the oilcloth banner on the roof of the car. The bald forehead, which seemed suddenly naked when Mr. Gillespie took off his glasses, was bright pink except for a sprinkle of liver spots where his hairline had been when he was younger. It was gentle and full like the forehead of an infant.

"Junior Lester," he said, climbing in, "boy evangelist. Our sign surely tells them who we are." Even though the car was like an oven, it was a relief to get in out of the sun. He turned and smiled fondly at Mama Lester. "Where's Junior?" he repeated.

"He went onto that there rise, Mr. Gillespie," said Mama, "to pray for a good meeting." As she nodded toward the knoll where Junior had gone, the perspiration on the soft white roll of flesh beneath her dimpled chin caught the light from outside and glistened like strings of pearls.

The knoll toward which Mama nodded was crowned with a huge live oak. From the vertiguous spread of its branches hung a dense canopy of Spanish moss. Within the canopy, the deep shade seemed curiously forbidding—not cool or inviting at all. Mr. Gillespie hoped, if that was where Junior was, he would come out of there. Wherever he was, he wished he would come on. After a bit Mr. Gillespie repeated that the sign surely told people who they were. He sighed.

Impulsively Mama Lester covered his hand with her own, pressing down upon the bony knuckles with sudden passion. But when Mr. Gillespie sought to remove his hand from the wheel and take hers she withdrew it and picked up the fan in her lap—a Sunday school fan from Supchoppy with a picture of Jesus on it praying at a rock in the Garden of Gethsemane. She whipped the air as if it were eggwhites and scowled when Mr. Gillespie pecked her on the cheek. If she was lucky—and she knew she was—to have a gentleman friend like Mr. Gillespie and a son like Junior, it was also true that the Lord had not yet seen fit to open Junior's heart to her and Mr. Gillespie's terrible loneliness. Until He did, Mr. Gillespie would just have to keep his hands to himself. Mama Lester worshipped that boy.

In fact it was this worship, really, that had made her reach for Mr. Gillespie's hand. She herself was peeved with Junior, him not being here so that they could go on now Mr. Gillespie had finished. It was hot. Beneath the wet curls that clung to the back of her neck, her prickly heat burned. Her flowered organdy was soaked. Heat did not agree with her. Nevertheless, Mama Lester could not bear disapproval of Junior, even her own, which she was likely to regard as some weakness in herself, and when Mr. Gillespie had only said again that their sign surely told people who they were he had shown her the way to patience. He had spared her an expression of resentment she would have regretted later. Besides, Mr. Gillespie sounded so genteel the way he said *surely*. Her heart filled.

A little reading from the Scriptures being always a great comfort to them both, Mr. Gillespie took up the Bible which lay on the seat between them. As usual he began reading wherever the Good Book fell open. That way, it seemed more like a special message, even if the message itself was often hidden from them. "Thus saith the Lord," read Mr. Gillespie from Isaiah. Mama loved to hear him read: he always sounded as if he had just waked up. The timbre of Mr. Gillespie's voice *was* good. While resonant and firm, it seemed to carry with it whispers of personal tragedy and shy kindness.

> *The labour of Egypt, and merchandise of Ethiopia and of the*
> *Sabeans, men of stature, shall come unto thee, and they shall be*
> *thine: they shall come after thee; in chains they shall come over,*
> *and they shall fall down unto thee, saying, Surely God is in thee;*
> *and there is none else, there is no other God.*
>
> *Verily thou art a God that hidest thyself, O God of Israel, the*
> *Saviour . . .*

Suddenly Mama burst into tears. And when Mr. Gillespie hastily put the Bible down she fell into his arms and wept like a child. "Oh, Mr. Gillespie! Oh!"

Mr. Gillespie held her close, patting the damp organdy on her back. Tears filled his own eyes, and he kissed the damp, plump flesh at the nape of her neck tenderly. Into her ear he whispered, "Praise the Lord!" Her answer came quick and muffled, "Praise the Lord!"

It was no more given to Mr. Gillespie to understand Mama than to understand the Word of the Lord. He accepted both without question, for the long thirst which he had gratified with liquor for so many years now found true refreshment in this late love, at once intensely physical for Mr. Gillespie and serenely spiritual. In the better part of a lifetime he had spent as a night clerk in Tallahassee at the Andrew Jackson, he had lived entirely without either of these essential realities, existing only in the ghostly oblivion of cheap whiskey. Whenever, in fact, he handed a guest a key he carefully tucked the key itself against the room tag so that it wouldn't dangle and held the key and the tag both by the tip end for fear he might accidently touch someone. In these, his own contacts with people, he was that afraid. Now, if only for his incarnation into this wet and heavy world of physical reality, Mr. Gillespie was eternally grateful. Every day, after God, he thanked Mama Lester and Junior. Gently he moved his hand so as to touch the mole on the plump, sweating slope of Mama's shoulder.

The incarnation of Mr. Gillespie was indeed something of a miracle. It began with the touch of Junior's forefinger when Junior and Mama checked in at the Andrew Jackson last spring for a revival at the Filmore Road Tabernacle Pentecostal Church. Mr. Gillespie was drunk. By twelve, when they came in, Mr. Gillespie was always drunk, which meant simply that he moved a little more slowly and deliberately than usual. Otherwise, he might have avoided Junior's grab for the key as he held it out for the elevator operator who doubled as night bellboy, but he didn't. And the shock of this unfamiliar contact was enough to sober him momentarily so that he listened with a solemn show of interest as Mama confided that she had been in hoe-tel work before Junior was called. She was the sixth floor maid at the Gulfside in Panama City ever since her husband left her when Junior was still a baby. Only she didn't like it—the things she seen, oh! She ended by inviting him out to the meeting the next night to hear Junior preach. Whether it was the idea of a boy preaching or simply his uneasy desire to get rid of her before she smelled the whiskey he didn't know, but anyway he found himself slowly and deliberately promising that he would be there.

"I declare I don't know what come over me, Mr. Gillespie," explained Mama Lester, as she withdrew from his embrace. It seemed to her now that what had flitted through her mind could hardly have explained such an outburst. "Always the same," she had thought, "Egypt and Ethiopia and the Sabeans—never any message!" She dabbed at her eyes with her handkerchief and mopped her wet cheeks. "Hallelulia," she whispered hoarsely. "Praise the Lord. *Where's* that boy, Mr. Gillespie?"

"Heaven only knows," said Mr. Gillespie with a chuckle. That boy was a mystery to Mr. Gillespie. He had come into Mr. Gillespie's life like the children of Joel: "And it shall come to pass in the last days, saith God, I shall pour out of my Spirit upon all flesh; and your sons and your daughters shall prophesy . . . !" Yet at eleven he could not be trusted in a strange bed without his rubber sheeting. Sometimes Mr. Gillespie thought him a little willful too. And jealous, terrible jealous.

"Junior!" cried Mama Lester. "*Junior Les-ter!*" She lowered a single fat white leg to the ground and then heaved herself out, emerging from the car like dough that has risen and spilled over the lip of its bowl. "*Junior Lester!*" As she turned back to Mr. Gillespie, who was still in the car, she was suddenly anxious. "You don't reckon anything has happened to him, Mr. Gillespie?"

Mr. Gillespie got out and called too, but there was no answer—only the still, foreboding tree with its airless shadows within the motionless beards of moss. Where could the boy have gone to? Reluctantly Mr. Gillespie descended into the drainage ditch at the side of the road and made his way through the wire grass and briars, the jack oak and sassafras, up the slope of the knoll. He eyed with care each fat, fallen stick that lay suspiciously undulant and spotted with spores of lichen in the long grass—this was snake country.

Once when he stepped on a stick he hadn't seen and it rolled under his foot like something alive, striking against his heel, he was so startled he jumped back into the enveloping branches of a small persimmon. Then as he extricated himself from this, pawing at the cobweb that had clung to the back of his neck, he thought he heard something that was almost as upsetting as the buzz of a rattler would've been: he could have sworn he heard a snicker. But he listened a moment and decided it was only the dry rustle of the leaves of the persimmon as its branches resettled. He pushed on, ashamed of himself for having thought, even for a moment, what he did.

At the tree he paused before the curtain of moss. He knew it was crawling with chiggers. He hated to even touch it. Remembering Mama, though, sitting out there in that hot car, he parted several of the thinner strands and ducked quickly inside. "Junior?" he called, in a voice that was hardly above a whisper, "Junior, are you in here?" In the sudden darkness he couldn't see, he could scarcely breathe. He was about to turn at once to go when he heard it again: somewhere above him Junior was hiding and laughing at him.

As the serpentine trunks, which are often separate and only twisted together at the base of the tree in live oaks, became gradually visible, Mr. Gillespie stalked to the base for a more comprehensive view of the massive, low-hanging limbs that spread out above him. "Junior!" he demanded, "where are you?" Another snicker told him.

There, out on the limb just above where he had been standing, sat Junior. From his chin hung a long grey beard of Spanish moss. In his fist he clutched a bouquet of wilted foxglove. With uncertain bravery he began to swing his feet back and forth, and as Mr. Gillespie stared, speechless, he began then to scowl. "I seen you," he said, scowling down at Mr. Gillespie like some Blakean Jehovah, at once infantile and ancient, "you and her," he added, "a-lovin' each other up. I see you."

"Junior Lester!" exploded Mr. Gillespie at last, "do you want them chiggers to eat you alive?" It seemed a foolish thing to say, even to Mr. Gillespie, but it was the only thing he could think of because his thoughts were entirely given over to the sudden realization that he needed a drink. Not once since he had been saved had he burned with such a thirst.

"I seen you," repeated Junior.

"That moss is crawling with chiggers, Junior! Take it off! Take it off right now and come down from there!" Mr. Gillespie had never spoken to Junior quite like this before. In some vague way it was the beard that made him so angry. "Come down from there, Junior Lester, right this minute!"

Now it was Junior who was speechless, surprised and a little frightened by the authority in Mr. Gillespie's voice. His scowl began to wilt, and then he began to cry.

"There's no need to cry," continued Mr. Gillespie firmly. "It won't do you any good at all." Even as he said this, Mr. Gillespie knew he had gone too far, because it wouldn't do to take him back to Mama crying. Mama wouldn't understand at all. "I'm only trying to get you to come down from there," he added.

"You're trying to make me fall off this limb," said Junior, as if sensing the direction of Mr. Gillespie's thoughts. "That's what you're trying to do!" He was standing up now, making his way back along the limb with his arms spread wide like wings for balance.

"Junior!" cried Mr. Gillespie, "how can you say that?" He begged the boy to stop where he was and to sit down and let himself down into "Mr. Gillespie's arms," speaking of himself in third person as he occasionally did in especially affectionate moments. And now, for some reason, he really did need a drink.

But Junior ignored him, walking the limb with his arms tipping perilously to first one side and then the other. At the base, Mr. Gillespie offered his hand, but Junior jumped, with his shirt tail billowing out behind him and his beard flying. He landed at Mr. Gillespie's feet as nimble and surefooted as if he had floated down. Quickly rearranging his beard, he stepped up to Mr. Gillespie with flashing eyes and his hair awry. He was covered from head to foot with bits of bark and flakes of lichen that were like ashes. "'Let them be confounded,'" he said, wagging a vengeful finger, "'and put to shame that seek after my soul: let them be turned back and brought to confusion that devise my hurt!'"

Mr. Gillespie was not sure now at what point he had so completely lost that moment of new-found authority, but lost it he had—he knew this. And now all he could think of was a drink. He was afraid. . . . He would've liked to ask Junior to pray with him. Now, before it was too late. Here, in this place, he would make a new covenant with the Lord. But how could he now? He had only to look into Junior's eyes. . . . "You're a sight," he managed to say to Junior, but with a voice as hoarse and unsteady as a boy's. "Fix yourself," he added, "you don't want Mama to see you like that." He turned quickly away, but not before he had seen the furious scowl on Junior's childish features become a strangely lidded, frightening smile.

"Praise the Lord!" cried Mama from the roadside when they emerged from the curtain of moss, "Glory Hallelulia!" She was so relieved that nothing had happened to Junior she seemed to have forgotten entirely her discomfort and resentment. "Lord have mercy," she cried when she saw his beard, "ain't he something now? Ain't that the cutest thing you ever seen, Mr. Gillespie? For all the world," she said, "like a little old man!" She hugged him happily to her and closed her eyes against any love greater than this. "Praise the Lord," she moaned.

Mr. Gillespie ducked around to his side of the car and got in without telling her that he had found Junior hiding from them up in the tree. He even managed to return Mama's proud smile when Junior assured her the Lord would give them a good meeting. He thought about it though. All the way into Tallahassee the image of Junior up on that limb in his beard kept coming back to Mr. Gillespie—this and the taste of whiskey.

As they approached the outskirts of Tallahassee from the south, they passed a piano painted red and mounted up on posts in a newly cleared lot where the stubs of cut pines were still yellow-white and sharp as gator teeth. A tarpaper shack set back on the lot bore a sign MUSIC SCHOOL. After several miles of flat fields of jack oak and pine, black-water marshes scabbed with algae and sway-roofed shacks buried beneath green mounds of cudsue, they began to come to little frame houses with chartreuse window blinds and telephone wires that sagged from brown-glazed insulators attached to the side of the house. In a tiny yard of packed clay farther on stood two monumental boxwoods, dwarfing the unpainted Negro shack behind them. From a tub beside the porch steps leaned a cross of orange crating with WORMS crudely lettered on the cross piece. Fruit stands and country-store filling stations began to appear on either side of the road, along with frequent billboards advertising automobiles, gasoline, and eternity. When they had crossed a railroad siding they were in the city limits, where huge storage tanks of oil and gas gleamed mercilessly with fresh coats of aluminum paint. Second-hand furniture stores displayed beds, chests of drawers, rockers, and mirrors out front. Across the road from the Tabernacle, to which they came at last, was a field of rusting automobiles. Above it swung a towering crane arm with a scoop dangling from it by a slender cable. A man with some kind of helmet on sat in the closed mandibles of the scoop, looking down, as the cable swayed with the crane arm.

Mr. Gillespie turned into the parking lot between Teague's Welders and the Tabernacle, aching with a vague anxiety that had grown upon him with each mile closer to Tallahassee. It was more than wanting a drink and being afraid of what would happen if he took one, though this, God knows, was a part of it. He didn't know what was the matter. And even though this was the place where his new life in Christ had begun five months and three days ago today, when the Lord first sent His Holy Spirit to such as him, Mr. Gillespie could hardly persuade himself to get out of the car and shake hands with Mrs. Billy Jo Fain, who came out to welcome them. He even dreaded the thought of the meeting tonight. In fact he suddenly admitted to himself something he had avoided for weeks: The Holy Spirit had not really entered into him since one night in July, over a month ago. Lately his speech was only his own jabbering, in the *hope* the Spirit would come. "Praise the Lord," whispered Mr. Gillespie to himself.

"Praise the Lord!" cried Mrs. Billy Jo Fain, because Mama had just been telling her how proud she and Junior was to bring Mr. Gillespie back without a drop passed his lips all summer. "Glory Hallelulia!" Mrs. Fain wrung his hand with joy. She then turned to Junior, who allowed her to take his hand, but held himself stiffly apart and avoided looking at her when it appeared that she was about to embrace him. While she talked on about the souls Junior had brought to Christ, Junior fixed his gaze on Mr. Gillespie, permitting the suggestion of a smile to lift one corner of the pout that swelled his lower lip. Finally when she released his hand Junior looked at her and nodded and quickly looked away again. "Well," said Mrs. Billy Jo Fain, "no sense in us standing out here in the hot sun, is they?"

But this was the smile, Mr. Gillespie told himself, of one man to another at the way women carry on. He was sure of it, and his spirits lifted. "Don't reckon so," he said, with a chuckle the women wouldn't understand, "huh, Junior?"

Junior was watching the man up in the scoop across the road and didn't seem to hear at first. But then he turned around and nodded. As the women moved along the walk to the Tabernacle, he fell in behind with Mr. Gillespie. He wanted to know if Mr. Gillespie had seen the red piano and why the man was riding in the scoop. He was as full of questions as any twelve-year-old, thought Mr. Gillespie, and you wouldn't know a thing had happened this morning. "Well" said Mr. Gillespie, "when they lower it to the car they want that man will jump out, you see, and hook them chains around the car so as they can lift it."

Inside, Mrs. Fain explained why she was so anxious for them to see what they had done: with the new expenses she couldn't figure how her poor flock could offer Junior the same guarantee as before. Would keep and $25.00 do? At this point, Junior, who had been over admiring the red velveteen cushions on the new chancel chairs, rejoined them and said, yes, it was privilege enough for him just to be able to preach the gospel to his elders—he wasn't trying to get rich off his preaching. "'It is easier for a camel to go through the eye of a needle than for a rich man to enter the kingdom of heaven,'" he added.

"Amen," said Mrs. Fain.

Mama stared in shocked disbelief.

"Junior," Mr. Gillespie pointed out gently, "if you want to preach the gospel in Valdosta too, come Friday night, we'll have to have money for new tires."

Then she and Mr. Gillespie both commenced to tell Mrs. Billy Jo Fain how tight money was with them, their surprise at Junior's butting in only adding fuel to the fire. So Mrs. Fain finally agreed to $50.00 and took them out to the Old Nursery, which had been newly partitioned off into two sleeping rooms, with a bath between, and a kitchen on the end.

They passed a young apple tree in the back yard and Junior plucked one of the small green apples from its branches. "Boy!" snapped Mrs. Fain, "leave them apples alone."

Junior made a face, having tasted it, and then with a major league hop, skip and jump he threw the apple over the roof of the Nursery.

"Ain't it nice?" asked Mrs. Fain, remaining outside when she had opened the kitchen door for them. She smiled broadly.

"It's real nice," agreed Mama leading the way inside.

But as soon as Mrs. Fain was gone Mama turned on Junior and de-manded to know what on earth had possessed him to say a thing like that. Junior only smiled and pouted and acted as if he didn't know what she was talking about. Mama was furious. Mr. Gillespie, though, had already begun to reconsider, because, when you stopped and thought about it, probably it was just the thing that decided Mrs. Billy Jo Fain to agree to fifty. Only he couldn't believe Junior was *that* clever. He tried to catch Junior's eye again, as man to man, but Junior only stalked away into the next room, disgusted with them both. Wearily Mr. Gillespie returned to the car to bring their things in.

When he got back Mama was standing before the brightly lighted interior of the refrigerator. "Potato salid," she said, "it's always potato salid." She closed the door, and moving over to the table she let herself down onto a chair where she sat staring vacantly at the dime store picture of Jesus hung, crooked, on the wall before her.

When he had put the suitcases down Mr. Gillespie took the chair beside hers and reached out to console her with a gentle pat on the thigh, drawing comfort from the mere touch of the wrinkled organdy and the warm dough of the flesh beneath. Mama seemed to find contentment in the weight of his hand, sighing as she turned to him to count his liver spots. She liked to do that. She would touch each one, then stroke his forehead. When she repeated "potato salid," they both smiled.

"Is there anything to drink in that box?" It was Junior scowling first at the refrigerator and then at Mr. Gillespie's hand in Mama's lap. "I'm thirsty," he added, "aren't *you*, Mr. Gillespie?"

Aren't YOU, Mr. Gillespie? What did Junior mean by that? Mr. Gillespie turned and stared at Junior, who then took a quick step toward Mama, putting his hand out to the other side of her chair, where he stood with his head to one side smiling as if for a publicity poster.

"Koolaid," said Mama, hoping it would sound inviting because she had already begun to accuse herself of meanness for having spoken to Junior the way she had about the money.

Mr. Gillespie could not believe Junior would tease about a thing like that, not about drinking. It was just *him* and him having only one thing on his mind made him think a thing like that. "Junior?" he asked, "why did Jesus say to the fig tree, 'Let no fruit grow on thee henceforward forever'?"

Junior frowned. His clear brown eyes clouded with suspicion. This was obviously not what he had expected from Mr. Gillespie. He went to the refrigerator where he lifted the Koolaid out before answering: "It's not for us to question the Lord, Mr. Gillespie."

"Amen," said Mama.

Mr. Gillespie sighed. Junior hadn't understood that he was only trying to put things right again.

"Ugh!" Junior spit the Koolaid into the sink and bent over it spluttering. Then he poured the rest of the glass into the sink, watching with satisfaction as it disappeared, gurgling, down the drain. Suddenly his face brightened. "Mama," he cried, "can Mr. Gillespie go get us some Doctor Pepper?"

Mama looked at Mr. Gillespie and shook her head. "Mr. Gillespie's tired, Junior."

"Please?" He went to her chair and put his arms around her neck, watching Mr. Gillespie as he leaned to kiss her on the cheek. "Please?"

Mr. Gillespie swallowed uneasily. All he would have to do for a fifth of liquor would be to keep on going, down to the Andrew Jackson, and he had no wish for such temptation to be put before him. He avoided Mama's eyes as she turned to ask him if he minded. "Surely," he said at last, "but why don't Junior come with me?" Though Junior didn't want to go, Mama insisted, because she was going to take a bath and lie down for a while.

As they went out Junior hung his head sulkily and kicked at the sparse tufts of crabgrass, stirring up small clouds of dust that only made Mr. Gillespie thirsty to look at. He also plucked another apple and threw it over the Tabernacle. Recalling how friendly Junior had seemed before, Mr. Gillespie couldn't understand what had happened. This hurt Mr. Gillespie, because only thirty minutes ago he was thinking how they used to go cane fishing in June, wondering if he and Junior couldn't slip off tomorrow morning down to the Wacissa. He dropped his arm around the boy's shoulder. He would just tell Junior the truth about why he wanted him along. But Junior shook off his arm.

"Junior, look—" the words died in his throat. He could see it was no use. "Say, Junior, how would you like to go fishing tomorrow?" In the way the back of Junior's curly head lifted, Mr. Gillespie could see that he had surprised him. But then his head bent stubbornly forward again, and he wouldn't answer. "Junior?" Mr. Gillespie's voice dropped lower, "I want you to go with me after the pop, son."

"I'm *not* your son!" cried Junior. "And I'm *not* going with you!" He ran to the side door of the Tabernacle where he turned in the doorway and explained angrily: "I need to meditate on Him for tonight." As he stepped back, drawing the door after him, it seemed to Mr. Gillespie for a moment that Junior smiled from within the deep shadow of the Tabernacle— the same frightening, lidded smile as before at the tree.

The darkened interior of Teague's Welders was lit with the spitting tongues of welders' torches as Mr. Gillespie pulled out into the highway. Mr. Gillespie looked the other way: his own tongue was fire enough. Then when he passed a store where he could have bought Doctor Peppers, he kept going. On South Baptist Avenue as he neared town he passed the fairgrounds where a ferris wheel turned slowly in the sunlight, its seats rocking. Then at the Andrew Jackson Mr. Gillespie pulled over to the curb across from the hotel and sat a moment, still rigid, still holding tightly to the wheel as if to his decision—for he had made up his mind exactly what he would do. Back at the Tabernacle it had come to Mr. Gillespie like a revelation that Junior *wanted* him to go back to his bottle. It was a terrible thing to have to believe. But it was the truth. And on the way in Mr. Gillespie had thought it all out very carefully: he knew what he would do. Trance-like, he crossed the street and entered the Andrew Jackson.

For ten dollars, Doc Pugh, the hotel doctor with an "office" in his room, was glad to give Mr. Gillespie a couple of signed health certificates. In a wistful cracked voice he kept saying Mr. Gillespie was a "new man, a new man." Mr. Gillespie would've liked to stay and "witness" for his old friend, but he was afraid. He didn't feel safe until he was once again outside on the street.

At the Courthouse they didn't want to issue the license without Mama there to sign it too. He wouldn't leave, though, until finally they gave it to him to take out to her to sign. Walking back to the car, which was still parked across the street from the Andrew Jackson, he had his worst time.

With the license in one hand and a carton of Doctor Pepper in the other, Mr. Gillespie collapsed into a chair at the kitchen table, exhausted.

After a while he got up and went to the wall and straightened the picture of Jesus. Then when he returned to his chair, he put his head down on the table to rest, the plastic top as cool as marble.

"Where's Junior?"

Mr. Gillespie lifted his head from the table and looked up: it was Mama, standing in the door into her room in her slip. He told her that Junior hadn't gone with him, he supposed he was still over at the Tabernacle meditating.

"Oh, Mr. Gillespie!" cried Mama, padding quick and weightless in her bare feet to where he sat. She seemed to know at once what he had been through. "Why didn't you tell me? Why didn't you tell me, Mr. Gillespie." She embraced him, pressing his head to her breasts, and Mr. Gillespie slipped his arm about her waist, thankful to the Good Lord who had gone with him into the very furnace of his fiery thirst and brought him safely out again. "Praise the Lord!" moaned Mama. "The Good Lord was with you, Mr. Gillespie."

"Mama," said Mr. Gillespie, "look what I brought you." He held up the license for her to see.

"Oh!" Mama gasped. Her eyes opened wide, and she stared at the little black rainbow of print that said MARRIAGE LICENSE as if it might be a summons of some kind. "Oh, Mr. Gillespie, you know you shouldn't have done that. I declare. Oh!" There were tears in her eyes as she clutched Mr. Gillespie's head to her bosom again and began to sway from side to side. Mr. Gillespie didn't know whether she was laughing or crying, and neither did Mama. "I declare," she said, "I declare."

Mr. Gillespie put his arms about her waist, happily allowing himself to be held like this until suddenly the image of Mama holding Junior just this way came back to him and he sought clumsily to stand up and take her in his arms.

But Mama stepped back. "No, Mr. Gillespie," she said, with a kind of frightened determination. "I just can't. Not less'n Junior will marry us. You know my heart is set on that."

"But Beulah,"—it was the first time he had ever called her by her given name—"he won't marry us. You know he won't."

"I can't help it, Mr. Gillespie, I just can't help it. My heart is set on that." Then abruptly she shushed him, eyes growing wide and fearful.

"Psst! He's coming!" She slipped from his arms, snatched up the license, and disappeared into the bedroom.

Wearily Mr. Gillespie turned to the refrigerator to take out an ice tray for the Doctor Peppers. The trays were stuck, and he was still trying to pry one loose when Junior came in, behind him.

"Where's Mama?"

Mr. Gillespie nodded toward the other room without turning from the refrigerator.

"I thought I seen her in here."

He finally managed to shake a tray loose, carrying it to the sink where he ran water over it before he tried ejecting the cubes. Then he took down three glasses and dropped the ice cubes in, one by one, three to a glass. Turning around, he knew that now was no time to ask Junior, but he could not seem to help himself. "Junior," he asked, "when are you going to marry your mama and me? I want to know."

Junior scowled. His clear brown eyes clouded unhappily. "When the Lord tells me to," he mumbled.

"When is the Lord going to tell you to?" asked Mr. Gillespie almost angrily.

Junior's eyes cleared, bright and sparkling with sure indignation. "Shall he that contendeth with the Almighty instruct him? He that reproveth God, let him answer it!"

The ice in the glasses which Mr. Gillespie still held in his hands began to rattle noisily as his hands trembled now. Embarrassed, Mr. Gillespie stepped quickly to the table with the glasses. He sighed. There was no use to try and reason with Junior. He had known this before he asked. He put his hand to his mouth and sucked at the blood in his palm where he had skinned it messing with the ice tray. Then he opened the Doctor Peppers, somewhat calmer now.

Junior wasn't satisfied. "'It hath been said,'" he added, "'Whoever shall put away his wife, let him give her a writing of divorcement. But *Jesus* says, That whosoever shall put away his wife, saving for the cause of fornication, causeth her to commit adultery; and whosoever shall *marry* her that is divorced committeth adultery.'"

As Mr. Gillespie stared at the Doctor Pepper in his glass, his stomach all at once rose up against it and he could no more have drunk it than he could a full glass of 666. Queasy and exasperated, he put it down and walked out, having to go outside in order to get to his room on the end since he couldn't go through Mama's room. Here he took off his glasses and lay down on his unmade bed to think, praying that the Lord would not allow his heart to be filled with hate for any that were in His image. Then when he found that this was not to be given to him without a struggle, he got up, put his glasses on again, and opened his Bible, being careful to read at the first verse his eye fell upon:

At the same time came the disciples unto Jesus, saying, Who is the greatest in the kingdom of heaven?

And Jesus called a little child unto him, and set him in the midst of them,

And said, Verily I say unto you, Except ye be converted, and become as little children, ye shall not enter into the kingdom of heaven.

Whosoever therefore shall humble himself as this little child, the same is the greatest in the kingdom of heaven.

And whoso shall receive one such little child in my name receiveth me.

"Amen!" cried Mr. Gillespie aloud. "Praise the Lord!" He fell onto his knees and thanked the Lord for sending him a message in his pride and his wicked resentment of a little child. When he arose from his knees he would have rushed to tell Junior of this message the Lord had sent him, but all at once his knees were like water and he began to tremble again, violently. Besides he had just remembered the dry cleaning. Somebody would have to take that in.

At 7:00 the gooseneck over the REVIVAL sign in the yard went on, at 7:30 the lights in the crosses and the inside lights. The three fiery crosses of glass brick, set into the facade that rose in tiers like a child's block house at the front of the Tabernacle, glowed a blood red, for red bulbs were used in the cross lights. They cast a red light onto the faces of the crowd gathered about the stoop and even onto the three dead palms along the highway. Now the crowd began drifting in. Old women, moving slow, with their wrinkled necks out. Old men, shrivelled, but stiffly erect like prisoners in some vague battle they could not believe they had lost, never having fought it. A few young women, thin, looking around. Young girls with bad eyes or poor complexions, inclined to be stout. No boys over twelve. Few men, these few guarded and uninquisitive, wanting only to get to a seat and not be seen. Some small children and infants, solemn-eyed, as if expecting a slap.

"It's a good crowd," said Mrs. Fain, turning around to Mama with a quick, muscular smile. She was at the lectern, which served as pulpit. Behind her were Mama, Junior, and Mr. Gillespie, seated on the platform in three throne-backed chairs of blond oak with bright red cushions. Everything was blond oak and new: the chairs, the Hammond organ, the lectern, the pew benches, and the wall plaques showing attendance and offering.

"Praise the Lord," said Mama. Then after a quick appraisal of Junior's handkerchief, bow tie, hair, and shoes, she leaned across in front of him to whisper to Mr. Gillespie that she was certainly glad he remembered the dry cleaning. (It had turned out that Mr. Gillespie had to make another trip into town to get their clothes pressed.) Mr. Gillespie nodded with slow, deliberate gravity.

First they sang "One Rose":

Don't send me any flowers
When I pass on
Just one rose for Jesus
When I pass on. . . .

Then Mrs. Fain told them about what a successful revival they had last year when Junior preached and how she hoped this one would be a success too because she had promised Junior's mama a set of tires so as he might carry the Lord's Word on to Valdosty next week. When she was through she introduced Mama, who told them how Junior was called at camp meeting two years ago, with him only nine when Mr. Bingham from Supchoppy laid on his hands and declared Junior was a witness to the power and the glory of God's Holy Spirit. (*Amen! Praise the Lord!* came sprinkled cries from the assembly.) She told how it was all she could do to keep Junior in school on account of him wanting to go forth and preach the gospel in all the world like Jesus told the eleven. (*Amen! Praise the Lord!*) She followed him for two summers wherever the Lord called, and now—praise be to God!—Junior had a church of his own in Lynn

Haven, and they travelled about only when they was specially invited like tonight. "And for you folks tonight," Mama concluded, "we have a special guest I am sure will open your hearts to the glorious power and the everlasting mercy of Our Savior Jesus Christ when he tells you what Our Savior done for him in this very Tabernacle last Spring. Tell the folks what He done for you, Mr. Gillespie!"

Glory Hallelulia! Praise the Lord! Oh yes, Lord!

As Mr. Gillespie rose and walked to the lectern with very slow and very solemn dignity, a hush fell over the assembly. He took hold of the stand with both hands, then half turning with a slight bow to Mama, he said, "Yes, I'll tell them what He's done for me, Mrs. Lester. Surely." He faced the assembly. He paused. Then in the whispering resonance of his best voice, which seemed charged tonight with a special tragedy, a special kindness, he spoke with slow and deliberate emphasis. "He *saved* me. He saved me, and privileged me to work for Him in the company of two of His finest servants. That's what he did for me!" Mr. Gillespie paused to reach back and scratch himself under the shoulder blade, his elbow protruding like a broken wing.

Amen! Praise the Lord! Glory Hallelulia!

Mr. Gillespie went on to tell them what a lonely life he had led until a kind word from Mama to a miserable drunken sinner like himself had brought him into that very door five months and three days ago today, drunk. So drunk he hardly knew where he was. (A young woman wailed, and gasps of surprise and pity stirred the assembly.) Mr. Gillespie pointed to the very bench in back where he had staggered to a seat. (Every head turned.) Then with a slow, awesome sweep of his arm, he pointed now at Junior. "But this boy," he cried, "this child before you now, preached like I'd never heard preaching before. Like Peter and John in Jerusalem, when the high priests told them they couldn't preach no more in Jerusalem, this boy was filled with the Holy Spirit and spoke the Word of God with boldness!" Mr. Gillespie dropped his arm now to scratch along the inside of his thigh.

Slowly and deliberately, with occasional pauses to scratch his chigger bites, Mr. Gillespie finished the story of how the Spirit had come to him also when he turned to embrace his neighbor as Junior had told them to and what a joy it was to discover God's mercy in sending His Holy Spirit to such as him. He told them about his return to the hotel where in the middle of his transcript he walked off and left his desk and his bottle under the desk, going up to Mrs. Lester and Junior's room to pray all that night and to make a covenant with the Lord to serve Him all the rest of the days of his life and never again to touch strong drink—

Praise the Lord! sounded one of the men's voices, deep and agonized. The women wailed afresh. *Praise the Lord!*

Mr. Gillespie himself seemed to choke up with emotion, visibly sagging as he stood there before them, holding onto the stand now with both hands. He paused. He moistened his lips. He turned first to one side and then to the other, slowly, as though suddenly he had forgotten where he was or was looking for some way out. He looked at his audience. He carefully moistened his lips with his tongue, to go on. He whispered, "But—"

A young woman on the front row seemed almost to scream.

There was another long pause in which Mr. Gillespie only stood there, holding onto the stand, looking at the young woman as if he had to decide why she had screamed before he could go on. He scratched at the place on his back. He moistened his lips. "The flesh," he whispered, "is weep." Again he paused. Something was wrong. He scratched himself. He thought very deeply for a moment, and then he knew: "Weak," he corrected himself in a whisper that trailed off into silence while Mr. Gillespie stood there, still facing his audience, holding onto the stand. . . .

In the intense hush that had fallen over the assembly now Junior was heard to whisper to his mama: I *knew* it! Then suddenly he was there at the stand beside Mr. Gillespie, his eyes shining, as he cried, "Fall *down*, Sinner! Fall down on your knees before your God and confess your sins! *Pray*! Pray for His Forgiveness—you're *drunk,* Mr. Gillespie!"

The hush was shattered with a single explosion of cries and screams as though a child having tired of his block house had put his mouth to the door and shouted.

As Mr. Gillespie sank to his knees Junior seemed to descend upon him on some invisible ferris wheel, rocking in the lights as he came down with beard flying and his voice roaring in Mr. Gillespie's ears. Now he was floating off, up and away again with his long grey beard flying and a bouquet of foxglove in his hand. Mr. Gillespie cried out in confusion. It had all happened so quickly. He had simply run out of the strength to concentrate. He didn't understand. Junior's voice was close again.

"Do you confess your sins before Almighty God?"

"Yes, Lord," moaned Mr. Gillespie. Now Mama was there on her knees beside him, her arm around his shoulders, repeating after him, "Yes, Lord."

Yes Lord! came a thundering echo from the wailing, still frightened assembly.

"Have you broken your covenant with the Lord?" shouted Junior, brushing the hair out of his eyes and jumping up and down in his excitement.

"Yes, Lord," said Mr. Gillespie

"Yes, Lord," repeated Mama, "he has."

The assembly moaned.

"Have you defiled the lips that He gave you for His worship with the stink and fire of alcohol?"

"Yes, Lord," confessed Mr. Gillespie.

"Yes, Lord, he has—when he went after the dry cleaning."

"Is this the first time since you made your covenant with the Lord?"

"Yes, Lord."

"Yes, Lord, it is."

"Do you repent your sin, you miserable sinner?"

"Yes, Lord, he does." Mama's voice in his ear as she held him close was full with love and faith.

Praise the Lord! came the cries. *Glory Hallelulia!* shouted others. *Save him, Lord!*

"Save him, Lord!" shouted Junior, stepping forward to lay his hands on Mr. Gillespie's head. He looked up and cried again: "Save this miserable sinner, O Lord! He has confessed his sin and repents, O Lord!"

Praise the Lord! Glory Hallelulia!

"Send down your Holy Spirit to this flesh, O Lord, that his sins may be washed clean for Jesus Christ's sake!"

But it didn't come. Instead came the image of Junior sitting up on that limb of the live oak tree. And Mr. Gillespie cried out in the agony of his doubt. Mama clutched him to her, moaning.

"Sinner, do you believe?" shouted Junior wrathfully.

Mr. Gillespie lifted his eyes to the stage light overhead, blinded, in his plea for the mercy of belief. Then there again in the flood of light appeared Junior: the beard flying, eyes flashing. Mr. Gillespie closed his eyes. He bowed his head. "Yes, Lord," he whispered, "I believe." At once, as if his very blood were turned to light, Mr. Gillespie was filled with a glorious discovery of his own unworthiness: His resentment of Junior was only rage against his own sinful thirst; even his determination *not* to drink was pride; his love for Mama, an awful lusting after the flesh; sneaking back with that bottle to his room, the weakness of an unregenerate sinner. And trying, for Mama's sake, to go through with his testimonial was a dark hypocrisy God alone could forgive. While this light, this throbbing unbearable pulse of light brought tears to Mr. Gillespie's eyes that streamed down his cheeks, it also filled him with a frightening joy—a bright incredible realization that God in His unbounded mercy could forgive even him. "*Yes Lord!*" shouted Mr. Gillespie. "*I believe, O Lord!*"

"Yes Lord, he believes!"

O yes, Lord! Yes Lord! roared the assembly, moaning now in unison except for the intermittent screams of the young woman.

"Do you in your heart desire a new life in Christ?" shouted Junior. He bent over Mr. Gillespie now, bright brown eyes wide and shining, his lips spread in a proud and blissful smile. His eyes rolled heavenward as he dropped his hands dramatically to Mr. Gillespie's shoulders.

It was then that Mr. Gillespie knew the Holy Spirit was entering into him. It split his bones apart as he leaped to his feet, trembling. It set his tongue to dancing in an unknown language. After this he seemed to be in a dream as he turned to Mama with open arms, feeling the Spirit flow into her body from his own as she too began to tremble and to speak. He could hear Junior's voice as he preached a sermon about Jesus coming in a golden crane, but it was like a voice in a dream, disembodied and distant in the darkness. He couldn't seem to discover where it was coming from, and even though he was listening closely he knew that he didn't hear it all. The part he heard was glorious, glorious. Jesus, Junior said, would come again, riding in the golden scoop of a golden crane, riding high above everybody's head till He looked down and saw one that was saved. Then Jesus would give the signal and God would lower that crane, that golden crane, so Jesus could step forth and bind His loved one with that golden chain, binding His loved one around and around with that golden chain. And when His loved one was bound secure in that golden chain, dear Jesus would give the signal again, and away they would swing off to heaven in that golden crane, in that golden crane . . .

Mr. Gillespie wasn't sure when it was that the final pandemonium broke loose, with everyone surging forward to be saved by the touch of Junior's hand. He knew only that it was like something faraway, faraway. And it was the loving-sweet cry of Mama's fulfillment that was close in his ear as he awoke with her beneath the apple tree in the soft light of the scoop of a new moon, tipped high in the sky above them.

"Heavens!" cried Mama, "what have I done?"

Lawrence Dorr

Lawrence Dorr (1925–) is the pen name of Janos Shoemyen, a man who has seen more than his share of adversity. He once said, "If I couldn't write, I would go crazy from all the horrors I've seen. When I put them on paper, they become stories and are inside me no longer." Born Janos (pronounced "Ya'nosh") Zsigmond Shoemyen in Budapest, Hungary, he grew up in a cultured, affluent family in a peaceful world that World War II brought to a sudden end. After the war, during which he served on the Eastern Front, and after the Communist takeover of Hungary, he became a political refugee and fled to Austria, where he worked as a masseur, an orderly in a mental hospital, a French Foreign Legionnaire, and even the front half of a zebra in a circus act.

In 1950, he married an American occupational therapist in England and moved with her to the United States, eventually winding up in Florida. He worked in Frostproof as a Protestant missionary, in Sebring as a ranchhand, and in Gainesville as an editor at the University of Florida. For a pen name—which he adopted after an editor told him his magazine would publish only American authors—he chose "Dorr," from his mother's last name, D'Ore, and "Lawrence," from a character in a Hungarian novel he wrote as a teenager.

He has published two collections of short stories: *A Slow, Soft River* (1973; republished as *The Immigrant* [1976]), which includes the following story; and *A Slight Momentary Affliction* (1987). Dorr used to write in German, Hungarian, and French, but currently he writes only in English and does not translate from Hungarian into English. Today he lives and writes on a twenty-acre horse farm in Alachua, Florida, with his wife, children, and grandchildren.

"A Slow, Soft River" is, like many of his short stories, autobiographical in that he and his son used to spend the days before Easter canoeing on the rivers of north Florida. The story contains a moving contrast between the idyllic Itchetucknee River and the grim hospital life the character Stefan is enduring. "Stefan" was based on a friend of Dorr's who was dying of an aneurysm; he had been a father figure for the protagonist's (Dorr's) son because he ("Stefan") could teach the boy American sports that the boy's father (Dorr) could not.

The Itchetucknee, which flows into the Santa Fe River, which in turn flows into the Suwannee River, which flows into the Gulf of Mexico, reminds the protagonist of life's flow and that our lives are always moving toward a final destiny. He comes to realize that death, while inevitable, is not the final end.

A Slow, Soft River

Lawrence Dorr

THE GIRL WAS driving the car up the slope, bouncing over the ruts gouged out by the run-off; then stopping a second, she waved. The man and the boy didn't look up from loading supplies in an old wooden boat half floating on the Itchetucknee. The river was cold and clear and smelled of the fish that swam close to the bridge, their heads pointing upstream. They were silver or black, nothing in between, with tails going like slow metronomes.

The girl turned onto the highway. When the man heard the car crossing the highway bridge he lifted his hand and wiggled his fingers in farewell. The boy waded into the river. Hunching over the transom with the outboard, he looked like a stork fishing.

By next year, the man thought, he'll be taller than I am. The boy was sixteen and he forty-five.

"Daddy," the boy said, straightening up, "we are ready to leave now."

"Sam," the man called. "Sam."

From under the bridge a big, gaunt black and tan hound sauntered down to the boat. He had a false joint in his hip that made him drag his right hind leg. He came to the man and put his muzzle in his hand.

"Samuel," the man said. He felt love rising in him like a great shout that spread over the giant water oaks, the face of his daughter in the car framed by dark hair, her emerald eyes smiling goodbye, the wind on the pale green sea of the river with its island-pools of blue, his tall, strong son; and Sam. Sam who had been found two years ago in a Georgia swamp on the verge of death. He lifted his arms as if he wanted to breathe in the blueness of the sky.

"Praise the Lord," the boy said matter-of-factly. "Get in, Daddy."

"Do you feel it too?" The man was astonished as if the boy had suddenly spoken in Chinese.

"I don't know why I shouldn't. I'm normal."

They floated under the highway bridge, then shot through the culvert under the railroad tracks. There were some houses on the left bank, but nobody in them. The river turned and widened. A congregation of ducks bobbed on the ripples. They were white ducks with one blue-wing teal in the midst of them. Out of sight a heron sounded deep bass. The ducks tuned up. Then as if the conductor had come in, there was a sudden silence. Sam stood up in the boat and, lifting his head, bayed.

"That was an otter," the boy said. Some turtles plopped into the water, one after the other. Sam lay down again.

"I feel the same as when I listen to Bach," the man said. "I am lifted up, I am soaring, and I am almost bursting with joy. . . . But it is all orderly."

"You can't orderly-burst-with-joy," the boy said.

"We better crank up." The man was looking ahead where the Itchetucknee ran into the Santa Fe. There was a large object caught in the turbulence, coming up and going under again like a drowning man.

The engine started with a shriek, then the boy slowed it down to a pleasant purr. They went around the obstacle. Close up it was only a tree trunk that turned with a nice even speed. A roller in a well-oiled machine.

The Santa Fe was wider and darker and so swollen that it hardly moved between the banks of moss-covered trees. The boy speeded up. Two long waves left behind by the boat rushed the banks like charging cavalry, then broke up into shiny fragments among the tree trunks. Dry land was nowhere in sight. The man turned his head to the other side. A new charge just broke among the trees, flashing here and there like pieces of broken mirror. Without warning he saw his friend Stefan on the hospital bed with his eyes half closed as he had been the last six weeks, breathing through a hole in his neck, his chest heaving. Then the sun came out, illuminating the spaces among the trees. The green patent-leather leaves of a huge magnolia reflected the light upward.

A garment of praise for the spirit of heaviness, he thought.

The boat changed direction, then got back on course. The boy had just finished taking off his shirt.

"Aren't you cold?"

"I wouldn't have taken it off it I were," the boy said.

"Vanity," the man said. "You want to get tanned, somebody else wants to bleach out. It's all vanity."

"If we all have it, you must have it too, Daddy."

"I have it moderately. On some Sundays when it is cold enough to wear my suit which I got to go to England in, I think, aha, not bad at all, but your mother will say: 'It's all right if you don't put on any more weight.' And I quit saying 'aha' till next winter."

"I remember when you bought that suit. I was five years old."

"That can't be."

"It was when I was starting school in England."

"And I am still not famous," the man said, "but at least I can get into my old suit."

"You look great in it, Daddy."

The man accepted this with a slight bow. He remembered how he stood in the door of the intensive-care unit not knowing if he should go in, conscious of his good suit and the nurses who were looking at him. But it didn't last long, this male pride, because he saw Stefan and understood that the rhythmic clicking he heard came from a green plastic pump attached to a hole in Stefan's neck. Stefan was pale, his unseeing eyes half open. For a crazy moment he had almost expected Stefan to ask him to have something to eat or to drink wine. He always did. But there was nothing other than the sudden awful silence of the pump. He was holding his own breath, wanting to share the pain; then the pump started and Stefan's chest expanded. The rhythm of the pump was back for a while, then it stopped again. He had reached out and laid his hands on Stefan's head.

"Do you want to fish?" the boy was shouting over the noise of the outboard. "Now that the sun is out I can see the fish." He cut back the engine.

"They prophesied rain," the man said, "but it doesn't look like it. . . . I'll just sit and watch you fish."

They anchored under a large oak. The boy cast; the bait falling like a meteor plopped into the river. Sam checked the sound. The boy reeled in and cast out again. Some ducks came in over the trees and settled on the Santa Fe.

"It's good to be away from the world," the man said.

"This is the world, Daddy." The boy reeled in again.

"I am glad that at least Sam can't talk back," the man said. "I am talking about this place where we can see and smell the sun."

"Yes," the boy said.

"I think it's all right for us to be here."

"Why wouldn't it be all right? We can't do anything for Stefan except pray."

"Even so, I saw Stefan at the nursing home and you didn't. There is no pump beside his bed now and that awful clicking is gone, but in a way it is worse. He struggles for each breath, and when I squeezed his hand there was nothing. In the hospital at least he squeezed back and I always thought of it as Stefan in a sunken submarine answering my knock, saying: 'I am here, I am here, I can hear you.'"

"I looked it up," the boy said, putting on his shirt. "The veins contract first to prevent too much bleeding, but if they don't relax after a certain time that part of the brain dies."

"Stefan was just lying there sweating," the man said, not smelling the sun, the river, and the fishes anymore, "and his pillow showed the damp outline of his head."

"I don't want to think of him that way," the boy said. "I always see him playing golf standing on that very green grass." He cast, the line flying out toward the other shore with a satisfying sound. The man saw Stefan, but he wasn't playing golf. He was sitting in his living room, in his dark green armchair next to a large candlestick with papers strewn around him on the carpet. Just two hours before the stroke.

"No bother at all," Stefan said. *"While I read it you eat something. And have some wine."*

"I have a nibble," the boy whispered. He leaned forward tensely, watching his line. "It's a bite, real heavy."

Play it, the man wanted to say, but he didn't say anything. The boy was a fisherman; he wasn't. He remembered his own fishing in the Danube with a cane pole and the dozens of fingerlings he pulled out from its olive-colored water. He also remembered his father's smile that said: this is all right for a little boy but men, our kind of men, hunt.

"A fighter," the boy shouted, reeling in and letting out the line again. "A fighter." The fish leaped clear of the water then went down making the reel scream like an ambulance. "I am pulling him in now," the boy said. He turned the reel, his torso leaning forward in the attitude of a Protestant at prayer.

"I'll help you land it," the man said.

"I can manage, thank you." He stood up and lifted the fish into the boat. The fish, it was a bass, fell to the floorboard with a thud. The boy took out the hook. The bass kept on flapping on the board, then lay still. The man was watching its gills pumping in and out, in and out.

"Let's turn it loose," the man said.

"Why? It's a perfect eating size. It must be at least five pounds."

When the boy was younger, he cried easily. The look he gave now was a man's incredulous stare. I couldn't tell him, the man thought. Besides it would be all wrong. Pagan. An exchange with the god of the river.

The fish flopped once, then lay still. Suddenly it lit up as if a light had been turned on inside it.

"It's beautiful," the boy said. "It gave a good fight."

అు   అు

By carefully navigating among the cypress knees and tree trunks, they reached the shore under a bluff. In the silence of the switched-off outboard the tea-colored waves sounded like heavy breathing.

"I like to look down on the Suwannee," the man said. "This is how a flying heron sees it."

The boy laughed. "A two-hundred-pound heron. You would need a steel reinforced kingsize nest."

The bluff's floor was flat and covered with dry grass and the contorted trunks of live oaks. Sam checked out the place by circling around it. The man set up the tent. The boy chopped wood, built the fire, then neatly arranged his cooking tools on a stump.

"How do you feel about fish soup?" he asked.

"With plenty of paprika," the man said. He walked down to the edge of the bluff and looked down on the Suwannee. Its color alternated between royal blue and green with the edges saffron. There were no boats going in either direction. Some ducks dove, then bobbed back to the surface. Sam came to stand against the side of his knee.

"Sam thinks this is a good place," the man said. He saw Stefan's saffron colored shoes that he still wore even after shaving off his guardsman mustache and returning to his more conservative look. "I might get a crew cut," Stefan had said. "That would make me avant-garde now." But he didn't. His hair was damp and matted on the pillow. "A nice full head of hair," the nurse had said.

"Do you want to taste the soup, Daddy?"

It tasted perfect and he slurped another spoonful. "Who is to put a price on the joy of sitting here tasting your fish soup?"

"Some rivers had to be dammed up because people needed electricity. You can't damn progress, Daddy."

"I don't. I wouldn't be here without it. I was pretty badly shot up in the war. It isn't that at all."

"We can eat now," the boy said.

"Anything for Sam?"

The boy gave the dog a few uncooked hot dogs. The man watched the dog. When Sam ran he looked perfect. Only walking and sitting showed his crooked hip joint. We are both here, the man thought. It could have ended for Sam in that swamp in Georgia and for me at the border, under the barbed wire.

"Benedictus, benedicet."

"Deo gratias," the boy answered.

After washing up, the man climbed back up the bluff. He put the cooking utensils away and sat down on the blanket in front of the tent. For the last six years he and the boy had left on their annual boat trip on the Thursday before Easter. On Good Friday they would have a service of their own and be back at church on Easter Day. But this time it was different. He couldn't wait another day and he needed the strength of his son. The boy was whole while he was bruised and battered, only hoping to be made whole. The boy knew that with God everything was possible; he only hoped.

"John," the man said, "let's have our service today. It's because Stefan . . . we are out here and he—"

"I thought about it," the boy said. He stepped into the tent, got the prayer book, and sat down on the blanket.

"You read," the man said. "I left my reading glasses at home." He loved to hear the boy read, and besides, his own accent made him uncomfortable knowing that it would ruin something precious. The boy opened the prayer book.

"Now before the feast of the passover, when Jesus knew that his hour was come that he should depart out of this world unto the Father, having loved his own which were in the world, he loved them unto the end—"

The man listened, already thinking of tomorrow when He would be led to Pilate and shame and rejection and torment so that he, sitting here on a dog-smelly blanket, could be made clean and whole again.

"—For I have given you an example, that ye should do as I have done to you." The boy closed the prayer book. "Lord, we lift up our friend

Stefan like those men who took the roof apart so that You could see their friend. You know what to do. We don't. Thank You."

"Amen," the man said, feeling peace carrying him along like a slow, soft river. He knew that he didn't have to worry about Stefan anymore.

The boy put away the prayer book in the tent and came back with a cigar.

"I didn't know that you were smoking. That cigar's at least six months old."

"I don't," the boy said. "Stefan taught me to blow smoke rings. They would float beautifully out here."

This time the man didn't ask the boy if he felt it too. He looked at his watch. It was four-thirty.

Just before dusk, the boy, who was fishing sitting in the tied-out boat, called him. There was a snake swimming across the river from the other side.

و   و

The rain began at noon Friday, and it was still raining when they pulled out the boat at Fannin Springs. The wood around the boat ramp smelled like mushrooms. There were cars crossing the battleship grey bridge at long intervals, messengers from another civilization. In the pause the only sounds were the rain splashing on the Suwannee, the river itself, and Sam's running on the wet leaves.

The boy was stacking up the camping gear with an economy of move-ment. He had done this so many times that he could do it with his eyes closed. The man was standing facing the bridge, waiting. He was happy. The trip was accomplished, to be cherished and savored in detail and compared to other trips till next year when another would be added. He was waiting for his wife to come with the car and boat trailer, waiting with the same gratefulness to catch a glimpse of her face as he had waited long ago in an English church. There was peace in this waiting, a healing where nothing of the bigger world intruded so that when in time he would turn on the car radio he would not be crushed by the hate and despair.

"Here she is," he said. The car rumbled across the bridge, the empty trailer bouncing behind it. The trip was over. "John, go and back it down for her."

He watched them embrace; then the boy got in the car, turned it around, and backed it down. She was walking toward him with Sam, who had joined her. In his happiness he didn't notice the tightness of her face, only that she was glad to see him.

"You haven't changed," he said.

"Why would I change in two and a half days?" She put her arms around him. "You smell like a wet dog."

They loaded the boat and the gear and were off. It began to rain harder, coming down in grey sheets. The bridge rumbled under them, then they were on the highway. The boy was talking, telling about the trip from the beginning—the way they shot through the culvert under the railroad bridge and about the flock of ducks with one blue-wing teal in the midst of them. When he came to the fish he caught, the man remembered Stefan.

"How is Stefan?" he asked, interrupting the boy. He wasn't worried about him. He asked almost out of politeness. Even when she touched his arm he wasn't prepared for anything.

"He is dead," she said.

He heard the boy say "no" and his own fist crashed down on the steering wheel. The pain in his hand was the only feeling he had in the general numbness until he began to think and anger filled him against himself, against the river, against Thursday when at four-thirty he and the boy sat on a bluff hearing and feeling and trustingly celebrating like two madmen in the wine cellar of a bombed-out house. Then everything stopped. He drove on, peering through the windshield, noticing the curve in the road, an abandoned shack, a forlorn cow with her calf at her side. He marveled at himself that he could go on driving when life had lost all meaning because if Stefan was dead then God was dead also or He never had been in the first place and he had lived his own life for the past twelve years in a mental ward, hallucinating. There never had been a dialogue, a blessing and saving, a Body and Blood, and he was alone in an existential nightmare.

"There was no way I could contact you, and Jane wouldn't let me anyway," she said. "The women were in the room praying when suddenly Stefan sighed and relaxed. He was gone. He died on Thursday at about four-thirty."

Relief came with a rush and with it the accustomed and bearable seasons of joy and sadness all marching toward glory that was and is and ever shall be.

"Forgive me," he said. He began to cry.

Marjory Stoneman Douglas

Marjory Stoneman Douglas (1890–) has lived in Coconut Grove, Florida, since she moved to the state in 1915 to obtain a divorce and to become better acquainted with her father, who had moved to Miami to start the city's first morning newspaper. Although she is best known for nonfiction works like *The Everglades: River of Grass* (1947), *Hurricane* (1958), and *Florida: The Long Frontier* (1967), as well as novels like *Road to the Sun* (1951), *Freedom River* (1953), and *Alligator Crossing* (1959), readers have become more familiar with her life with the publication of the autobiographical *Marjory Stoneman Douglas: Voice of the River* (1987). They also have come to know her short stories through *Nine Florida Stories by Marjory Stoneman Douglas* (1990), published to coincide with her one-hundredth birthday on April 7, 1990. The story that follows, which appeared in *The Saturday Evening Post* (December 21, 1935), deals with a theme she has espoused for eighty years: we must stop the indiscriminate killing of birds.

In *The Everglades: River of Grass* she also wrote about the fragility of the bird population: "The killing of plume birds had continued to scandalous proportions. In New York, one millinery wholesaler alone bought two hundred thousand dollars' worth of plumes. It was not only the egrets. Bright-colored birds of every kind were trapped and sent in cages to Havana or New York. Women even wore dead mockingbirds on their overloaded hats." She authored other works about the birds of the Everglades, including the fictional "Plumes" (1930), about the rampant slaughter of birds; the nonfictional "Wings" (1931), about plume hunters; and *The Joys of Bird Watching in Florida* (1969), about the harm that pesticides can cause. Her writings, speeches, establishment of the Friends of the Everglades (with membership currently exceeding two thousand), and lobbying of powerful politicians have done much to preserve the Everglades for generations. Those who have come to know her admire her determination and perseverance to save the natural beauty of south Florida.

The bird that she wrote about in this story, the ibis, was a favorite target of plume hunters in the nineteenth and early twentieth centuries, before laws banned hunting the birds. The Everglades has three varieties of ibis: the glossy ibis, which appears black at a distance; the white ibis, which some people incorrectly call a curlew; and the wood ibis, which is the only species of stork living in North America. The protective laws passed in this century have done much to restore the ibis to its rightful place in our environment, and one can see thousands of them soaring over the Everglades in huge flocks, with their outstretched black-tipped white pinions and their extended neck and legs presenting an unforgettable scene to the lucky spectators down below.

A Flight of Ibis

Marjory Stoneman Douglas

He had found the hidden stronghold of the ibis at last. A long way off, through a break in the rampart of mangroves, beyond the saw-grass country and the country of dwarfed and ghostly cypress through which he had struggled all day, he had caught sight of a few white bodies already resting on the treetops. Now he clung to an arched mangrove root and peered out across the small lake, where, in the last shafts of sunset, the ibis in white hundreds came planing down to the branches from their far, serene courses in the sky. Exultation lifted his heart above fatigue and the dulled failure of these last years.

For the hunters of ibis meat that, salted, found a market up and down the west coast of Florida and in Cuba, had not found this place yet. He had already come upon two rookeries of egrets shot up by the plume hunters in the spring breeding season, the nests full of dead fledglings, the piles of stripped adult bodies left rotting for the buzzards and the ants. He knew well the ruthlessness of the men who made their living on the fringes of the Everglades. This was one of the last great flocks of ibis which he now stared at, almost in unbelief.

The ibis had hidden their nests carefully about this tiny lake, lost in the deepest of the mangrove forests above the slow salt-water courses that led to the Gulf. They had reared their young here safely in the spring and now returned nightly from the feeding grounds, their great black-tipped white pinions soaring stately above the lesser flocks of blue and white herons, the surviving ribands of snowy egrets.

They settled now, in the late light, the ease of flight relinquished, their bodies balanced clumsily on their awkward stork legs, their long curved beaks clapping and croaking. The mouth in Joe Harper's worn young face twitched with excitement and with hope. If he could only catch that last moment when the wings marked the violet sky with shifting patterns of curved, incredible beauty. If he only had a good camera. If he only had more than this last one roll of film. Because everything in the world depended on the pictures he would get at dawn.

Back on the more solid land at the edge of the saw grass, from the semblance of path he had hacked out in the mile-long tangle of mangrove, he sat all night by a tiny smudge fire, among screaming mosquitoes, worrying about the quality of the light at dawn, exposures and timing, distances and camera angles. These must be the greatest photographs he had ever made. He must show that man from Washington, back in Miami, that Joe Harper was still a great photographer. They had to be perfect, or he was done for. He had hardly a cent left, not just for food, but for more film. This one chance had come to him after two years of no work, of illness, of discouragement. The tiny eye of his fire was lost in the enormous dark and silence of the Everglades. He brooded over it, thinking desperately of what he had been, of the woman he had loved, who had forgotten him. He had no business to think of that any more. He had no business to think even of the face of that girl back at the Trail station whose smile had warmed him.

Three hours later it was all over. He had used up his film in a frenzy of concentration. But what shots! What beauty! At the shack that he had for two months occupied in a group of ruined buildings on high pineland, he stopped, exhausted, cooked bacon and coffee and threw himself on his cot for an hour of sleep. When he woke he stretched his sore muscles, pulled on wet boots, and in the late afternoon went out to the old road that curved for ten miles to join the Tamiami Trail by the Miller's River station. The driver of the bus from Tampa would take his film in to the photographer who had promised to develop them. The man from Washington had promised to wait for them, to send him new film if they were any good. And as the first glint of telegraph wires showed where traffic whined in the distance, he found that he could not wait to tell Mary Sue what he had discovered. He was too tired and too excited to remember that he had meant never to think of her at all.

She was standing at the gas pump, servicing a westbound car as he came up from the Old Road to the hard black surface of the Trail. The curves of her little body, under her white blouse and her clean white shorts, were lovelier to him, seen again suddenly, than the curves of wings.

She turned and smiled at him easily, and his breath caught. She was brown and sleek as a small deer. Her eyes startled him again with their clear blue, under her smooth brown hair.

Women could be the devil, but Mary Sue was—she was—"My love . . . thou hast doves' eyes"—my love—

Good Lord, he couldn't be in love with her. The thought, the sensation, stung him like a pain. He had no time for love, no place for it, he had told himself before. It was not to be thought of for a moment. It was his fatigue, or his excitement. He sat in a chair under the overhang staring at her, his thin legs stiff in their stained trousers, his torn shirt stirring in the wind that ran cool fingers over his painfully beating heart. If that bus would only come he would plunge back instantly into his solitude and sleep this thing off.

She had smiled at him over her shoulder, after the car had gone, and strolled idly out to the middle of the hard roadway that was flung straight as a sword from horizon to horizon, cutting through the distance, the ancient vastness of the unconquerable Glades. She looked east carelessly and then stared west, her hair blowing and curling a little, her lips parted. She was waiting for something, and waiting breathless and aquiver. He saw that plainly, and the panic of his sudden knowledge that he loved her was shot with the pain of jealousy that she was looking that way for something, somebody, not himself.

Henry Martin racketed suddenly from eastward, curving his motorcycle up to the steps. He had been a good friend of Joe's from the beginning, when he had trudged up here, all the way from Miami, to ask how you got into the deep Glades. He was the best of the three or four Trail police, careful about his work, cheerfully ignoring the pettiness of this job in contrast to the better days when he had been an engineer and a builder of this very Trail. He lifted his cap from his graying hair and dropped heavily into the chair by Joe's.

"Got your pictures, did you?" he said heartily.

"How could you tell?" Joe said, startled.

"You look as if you'd seen a miracle."

"Maybe I have," Joe said slowly. But his eyes were on Mary Sue.

It was Leroy Pennock she was watching for. She had turned suddenly and walked toward them, her face rosy, her brilliant eyes not quite seeing them, turned, the way a woman will, from something that has brought her heart to confusion, as Pennock roared up in that car of his, his black hair flying, his black eyes shining like drops of ink. She stood looking up as he spoke to her swiftly, tossed a careless hand toward her father, kicked his gas and was gone.

Henry Martin spat, once, among the marigolds. Leroy Pennock! Good heavens, she couldn't—

The heavy grinding bellow to westward was the bus from Tampa. Joe remembered his film and walked out to the driver. He was a good sort. He tucked the small roll that was Joe's future and his desperate hope carelessly into his pocket. . . . Sure, he knew the place; went right by it to his supper. . . . Sure. . . . Okay. Glad to. And Joe was left standing in the road, watching the bus become a spot in the shimmering steely distance.

The lonely length of the road reached west to a towering copper-and-brass sunset, east to the lavender smudge of night. Mary Sue's heels were tapping briskly in the lighted kitchen, and the smell of ham sizzling was potent over the night wind heavy with wet-leaf scents. Henry Martin asked him to supper. Hunger scoured him, but he dreaded seeing Mary Sue under the light. He dreaded his own emotion. He had had too much of it.

But the good food put new life into him, and Mr. Jennings' hearty interest over the telephone brought hope back with a swelling warmth. The man was enthusiastic about Joe's discovery of the ibis colony. By all means he must go back and work there. No matter how the first pictures came out, he said he would send out new film and flashlights for night work. What the Audubon Societies wanted was evidence of the ibis shooting. None of the people would testify. His supplies would be out by bus tomorrow, with prints of the pictures.

Joe turned from the telephone. Now he could go to work. It was all in the world that he wanted.

But he sat out in front beside Henry Martin again, dismayed at his own jealous concern about Mary Sue. Now, of all times, he needed not to think about her. But she had come down from her room upstairs in a clean little blue dress, with a white frill about her throat, her hair brushed and shining, her eyes absent. Leroy Pennock drove up presently, and she went out and got into his car. The man's dark careless face grinned over at him and at Henry Martin.

Henry Martin uttered a word or two like a growl in his throat, strode out after her and put his heavy-booted foot on the rusted running board.

"Just going for a little ride," Pennock said easily.

"You get her back here by ten o'clock or I'll start telephoning," her father said. They both had to watch silently as the car ground off.

When Henry Martin stumped back to his chair, his face was dark. "I don't like it," he said. "She's got no business going out with that guy. His father was killed in that battle two gangs of plume hunters fought down at Cuthbert Lake years ago. This one's got a boat he takes fishing parties out in, down at Everglades. Nothing definite against him, of course, or I'd turn him in. But it's the blood. They think they own this country."

Joe sat and worried, as helpless as he. Just like a woman, he told himself scornfully, taking up with a bad lot just because he was wild and good-looking and dangerous, worrying her father, getting into goodness knows what messes, the thoughtless little—But her face, with its gentle mouth and lovely eyes, the curving way of her arms, the little gay smile she had had for him, stayed with him all the dark miles back to his shack, and kept him from sleeping. And he needed his sleep.

MARY SUE MARTIN

Mary Sue was glad that Joe Harper had stayed to supper again, because, perhaps, her father would not notice her slipping out. She was going to meet Leroy up the road, so that her father could not be horrid again. Leroy was going to take her to a dance, and nothing, nothing was going to stop her. The two men could sit at the table under the light, poring over those photographs and charts, and talking about birds all they wanted to. They had nothing to do with this exultation that stirred in her, thinking of Leroy's dark burning face. No boy had ever made her feel like this, walking back from school with her in Miami. This was a man, sultry and exciting, and yet it was as if he were not a man but a force, making her feel powerful and beautiful, making her a woman.

The heels of her best slippers clicked on the black hard roadway, and she was not afraid any more of the dark, running to meet him. Those were his lights coming, she was sure. The lights picked her out suddenly and he came near and stopped. His head was against the stars. She couldn't help the little cry she gave at his sudden laugh. Then she was in the car beside him, with the night rushing away behind. Everything else but this dark excitement flowed away with it.

His long arm lay on the wheel and she felt his shoulder tinglingly beside hers. She could have driven on like this for hours. But they stopped presently at the long, lighted frame shack by the roadway, with music pouring out, loud and gay, and the heads of men and girls under the lights. She was shy about going in with him, because she had never been here before, but his hand was on her bare arm and all the girls turned to look at him. The girls wore bright cotton dresses and earrings and rouge, and stared at her. When he swung her onto the dance floor she trembled a little, and he felt it and laughed down at her with his eyes brilliant. "Purtiest gal here, sugar," he said, and she felt her face flushing.

He didn't, she had to admit, dance very well, or else she was not used to his kind of dancing. But his hands upon her were vibrant and it didn't matter. She liked it better when they sat behind a table in the shadows of the porch. He poured drinks out of a bottle he carried, and laughed when she made a face over hers. Men came around and slapped him on the shoulder, staring down at her. A girl in red put her hand on his arm, but he shrugged it off, his eyes returning to her face.

"Purtiest gal here," he was saying again. "Your pappy don't like me much. But we foxed him. You stick with me, sugar. I'll show you a time." She laughed a little, loving to see what spark she had lit in such a man.

They sat for a long time without dancing again. His face was near hers. He was talking about himself, about the money he made in the winter, about how fast his boat was, about the things tourist women said to him. They liked him all right, those rich Yankee women. There was one he bet he could have married, rich as mud. But he wouldn't have had her, not for all her dough, old dog-face thing. What he wanted was a nice sweet little gal like her, with her little hands and her cute, purty face. Little sugar baby. He caught her hands and tried to pull her to him. But there were too many people looking. She couldn't bear to have him kiss her like that. He was drinking a lot, but it didn't frighten her. He made her feel that she could do anything with him.

"You're my girl, ain't you, sugar?" he insisted. "Go on. Say it with your sweet li'l' lips."

She laughed and shook her head at him. "Don't be so silly," she said. "Why, I don't know you hardly at all."

"You got another boy friend, that it? I know. That thin guy that hangs out around your place. I could break him in two."

"Oh, no. That's only Joe Harper. He doesn't—I don't care a thing about him. He doesn't hardly look at me."

"I bet you're crazy about him," he went on, clutching her wrist. He was angry with her. His voice was loud.

"No, honest I'm not. And he isn't. All he cares about are his old birds."

He poured his tumbler full again from the bottle and looked at her, sidelong. "What you mean, birds?"

"Ibis. Things like that. He found a place full of them where nobody's been before. That's all he talks about."

"What's he know about it? He don't know nothing. Just a dumb Yankee. Where's he think he's found any birds?"

"Oh, I don't know. Somewhere west of Pinecrest. He says he's seen hundreds of them. Nobody can get there but him. Honest, that's all he cares about, and taking pictures."

"Any time I see you talking to him, I'm gonna walk right up an' bus' him in the face. Was it east of Chokoloskee, he said?"

"No, I don't think so. North of that, I guess. I don't know. I didn't notice."

"Birds," Leroy said contemptuously. "His birds, hey? Bet it's that ol' lake up by that ol' egret rookery. Why, I bet I—" He stopped and looked at her with his lids narrowed. His breath was heavy on her face, and a little pinprick of uneasiness came to her. Perhaps he had drunk a little too much.

He dragged her up to dance with him again, singing the tune in a wild, high voice, shouting at other couples over her head. He held her so tight that her face was pressed against his shirt front. And suddenly she didn't like it at all. She felt hot, and horrid. Her dress was crumpled, and the unaccustomed sip of drink she had had burned in her face. These girls around her were cheap and tawdry, laughing with shrieks back at Leroy's bawled witticisms.

Back at the table, watching him pour the last of his bottle into his glass and drinking it, she said quickly, "It's getting late. I want to go home now."

He turned his heavy-lidded face to her, squeezing her arm. "What for? Ain't you havin' a good time?"

"Yes, of course. But it's hot here. Let's go out and ride."

She hated this place. It had changed all that lovely feeling she had had. She didn't feel queenly any more, only cheap.

At first she thought it was better, riding back in the cool dark.

"I got so hot in there," she explained. "You don't mind, do you?"

He grinned back at her, throwing a heavy arm over her shoulders and pulling her over to him. She sat quiet, not protesting. But suddenly he stopped the car in the shadows and caught her closer, kissing her hard. She struggled, turning her face away. She hated his reeking breath, hated his mouth, hated the released savagery of his arms.

"You start this car right now and take me home, Leroy Pennock," she said breathlessly. She was frightened now. His arms were like iron, crushing her. This wasn't what she had wanted. "You stop," she said breathlessly again. He had torn her dress at the shoulder. He was savage and clumsy. She hit him in the face with her clenched fist. The lights of a car, coming at them, stopped him short.

"You little spit cat," he said viciously. "No gal's gonna high-hat me. Who you think you are, anyway?"

"You take me home," she said shortly, trembling with rage and with fright. "I mean it."

When he stopped before her own door, he grinned at her evilly. "Get out," he said. "I might have known you was a stuck-up. You and your pappy, thinkin' you're too good for us. You watch out. That's all I got to say. No gal's gonna do that to me twice."

She went in slowly, hating the feeling of being pawed over, hating the feeling of cheapness and of disillusion.

Her father had left the light burning over the table. She could hear him snoring in his bed upstairs. Joe Harper's pictures were on the table. She picked them up, trying to calm herself. They were so beautiful, so cool and clear and fine. The birds were marvelous. They made her feel worse than ever—dirty and miserable.

Just about dawn she woke with a chilling memory. She had told him about Joe Harper's birds.

She lay rigid, trying not to feel that she had told him what she had no business to tell, trying to calm herself and go back to sleep. But she could not forget the quick alertness in his eyes.

She got up quickly and went to the window. The dawn was just coming up, pale and exquisite, over the far black trees. Herons were flying far beyond there. Little birds, nearer, were stirring and crying in the swamp bushes. Joe Harper wasn't anything to her. He hadn't told her not to tell. But she had told. She had opened her silly mouth and said everything she knew, to a man who even then she should have known was not to be trusted. She felt like a traitor to something deep within her, something her father represented, something she should never have forgotten. Made her feel like a queen, did he? The more fool she, the fool.

She began moving quickly, in a tumult of self-accusation. She pulled on a shirt and worn trousers and high boots, grabbed her old straw hat and went hastily downstairs. She left a note for her father by the coffee-pot. He would have to get his own breakfast. It didn't matter if he didn't understand.

Outside, in the sweet freshness of the early wind, the old roadway was still shadowy. A sheet of tiny clouds to eastward was turning pure gold. She ran a little, cooling her face in the young air.

When she came silently down the grass-grown road that ran between high pine trees, past the shacks that had once been the village of Pinecrest, the morning was brilliant all about her. All the greens of bush and tree and grass were brilliant, dripping with heavy dew. Even the big white cobwebs were aglitter with dew, and the sky looked newly washed. Joe Harper would think she was crazy, coming down here like this, but once she told him, she would feel better. It was fine, anyway, all this open, silent, ancient country. There had been flock after flock of herons going over, and the whiteness of egrets was something to take your breath away.

She came upon him suddenly, crouching over a little fire with a frying pan in his hand, beside his shack. The bacon smell was delicious. She said gaily, "Is breakfast ready?" and was astonished at the look on his face as he turned.

"Mary Sue, what on earth—" he was saying, standing stupidly with the frying pan in his hand.

Her gaiety left her. Facing his direct and eager look, she was miserable. It was going to be a lot harder to tell him than she had thought.

"I had to come and tell you," she said uncomfortably. "I don't know what I was thinking of. But last night when I was out with Leroy Pennock, he found out—I mean, I told him without thinking. About your birds. I mean, where they are."

He stood absolutely still. It didn't seem to do any good, telling him. She didn't feel a bit better.

His face was slowly changing, becoming fixed, more quiet, more formal. "I hope you had a good time," he said politely.

She felt perfectly dreadful. "I didn't," she said. "It was horrid. I should never have gone. But whatever happened, I shouldn't have told him. I see that quite clearly. He's not to be trusted. I—I can't tell you how mean I feel."

"Do you think he—could tell where the place was, from your description?"

"I'm afraid—he seemed to have been there once before. Oh, Joe, I'm so sorry. If anything happens it will be all my fault. I can't tell you how badly—"

He wasn't listening any more. He was frowning, thinking hard. She stood watching him humbly. It was right that he shouldn't say anything to make her feel better. She saw suddenly that it was childish to expect that just saying you were sorry made everything all right. When you were grown-up you had to be responsible.

He stooped to finish frying the bacon.

"There's some bread in the house, in the box on the shelf," he said. "Will you get it, please? And another cup. You haven't had your breakfast."

She sat on a box, choking down a sandwich and a cup of black coffee. He was eating hastily. When he had finished he went into the house and came out with a revolver in a holster which he buckled to his belt, slung a camera and knapsack over his back. "I'd better be getting down there," he said, wrapping up the bread and picking up the water bottle. "Thanks for telling me, Mary Sue."

There was a kind of scorn underneath his politeness. She could have cried, staring up at him. But she deserved it. When he turned away she got up and stared after him. There was his machete. He ought to have that, and the rest of the bacon. And the coffeepot and coffee. He was striding off directly, as if he could not wait to get down there.

She went into the house and looked around her hastily. There was a sack with a bag of grits in it. She put in the coffeepot, everything else she could think of, slung it over her shoulder and hurried after him. "I'm coming, too, Joe," she said. "You can't carry everything. You oughtn't to be alone down there."

"There's nothing you can do," he said, turning to look at her. "It's a long hard way. You haven't any business—"

"It doesn't matter," she said. "You'll need somebody. Or I can come back and get help when I've learned the way. I promise you I won't be a nuisance. I've tramped around here with father. I—it's the only thing I can do to make up for it."

His face was set, eying her. She must show him she wasn't useless—she must. "All right," he said abruptly. "But you won't be able to keep up."

When he set off again she walked behind, humbly, at his heels.

The sack on her back was heavy, the machete heavy in her hand. The first mile or two of going was through the fringe of the pineland, among the waist-high palmetto. Rocks were uneven under her boots. She had to scramble to keep up with him. After that they threaded an open swale of saw grass, over dried mud that gave soggily in places. There was no shade here and the mounting sun beat down brassily on her head and shoulders. The saw grass was often higher than her head, shutting off the air, and the edges of the tawny stuff cut like glass when they brushed against her arms. She rolled her shirt sleeves down and learned to strike at tufts of it with her machete.

She must be sure to recognize every clump of palmetto, every island of tangled buttonwood or cypress, that they skirted. Her face stung with sweat and sunburn.

But by the fourth mile she was hitting a more regular pace behind him, adjusting the weight of the sack more easily. And she felt better because it was hard. She would prove to him that she wasn't useless.

By noon they were in the dwarf cypress and the going was cooler, if more difficult. Mosquitoes hung about in tormenting clouds, and they both swished branches about their faces. The white cypress trunks stood in a foot of clear water over uneven limestone. The tiny leaves were a mist of green all about, with air plants fuzzy on the branches. He had broken limbs and marked stumps before, so that she could see the trail ahead, or it would have been utterly confusing.

In places, the taller cypress made an impenetrable jungle which had to be skirted. She made additional marks with her machete, growing to hate the ghostly branches, the clumsy footage. The open spaces, for all their heat, were better than that. Here and there from the upper branches, egrets whiter than the cypress disentangled themselves from boughs and flew off with faint cries. Once she saw an ibis standing with clumsy bent knees at the very top of a tree no bigger than itself, its great body balancing ridiculously. But when it slid off into the air and the great wings spread and caught the wind it soared, higher and higher, so easily, so perfectly that she laughed with pleasure at the fine free thing.

He heard her and stopped to look back, as if he had almost doubted she was there.

"When we get through this we'll rest," he said, looking at her intently. Her face was streaked with sweat and dirt and dried blood where she had killed mosquitoes. There was an oozing saw-grass cut on one cheek. Her shirt was torn, her boots were soaked with water and mud. She knew exactly what she must look like. He was a strong and competent figure, going on ahead of her. It seemed to her that she had never seen him before.

When they came to the edge of the cypress, there was more saw grass and a green island of palmettos glittering in the sun beyond. On the south there was a place where they could sit down and look widely out over the sea of saw grass before them, blowing like a tawny sea under the plum-colored cloud shadows, reaching far to the sky edge on each side. He built a little fire and boiled coffee. It was nice, there in the wind, under the high impact of the sun. He gave her a little water to wash her face with and watched her gravely.

"I take that back about your not being able to keep up," he said. She couldn't help laughing with pleasure. They were less like strangers, sitting there together for a moment, silent in all that glittering, open world of sunny silence, savoring the salt and grass-sweet taste of the wind. She liked his grave brown face and his quietness.

But they couldn't rest there long. The worst of the way was all before them. They would be lucky if they reached it by nightfall, he said. She had had no idea it was so far. She struck out after him with a twinge of dismay. But she would see it through. She must. She couldn't possibly stop or go back now.

It was the hardest four hours she had ever spent in her life. The sun was cruel. There were places where the mosquitoes were so bad that if he hadn't shown her how to plaster her face with mud, she thought she would go crazy. Sometimes they had to jump from grassy tussock to tussock, out of mud that caught stickily at their heels. Sometimes they had to fight their way through almost impenetrable cypress, where the trail he had cut before was almost obliterated already by tough and wiry vines. The sack weighed heavier and heavier upon her aching shoulders. He had taken the machete, giving her the water bottle, cutting and slashing his way just ahead of her. And the open country amid the merciless saw grass did not seem much easier. There were times when it seemed to her that if she could only lie down right in the mud and cry, it would be everything she could ever ask of life. But she managed somehow—just somehow—to keep on behind the relentless, unfailing stride of his long legs. He was, she had begun to think, amazing.

They came out, late in the afternoon, amid a fringe of young mangrove trees arching their young roots on drier ground. Here was the campfire he had built before, and the dried armloads of branches and saw grass he had rested on. When he saw her face this time he gave a little exclamation of concern. "I'm crazy to have let you come," he said. "Here, drop everything. Lie down here. You're completely exhausted." He mopped her face with a wet handkerchief.

"I'm not," she said stoutly. "I did keep up." But it was delicious to get her boots off and drink a cup of lukewarm water from the bottle. They cooked bacon and ate hungrily.

The sunset light was staining all the sky over their heads. The mangrove leaves were glowing greener and greener. And toward that secret place, still behind the rampant mangroves at their backs, across the whole surge of the sky, the ibis, in long orderly ranks, were soaring home. It seemed to her then, for all her exhaustion, that she had never known anything like the exaltation and the whiteness of those wings.

"You see why I want pictures of that," he murmured, watching them with her.

"They'll be marvelous. There's nothing like them," she said in awe. They spoke softly, their heads together, as if nothing must disturb that vast flow of beauty, sweeping over them. The sky was ice-blue between great streaks and shafts of rose color, and the whiteness of the moving wings was the whiteness of a sea of foam.

"I'm going on now," he said suddenly. "There's a place I fixed where I can watch. You'll have a fire and you can sleep here. I'm going to take you back in the morning. I don't know what on earth your father will think of my letting you in for this."

She looked up at him slowly. He wasn't scornful now. He was worried about her more than about his birds. It was good to have followed him. This was the kind of man it was good to follow.

"Please," she said humbly, "I want to go there with you, too, Joe. I know I've been a nuisance. But I want to be with you there. I'm not tired. Please."

His face quivered a little with some feeling she could not quite understand. His eyes made her feel shy and curiously glad.

"You're a great girl," he said. "I didn't think there was a girl in the world like you. You've got a brave heart. Come along. I thought, the first time I found this place, that I'd like to—show it to you."

That mile or two of mangrove was the worst of all. You couldn't walk, you couldn't climb. The great roots arched as high as the lowest branches, with ooze and mud below. They moved forward along the way Joe had cut before by a kind of crawl, clinging to roots, swinging on branches. The tough interlaced boughs made a kind of darkness, darker because of twilight coming swiftly over the unseen sky. Her arms ached at the sockets with swinging and pulling; her legs ached at the hip joints and all along the muscles with balancing and jumping. He was behind her and beside her, holding her steady, catching and bracing her. She felt under her grip the hardness of his shoulder muscles. They rested against each other with equal panting breaths.

But there was light ahead at last, and the shine of water. They sat at the very edge on a great bough, leaning against tree trunks, hardly noticing that they still clutched each other.

The birds were there, masses of white, resting and stirring all along the face of the massed mangrove opposite. Their croaking, snapping cries filled the silence. In the last light the whiteness of their heavy bodies was like massed white fruit weighing down the branches to the water's edge.

Joe hung his camera and all his dunnage on the boughs about them and tried to make her comfortable. She wasn't tired any more. The air was cool. It was enough to rest, half against his shoulder, and listen to the settling birds and watch the rosy light diminish and the stars come out thinly. There was even a moon that gave out a white light that stirred in frost and silver on the water stirring under the marching wind.

They talked softly, as if suddenly there was everything in the world to be talked about, and they did not notice how often and how intimately they laughed. He told her all about himself, about the hopes he had had, and the long years of failure, and she murmured little words, consoling, eager words, by his ear. When they were silent, they were happy.

The thing that they had forgotten, that had seemed utterly shut out in the darkling place, happened suddenly. There was a series of muffled crashings at an unseen point across the lake. Birds stirred sleepily. Men's voices shouted. Almost before Joe's muscles stiffened beside her she realized that the thing she had only vaguely dreaded, for which she was responsible, had come.

There was a light at the other end of the lake.

"They've got a boat," Joe said to her harshly. "There must be a creek there that I didn't know about."

That was what Leroy had meant. She sat there stiff with horror. It was a place that he really had known.

There were two boats, or more. They could hear men talking plainly.

"Got the flares ready?" someone shouted. "There's hundreds of them over there!"

From the black wall of trees opposite, a ruddy blaze of light flared up. Dark figures of men lifted blazing branches. Two big flashlights swept white lanes along the branches, picking out the whiteness of the resting birds. A few roused wings swept by them. There were croakings and stirrings, sleepy flappings of great wings.

"They're dazzled. They can't see," Joe said. He scrambled to a footing on the limb, jerked at his revolver. The shots echoed over the lake. He had shot high, and his raging voice shouted, "You leave those birds alone! I've got you covered! Get out of here!"

There was a chorus of shouts, laughter and catcalls. Somebody shot a rifle high to the right of them, and the bullet cracked against a limb.

"It's that Harper!" a voice shouted. "We kin shoot too!" The flares from the farthest boat were right up against the bird-laden branches. A dark figure clubbed a bird that fell without a sound. Joe shot again, into the water. Three rifles answered.

When he felt Mary Sue's shoulder he started, as if he had forgotten her. "I can't shoot," he muttered. "They'll get you."

Mary Sue was sobbing dryly with resentment and horror. They were swinging their clubs constantly now. The birds were stupid in the light. The flares moved calmly along the tree front, and the birds, by the dozen, were dying and falling.

"Never mind! Shoot them! Please shoot!" Mary Sue cried, but Joe's hand was firm on her shoulder.

"I can't," he said hoarsely. "Even if they knew you were here. I haven't got many shots. It's hopeless."

"You've got flash cartridges," she said suddenly. "That'll scare them. Quick! They won't know!"

He jerked blindly at his knapsack, fumbling amid his apparatus. "By gosh, yes," he muttered. "I'd forgotten. . . . Here, hold this. . . . Steady now. You do it like this. . . . I've got plenty. When I say 'go.' Wait now. Keep steady. Keep steady."

He was crouching again beside her, working at his camera. One boat with the rifles was drifting nearer. The sounds of the clubs, of falling birds, of crashing branches, were loud beyond.

"Hold it over your head. High up. High up and steady. Lord, if we get this, we'll—" He called suddenly, "I warned you! You'll pay for this!" And, "Now, Mary Sue, give it to them."

The ghastly crackling light from the flash she held high over her head flared out over the whole lake. She saw the staring eyes, the white faces, the crouching figures of the men in the nearest boat, the figures in the other, their clubs held high, their hands full of birds, in one enormous, blue-white revelation. When, in the next moment, the light was swallowed in blinded darkness the lake was full of the men's startled shouts.

"Look out! What is it? Hey, get back! Get out!" They were falling over their oars in blinded confusion. The clubbing stopped.

"Here, quick!" Joe thrust a cartridge gun into her hand again. A boat was quite near now, by the sounds. When Joe said, "Shoot, Mary," and the weird light leaped again and Joe's revolver cracked, she was looking straight across into Leroy Pennock's aghast face. In the blinding dark again, somebody shouted in sheer panic. Joe's bullet had smashed into an arm.

"One more, honey! Give 'em one more!" Joe cried into her ear, and she held the flash a third time, and in the white explosion saw them frantically splashing back toward the place from which they had come.

When the lake was still again, and full of moonlight, and Joe had finished adjusting his camera, he hung his knapsack calmly on the branch, sat down beside her and caught her to him with a steady arm.

"Don't cry, baby; don't cry so. It's all right. We scared 'em. And, boy, what pictures I got. Not beautiful, darlin,' but oh, what evidence. Every one of their faces clear and sharp, and the clubs, and the dead birds. Don't cry. Oh, honey, what a girl you are."

His shoulder was beyond words dear and comfortable and consoling. There was no man in the world like him—no man. When she lifted her face from his arm, in the good darkness, he stopped talking suddenly and kissed her. He kissed her until she forgot everything but his nearness and that he loved her and that loving him was the best thing she could ever do.

Rubylea Hall

Rubylea Hall (1910–73) was born in Greenwood, Florida, and earned a degree at Florida State University in Tallahassee. She taught in Florida public schools from 1927 to 1932, worked with the Federal Emergency Relief Administration in 1932–33, at Camp Blanding in Florida in 1943–44, and in the Chemistry-Pharmacy Library at the University of Florida from 1944 to 1949. In 1959 she became director of consumer services for Q-Tips, Inc., in New York.

Among her Florida novels were three that dealt with historical themes. *The Great Tide* (1947), which won the Bohnenberger Award of the Southeastern Conference of Libraries for the best novel of the South in 1947–48, was about the doomed Florida town of St. Joseph during the 1830s and 1840s; St. Joseph, now a ghost town in Gulf County southeast of Tallahassee, was where Florida's first constitution was written, in 1838–39. Known as the wickedest city in the Southeast, the city was devastated by a yellow fever epidemic, a hurricane, and a tidal wave. Her *Flamingo Prince* (1954) dealt with the great Seminole leader, Osceola. Her *God Has a Sense of Humor* (1960) pictured two sides of a family growing up in the Florida Panhandle around 1900.

The following story, "Panther," comes from her book *Davey* (1951), the story of a young boy who resembled, according to Hall's note at the beginning of the book, "one of the many boys I knew during the years I was a backwoods schoolteacher in remote sections of West Florida, where malaria, hookworm, poverty, and ignorance constituted my greatest problems." The story is appropriate today because of concern throughout Florida for the panther. The last of the big cats east of the Mississippi River, the Florida panther is a large, long-tailed, light-brown cat that can reach a maximum length of seven feet. It resembles the mountain lion or cougar of the American West and is larger than the bobcat, which has a shorter tail and a spotted coat. Although panthers seldom attack humans, the big cats do hunt birds and mammals, especially deer, and live in and around the Everglades. Because motorists speeding along Alligator Alley between Naples and Fort Lauderdale have maimed several panthers that were crossing the road, authorities have built under heavily traveled roads panther tunnels that they hope will protect the animals.

Despite being placed on the Federal Endangered Species list in 1973 and protected by the Florida Panther Act of 1979, which makes the killing of a panther a felony, the number of panthers in Florida has declined to around fifty today. Each panther needs between 150 and 300 square miles of territory, and the state's rapid development makes the panther's domain smaller each year. Scientists still have hopes of protecting the panthers in south Florida and of returning some of them to their former range in north Florida.

Panther!

Rubylea Hall

MONDAY MORNING, bright and early, Pa had everyone on the place in the canefield picking up the freshly plowed cane stubbles from last year's crop which had frozen during the winter and were now a rotting, soured mass.

Jim was now using a turn-plow on the part of the field they had cleared, turning the rich soil once more before opening the furrows into which the cane would be dropped when they began planting tomorrow. If Pa had a disk to cut the soil and cane stubble, it would save a lot of back-breaking toil, but he argued that that was what he had so many younguns for.

Between the land where the potatoes were to be planted, and the runner peanut fields, where the hogs would be fattened, Tom and Amos were straightening the sagging wire fence, making it strong so that when it came time to turn the hogs into the field, they could not break through to the sweet potatoes.

"Pa!" Tom shouted. "This here fence is gotta have new posts. Ever' time we pull on 'em, they keep crackin' off. They're plumb rotten!"

Pa laid down his rake and crossed to the potato patch to examine the posts. Joe, keeping ahead of the younguns in plowing up the stubbles, stuck his plow in the ground and joined Pa at the fence.

"Shore could use some new posts, awright," Joe agreed, shaking one and looking down the long line where others wobbled dangerously. "Them hogs'll tear this down 'fore you kin say scat."

"They done that in several places last year," Amos reminded.

"Guess mebby you better start cuttin' some of them young cypress trees up the pond there next to the road," Pa agreed, mopping the sweat from his face and neck with a dingy cloth he took from his hip pocket. "They's a lot in that second hollow whut's the right size."

By the middle of the afternoon, most of the field was cleared of the stubbles, and Pa, figuring it would be best to wait until morning before opening the seed-cane beds, told Joe to take Tom and Amos and Davey and go cut the cypress fence posts.

On his way to the wagon-shed to get the crosscut saw, Davey stopped by the mule trough to wash the black soil off his face and arms, sticking his head quickly into the trough and wetting his wiry hair, which he plastered down with his hands, the cool water running down his neck and soaking his dirty shirt.

"Go git Pa's twelve-gage an' some shells, Davey," Joe said, beginning to draw a bucket of fresh water. "I'll git the saw. I heered a gobbler out that way 'tother mornin'. . . an' we might accidentally come 'crost 'im."

Davey ran toward the house, excited at the thought of finding a big turkey gobbler. There had not been one around in years, for Joe's and Jim's constant hunting had driven them farther into the river swamp, but one could never tell when they might venture back to the pond land. Each winter, the older boys usually managed to kill one or two back in the swamp, but never this close to the house.

He took the shotgun off its rack above the head of Pa's bed, thinking how he had always wanted to find a wild turkey and kill it; many times he had pictured himself coming home lugging a twenty-pounder, much to the astonishment of everyone on the place. Filling his pockets with shells from the sack hanging on the bedpost, he thought of the only time he had ever seen one when he had been by himself down by the river.

He had been on his way to see Mr. Ackry and had stopped at the big rock to rest a while, his thoughts following the swift flowing water as now and then he picked up a limestone rock and hurled it in midstream, listening to the splash and watching the circles of ripples. Nothing had been farther from his mind than a flock of turkeys. For some time he had been hearing the slight rustling of dry leaves back in the sandy gully, but had attributed it to squirrels in search of food. And then he had become aware of a contented "peep" now and then . . . like the turkeys at home made when they were feeding.

His heart had jumped and he had sat petrified, afraid to move, for he knew what it was; and they were coming straight toward him, on their way to the river for water. Clutching the lime rock tightly in his hand, he had waited, scarcely breathing, until they came into sight, picking up the pine mass that had fallen from the pine cones on the trees above. There had been five hens and a huge gobbler, not one of them aware of his presence, for the wind had been blowing off them toward him.

He had continued to sit there without moving so much as a hair until they were within thirty feet of him and then he had let go with the rock, directly at the big gobbler who at that moment had started to scrape his wings on the ground, bushing his brownish feathers and spreading his tail. Before he could bat an eye, the frightened hens and the wounded gobbler, with varied squawks of alarm, fled up the bank of the gully and ran like deer through the undergrowth.

Grabbing a cypress limb, he had gone in pursuit, hoping against hope that he could catch up with the one he had wounded. Turkeys had gone in every direction, and he had swung once at the big gobbler before it managed to get off the ground, its huge wings flapping thunderously as it gathered altitude and then disappeared like a streak of light to the safety of the other side of the river. He had been amazed that a bird so large could fly so swiftly. Heartsick because he had not had a gun with him, he had stood quietly listening to each of the hens flap her wings and take to the air. Later Jim and Amos had hunted the flock down and killed one of the hens.

He trotted down the lane to catch up with Joe and the other boys. No one had ever seen the gobbler again, and he had worried for a long time that the rock might have wounded him to such an extent that he had later died. It would have been best to have let him go free, since the blow had not stunned him enough to keep him from flying away.

Joe took the shotgun from Davey, loaded it, and threw the safety. He laughed, "Give a purty to git a peek at that critter. He sounded like a big 'un."

"Maybe he's my old gobbler," Davey said, "—the one I hit with the rock that time."

"Reckon it wun't one from Ma's bunch strayed off an' got lost?" Amos asked.

"Not likely. Wild turkeys sound diffrunt. Anyway, he'd come back 'fore now."

"I heard tell o' tame turkeys turnin' wild," Tom replied, "when a wild hen comes pokin' 'round. He jus' keeps follern 'er an' goes on off to the swamps."

"Sure do wish these swamp turkeys 'ud mix with some tame 'uns!" Joe said. "Them kind ain't so hard to git close to, bein' part tame. But these we got 'round here go like a streak of lightnin,' an' if a feller ain't there when they come off the roost, he's lucky iffen he ever gits a peek at one."

"That shore was a big bunch what walked up on me that day," Davey replied. "I thought they was buzzards at first . . . till the old gobbler strutted his wings."

Joe laughed. "I done kilt more buzzards than I kin shake a stick at, thinkin' they was turkeys. Sometime they act jest like a wild turkey, an' when you're huntin', expectin' a big gobbler any moment, you jest shoot first an' ask questions after'ard. Iffen you stop to think, that critter'll be a mile away 'fore you make up yuh mind."

"Whut I'd like to see," Amos said, "is some of them bucks Alvey claims his dogs run up back in December. He kilt one, but that's all anybody ever seen."

"They's plenty deer down that river," Joe replied. "I allers see several does with fawn . . . jest when I cain't shoot 'em. But then Alvey claims hit's not good to kill does . . . that 'fore long there won't be none a'tall."

"Doe tastes better' n buck," Tom asserted.

Joe stopped and looked about him, running an expert eye over the various clusters of young cypress bordering the road. "Guess we might as well start right here," he said, turning off the road. "Y'all look out for rattlers and moccasins. This is a good place fer 'em."

Davey watched the ground as he made his way through the tufts of wire-grass and palmetto clumps to the edge of the marshy land where the cypress were. Behind them lay the dark and gloomy swamp that bordered the northern edge of the pond.

"Reckon these cypress is as old as folks claim?" Amos questioned, looking at the silvery bark and spindly limbs just beginning to put out a fuzz of green.

"You ain't knowed a bunch like this to git grown, have you? Long as I kin remember these been just this same size," Joe replied.

"Teacher says they grow fast the first few years an' then they stop," Davey contributed. "They don't grow but a' inch ever' thousand years. Some of them big 'uns back in the swamp been here two hundred thousand years. . . ."

"Two hundred thousand years!" Tom scoffed. "The world ain't that old!"

Davey broke a water lily and sniffed its pungent odor. "One inch in ever' thousand years . . . an' some of them trees is fifteen feet thick. Figger it out for y'self . . . iffen you can. They been here since all this part of the world was covered with water . . . that's why them knees is growin' around;

they're the tree's lungs. They stick up out of the water and send air down to the roots. That's why cypress kin grow in water 'thout dyin.'"

Tom snorted, but Joe interrupted him, "Sounds reasonable to me," he said thoughtfully. "They's somethin' strange 'bout 'em . . . an' I shore ain't never seen a cypress tree git grown." He grasped one end of the saw while Amos took the other and they began to saw.

"Jes' think how many thousand years you fellers sawin' down." Tom sneered, grinning at Davey.

Joe chuckled. "We gotta have fence posts an' these kind don't rot so fast in this dirt we got around here. Anyway, they's plenty."

Davey sat on a stump, his bare toes dangling in the shallow water, and gave over to his flighty imagination, the steady hum of the saw like soothing music to his ears. He thought of the Indian story he had read once, the one about the little Indian boy who had gone hunting without his dogs. The sight of the towering cypress reminded him of it, for it had been cypress trees the boy had told his arrows to grow in to. That was how Indian lore explained the presence of the huge trees.

The little Indian had shut his dogs up and told his mother to watch the feather hanging on the wall, that if it turned green he was in trouble and she was to turn his dogs out.

Davey became the Indian boy, seeking his way through the great pine forests of Florida in search of game until suddenly, out of nowhere, a pack of wolves descended upon him. He quickly climbed a tree, but the wolves fell to cutting it down with their long white teeth. Just before it toppled over, he sprang to the branches of another tree, but the wolves cut that one down too.

In the meantime his mother had gone to sleep and forgotten the importance of watching the feather, which had turned a brilliant green. The dogs were frantic, rearing and barking, beside themselves with fear for their master who, not watching in which direction he was jumping, was moving closer to the edge of the pine wood toward the water where there were no tall trees.

When he saw there were no more trees, and the wolves were working on the one he was in, he suddenly remembered the ancient legend that some day a young chief would be born who would shoot arrows into the ground and a silver forest would spring up about him. Trembling with fear, he reached for an arrow, fitted it to his bow, pulled back on the stout thong, and let go. The arrow whistled as it sped through the air to the ground a few feet from the wolves.

"Grow, grow, my arrow; grow into a tall silver tree!" he cried the magic words. And instantly a silvery-looking tree sprang to life just as the one he was in began toppling. He leaped to safety, but the wolves began whacking it down. Due to its great width, it took them much longer. He fired another arrow into the ground and there was another tree. At last he was forced to shoot his arrows into the water, and much to his amazement, up came the tree, much more beautiful than the others had been.

Springing into the branches of this one as the wolves succeeded in cutting down the one he was in, he saw now that the animals could not follow him, that they gnashed their long fangs in defeat, snapping at one another in their anger. Then he heard the distant baying of his faithful dogs; his mother had wakened in time to turn out to his rescue. Happy that it was he who had fulfilled the prophecy, he fired the remainder of his arrows into the edge of the lake, crying the magic words as each new tree sprang to life. . . .

"You gonna set there dreamin' all afternoon?" Tom demanded. "Git holt of the end of this post an' he'p me stack it on dry ground."

Davey slid off the stump and caught hold of the post. Again and again he and Tom carried the sweet-smelling cypress posts to the pile which they erected so that air could pass between them until the wagon could be brought to haul them to the field. When the stack was higher than he could reach, they began a new one.

No one had any idea how long they had been working, when a piercing scream rent the air. Davey and Tom dropped the post they were carrying and stood as if frozen to the ground.

"What in the world was that!" Amos cried, his eyes darting first toward one and then the other.

Joe, his face suddenly blanched, stared in the direction the sound had come from. At first he had thought it had come from the direction of the house, and in that split moment he had lived a lifetime, for his first thought had been of Dilly, that something had happened to her or someone else at the house.

Davey, too frightened to move, stared at Joe. "It sounded like a woman's scream!" he blurted, thinking of Dilly too.

"Listen!" Joe commanded, for there was a weaker scream, one of pure terror . . . and it came from down the road toward the McKeevers'.

"That's Het!" Amos cried, bounding from the water and starting toward the road.

Then the piercing scream, that could be heard for miles, split the air again.

"My God, that's a panther's scream!" Joe cried, grabbing his gun and taking after Amos. Davey sped past them all, his heart pounding against his ribs, all fear of the panther forgotten. It had jumped Hetty, and all he could think of was the creature's claws tearing into her white flesh as they had the heifer, maybe eating parts of her before they could reach her.

He was the first one to see her as she rounded a bend in the road. She was running as fast as she could and screaming hysterically, now and then venturing a look over her shoulder. Then he saw the big panther coming round the curve.

"Thrown down yore bucket!" he screamed at the top of his lungs, which to him sounded no louder than a squeak. He saw that she had already pulled off her blouse and thrown it in the path of the panther, for, as Alvey had said, in case any of them ever encountered the creature, the surest way to escape it was to keep throwing pieces of clothing in its path. Each time it would stop because of the smell and tear the cloth to bits; then, finding out there was nothing to it, he would scream that terrible scream and take after his prey again.

She fled frantically toward him, as Joe, having outdistanced Tom and Amos, bounded close behind him, his breath coming in great gasps. Davey, with a new burst of speed, flew to meet her, for he saw she was too frightened now to hear his cries. Silly, stupid Hetty, who had ridiculed him the night the panther had scared him almost to death, was now too frightened to do the only thing that would keep the animal from pouncing upon her. He had known that night to keep the light in its eyes until he could get away, and she had known for weeks what to do in case the panther ever jumped her, but no doubt that had gone over her head like everything else he tried to tell her.

Reaching her as she collapsed in exhaustion, he seized the bucket of eggs she was bringing to Ma and flung them as far as he could in the direction of the oncoming panther. Then catching her under the armpits, he tried to drag her out of the way of Joe's gun.

"Panther!" ॐ 87

Joe, stopping where Hetty had fallen, took quick aim and fired at the panther as it pounced upon the bucket of eggs. Running forward, he fired the other barrel, but neither shot killed the panther. Joe had been too far away.

With a scream of pain, the panther whirled, stumbled, and then ran drunkenly into the swamp.

"You hit 'im!" Amos cried, running up.

"This old shotgun won't git 'im," Joe panted, "'cept at close quarters. Git to the house an' bring them dogs, quick, Davey!" He stooped anxiously over Hetty, who sat with her head propped in her hands, sobbing hysterically. He reached out and took her gently by the shoulder. "That wuz a close call, gal," he said. "Iffen we all hadn't been just down the road, he'd'a gotcha shore. Better thank Davey fer bein' able to run so fast."

Amos knelt in front of Hetty. "Did 'e git close to you a'tall?" he asked.

"I don't know," she wailed. "Fust thing I knowed I heard a loud cough an' then he was comin' adder me! I 'membered whut Alvey said an' throwed down my head rag. He jumped on it an'. . . an'. . ."

Joe patted her shoulder. "Stop thinkin' 'bout it an' git on down the road to the house. Tom, go with her till you meet Davey with the dogs. We gotta track that critter down this time iffen it takes all summer. He's wounded an' cain't git too far ahead of them dogs."

"I shore wish Alvey was here; he'd know whut to do," Amos said.

"They ain't no time to go git 'im," Joe retorted, getting to his feet. "I kin shoot as straight as Alvey Shanks ever could; I just ain't got a good rifle. That twenty-two might slow 'im down, but hit'ud never git him 'less you hit 'im in the right spot. You let me git close enough to 'im with this here twelve-gage an' I'll blow 'im to Kingdom Come."

Davey, fleeing down the road to the house, thought his heart would burst from running. Jumping the fence that enclosed the woods between the house and the pond, he sped across toward the chicken yard, shouting as he ran. Pa and Jim were hastily unloading the wagon, preparatory to taking off down the road to see what was happening. They had heard the panther's screams and then the gunshot. Ma and Dilly and all the younguns were gathered around the wagon, their faces drawn with anxiety.

"Hit's Davey!" Seth cried running to meet him.

"Whut's happ'n?" Pa shouted, coming to meet him.

"It was Hetty . . . the panther jumped 'er!" Davey cried, running past him toward the shelter where old Belle was tied.

Ma began to wring her hands, suddenly visioning Hetty lying mangled.

"He didn't get 'er," Davey shouted, fumbling in his haste to untie the rope. "I got to 'er in time to throw the bucket of eggs in his path . . . an' then Joe fired at 'im." He ran to the pen to turn out the coon dogs. "He wounded 'im, an' now we're gonna take the dogs an'. . ."

"Where's Het?" Pa demanded.

"Settin' side of the road when I left. Not nothin' wrong with 'er 'ceptin' she's scairt half to death . . . like me the night I come 'crost 'im lyin' under the trees.

"Pa, you reckon we oughter take this mule down there? Ain't no tellin' what that wounded critter might take a notion to do . . . or what he's liable to strike at. I'll go git the other guns; they ain't much, but they'll he'p out."

Davey unsnapped the ropes from all the dogs and turned them loose, running ahead of them and calling to each by name to follow him. Away they went, with Pa and Harvey bringing up the rear. The last thing Davey heard before the dogs began to yelp, was Ma threatening the other younguns if they dared follow.

Halfway to the place where they had been sawing posts, they met Tom and Hetty. Pa stopped to see if she was all right, but Tom turned and ran after Davey and the dogs.

Almost immediately, the dogs picked up the scent and were off like a streak, their deep baying resounding through the swamps.

Davey's excited, "Hee-ee!" as he shouted encouragement, almost matched their yelps. Then they reached the spot where the panther had torn at the tin bucket, where the shotgun blast had turned him into the woods, and then they were off again.

Joe's familiar shout came from deep in the woods, from the direction the dogs were headed. Davey and Tom raced after the dogs, and finally they came upon Joe and Amos looking carefully about them. The dogs, their noses to the ground, raced in circles.

"He come through here," Joe said. "We found a spot of blood on some leaves back there. His tracks was plain adder he hit soft ground."

Suddenly old Belle's yelps changed in tempo.

"That's it!" Joe shouted, starting on the run. "Belle's gittin' close. Look out fer all them big limbs . . . just in case that rascal's took to the trees an' plans to git one of us!"

Davey sped along casting anxious glances at large overhanging limbs now and then, for Joe was right; the creature could be crouched on any one of them, and, wounded like he was, he might attack without warning.

Then suddenly, before Joe had time to reach the scene where the other dogs had joined old Belle, there was a roaring snarl and one of the dogs yelled in pain. Then, of all the noise any of them had ever heard, there began the greatest: the dogs snarling and yelping, with the panther joining in.

"He's jumped the dogs!" Amos shouted. "He'll tear 'em to bits!"

At that moment all of them reached the scene, but Joe could not fire for fear of hitting the dogs.

"Do somethin'!" Tom yelled. "He's killin' my coon dog!"

"Cain't kill 'im no deader'n a blast from this shotgun could!" Joe snapped. "Looks like them dogs is givin' 'im tit fer 'tat."

First one and then the other of the dogs would charge in only to be slapped broad-sided by one of the panther's powerful blows. When one succeeded in closing in, the panther leaped, and it was only a matter of seconds before the dog was whipped, backing off to get up the courage to attack again. Once old Belle closed in and she and the panther rolled over and over, the other dogs joining in the fray, snapping and snarling, but keeping a respectful distance from the sharp claws. Succeeding in whipping even old Belle, the panther, its back to the trunk of a big oak, reared up on its hind legs and slapped at any of them, now bleeding from numerous rips in their sides and ears, who dared venture within reach.

At that moment, as if the creature had just sensed the presence of man, it snarled and spat defiantly, its yellowish eyes gleaming, and leaped over the heads of the tired dogs in a last effort to escape.

Joe, the gun already clamped to his shoulder, waiting for the first chance to fire without hitting the dogs, pulled the triggers of both barrels at the same time. The huge yellowish-gray body seemed to rise higher and then it struck the ground with a thud, its legs continuing to jerk spasmodically. Instantly the dogs were upon it, respectful of its sharp claws even though they could no longer slash at them.

"Belle!" Joe shouted, running forward. "Back!"

Tom and Amos, running forward, began to try to get the dogs away from the dying panther, of whom everyone was still wary, for it still struggled, its sides heaving. Joe, in his excited haste, fumblingly tried to reload the shotgun, dropping one shell after another in his excitement.

"Don't shoot 'im no more!" Davey cried. "He's dyin' . . . an' we wanna git his hide. That last blast done knocked a hole in his belly!"

"Stick 'im in the throat!" Amos shouted, fumbling in his pocket for his knife.

Joe, snapping open his long-bladed knife, plunged the blade into the panther's throat as he would a hog at hog-killing time. Instantly the ground was covered with the rich, red blood and the panther's legs ceased their quivering.

Pa came trotting upon the scene, exhausted from his long run, his gaunt frame heaving with every breath he drew.

"We kilt 'im!" Davey cried, running to meet Pa. "Joe got 'im when nobody else could . . . even Alvey Shanks!"

"Ain't nobody hurt?" Pa demanded, shuffling forward. He looked at the torn sides of the dogs.

"Nobody but the dogs," Joe replied, stooping to gather up the shells he had dropped, "and they ain't hurt too bad. Pa, that was some fight! You oughter seen it. Better'n any wildcat fight you ever seen!"

Pa knelt and looked closely at the beautiful, dead body. "Ain't he a beautiful thing!" he exclaimed. "Don't seem right to haft to kill 'im. But when one of them fellers turn killer, hit's the only thing kin be done."

"Reckon there's any more like 'im?" Amos asked, taking hold of the silky head and pulling it upright for a better look. "I shore ain't never seed anything like that!"

Pa got to his feet with an effort. "They cain't be no more like 'im . . . or folks 'ud been reportin' 'em 'fore this. My Pa use' to tell me 'bout big 'uns like 'im . . . that when he wuz a boy, these woods was full of 'em . . . wolves too!"

"Wonder why he come back up here . . . adder we chased him so far in the swamp?" Jim asked, lifting one leg and rolling the still warm body.

"He ain't fergot that heifer he kilt," Pa replied. "They kinda funny critters. They keep comin' back whur they start their killin'."

"How we gonna git 'im to the house?" Jim asked. "We wanna skin 'im. Iffen we drag 'im, we'll ruin his hair."

"Tie his legs together and poke a long pole through 'em," Joe suggested. "That way we kin carry 'im."

And that was what they did. With the long pole balanced on Jim's and Joe's shoulders, the jubilant procession started up the road to the house, each one talking excitedly about how the creature had acted, reliving every moment of the chase and fight.

"Git on the mule an' go tell Mr. McKeever," Pa said to Tom. "He'll shore wanna know the critter's been kilt."

And before night, folks had come from miles around to see the big panther, for the news had spread quickly, as such news could in that community.

A huge log fire burned in the side yard, where men and boys talked excitedly and swapped tall yarns of other big hunts, all the younguns on the place ran about shouting with glee, and before long the panther's hide was scraped free of all particles of flesh, rubbed with salt, and nailed to the side of the smokehouse to cure.

"Don't git too much salt," Alvey Shanks cautioned. "Hit'll make the skin brittle. You better keep a' oak smoke going . . . not too close to it . . . but close 'nough to keep the flies away. Them maggots, iffen they git in it, will eat it full o' holes 'fore you know it."

"We cure it jus' like a coon hide, don't we?" Joe asked.

"Yeah, but 'member you gotta bigger varmint here, an' hit's gonna take longer."

Mr. McKeever said he would like to have the pelt when it was cured; that he would give Joe five dollars for it . . . if the bugs didn't destroy it before it was cured.

It was a deal, and for weeks to come there was nothing more talked about than the dog and panther fight and the final killing that had freed the community of the menace.

"I allers knowed you was meant for some good, Joe!" Alvey Shanks laughed as he crawled on his horse to go home. "Shore wish I coulda seen it."

Joe laughed and waved them away. He was glad it was he who had had the opportunity to succeed where the others had failed.

Davey went to sleep that night with the same kind of thoughts. Hetty had come in for her share of attention, once she got over her scare, tossing her head when she denied having been frightened out of her wits. But Davey knew better; he had come across the panther at night.

Stetson Kennedy

Stetson Kennedy (1916–) was born in Jacksonville, Florida, and has spent most of his life in the area, especially on a small lake near Green Cove Springs. As a young man working in some of Jacksonville's poorer neighborhoods, he saw how some of his fellow whites mistreated African Americans, an experience that helped shape his future career as a strong defender of the ill-treated. Those readers who might be surprised at the brutality of the following story, which first appeared in the spring 1938 issue of the *Florida Review,* should realize that he wrote from firsthand knowledge of atrocities against blacks. As a youngster, for example, he witnessed the brutal bludgeoning of an African-American maid who objected to being cheated out of change by a bus driver.

While living in Key West during the hard times of the Depression and later working on the Federal Writers Project with Zora Neale Hurston and other folklorists, Kennedy collected folktales and folksongs that he incorporated in his writing and made available to other scholars. He later helped establish the Florida Folklore Society and served as its president, helping to incorporate folklore into school curricula. His *Palmetto Country* (1942) is what he calls a "barefoot social history" of the people who made Florida: pogey fishermen, cigar makers, Greek spongers, Bahamian Conchs, and turpentiners.

In the 1940s, realizing he could not enlist in the armed forces because of a back injury, he chose to fight fascism at home by infiltrating terrorist groups like the Ku Klux Klan, the Confederate Underground, and the American Gentile Army. He remained a member of the Klan until he went into court to testify against them in 1947. He also wrote three books about the Klan and about the racism still rampant in parts of the South: *Southern Exposure* (1946), *I Rode with the Ku Klux Klan* (1954; republished as *The Klan Unmasked* [1990]), and *Jim Crow Guide to the U.S.A.* (1959). In retaliation the Klan once burned the old, ramshackle bus where he lived, but he survived and has continued to battle them and other groups engaged in human-rights violations.

Kennedy's anti-Klan works, which philosopher Jean-Paul Sartre reprinted in Europe and therefore made accessible to foreign readers, were powerful indictments of American society. During the 1960s, Kennedy marched with Martin Luther King, Jr., in Alabama, Mississippi, and Florida and antagonized so many segregationists that the Grand Dragon of the Klan offered a reward of one thousand dollars per pound of Kennedy's posterior. Kennedy also knew—much to the consternation of the hooded group—the Klan's secret signs and passwords and had them broadcast each week on the Superman radio serial. While Kennedy was pleasantly surprised at how quickly much of the South became racially integrated in the 1960s, he remains dismayed with the degree of power racists wield today.

Color Added

Stetson Kennedy

THERE IT WAS. Al barely glanced at its freshly repainted letters.

NIGGER—IF YOU CAN READ
DON'T LET THE SUN SET ON YOU
IN ORANGE MOUND

"Ah'd better keep rollin," he thought, "iffen ah'm gon git mah feed an git outa town foh dark. Dis heah truck's gittin in mighty bad shape."

He slowed down as he approached the side road from Spring Junction. He had the right-of-way, but no brakes. A white woman in a new sedan dashed out onto the highway, just in front of him. Driving over to the shoulder, he managed to escape an immediate collision. "Damn! Wy doan she move ovah? Ah gotta git back on de road—gon hit dis culvert! Wreck mah truck *sho!* Ifen she'd ony move a little ways—maybe ah makes hit anyhow—*gotta try!*"

He waited until it seemed his front wheels would strike the culvert—then cut sharply back to the pavement. He heard the grating, felt his truck shudder as it scraped the rear fender of the sedan. "Whoeee! Now ah pays de bill! Huh! Smilin! She come neah killin us bof, an mus ain ebm seed me til now. *She's drivin on!* Well, dis is de fus un ah ain paid foh, mah fault or no."

Rattling along at twenty-five miles per hour, he began to whistle. A car drove up behind, came alongside: "Pull ovah, niggah!"

He pulled over. A bony red-faced man wearing overalls and a worn blue serge coat jerked him out of his truck and shook him.

"Whadn hell ya mean runnin inta a white lady's car an trying ta git way? Ya oughta be skinned alive! Whur ya from?"

"Garnet."

"Wal—get back in yer truck. Yer goin ta jail. Drive inta Jedge Mullis' Seed Store—know whur hit's at?"

"Yessuh—but please doan run me in Boss—*please Suh*. Ah ain—"

"Shet ep an git in yer truck!"

Al drove slowly into Orange Mound, the man following close behind. They stopped in front of the seed store and the man caught him by the back of his shirt and shoved him inside.

"Jedge, this hyear niggah run inta a lady's car out on the highway an diden stop atall. Kep right on going. He musta been doin sixty. Tried ta git way fum me twicet on the way ta town."

Judge Mullis, also wearing overalls, was carefully weighing sun-flower seed into one-pound packages. He didn't look up.

"Ya guilty niggah?"

Al considered. If it hadn't been for him, there would have been a *real* accident. Still, if he said no, he'd be calling the man a liar—get beat on the head with a blackjack.

"Yessuh Jedge. Ah's guilty."

"Hundud dollahs er nine-ty days—take him on out ta the Farm, Chahlie."

Al got back into his truck, and Charlie followed him out to the Blue Jay Farm. Charlie backed Al's truck under a shed, and led him into the Superintendent's office.

"Wal Chahlie," said the Superintendent, "I ain seen ya since-t the woods was burned—bout time ya was bringin me somebody. Looks liak ya picked a big un. I'll be needin lots more liak him when I start plantin nex month . . . Whas your name boy?"

"Alphonse Brown."

"Ya means *Al,* doncha?"

"Yassuh . . . guess ah does . . ."

"Know damn well ya do! We doan feed no uppity-talkin niggahs out hyear! Come on an les git ya fixed up with a new suit a clothes."

"Yassuh."

"Whad size shoe ya wear?"

"Levens."

"Hyear's tens—bigges I got."

"Cap'n—how long is ah got ta serve?"

"Pends how hard ya works. Six months maybe."

"*Six munts?* . . . Cap'n—doan ah git no chance-t ta write mah wife?"

"Ya writes a letter a week—on Sundays. Taday's Tuesday."

Al thought a moment. "Tinnie's gon worry hasef sick tween now an Sunday. Ah'l ast her ta git me a lawyer . . . Sun's sho settin on me in Orange Mound . . ."

The Superintendent waited for him to put on his stripes, and then led him into the dining hall. The gang was eating at long board tables, watched by a guard who sat by the door with a shot-gun across his lap. They brought Al a tin cup of black coffee, and a plate filled with hash, boiled cabbage, and corn bread.

Al grinned at the Negro sitting next to him. "Is de vittuls allus as bad as dis? Hit's hardly fitten ta eat."

"Mosly hit's wus. How ya think de Supntendent gits hissef a new car ever year?"

"Does ah git a second helpin?"

"Not as ah knows of—evah heerd tell of one hawg savin somethin foh anothah?"

"No," laughed Al, "kaint say as ah is."

After supper they marched back to the stone cell building. Al was put with a little yellow negro called "Sugar-Hill."

"We in a helluva fix, ain we?" asked Al. "How long is you been heah?"

"Nigh onta six munts, areckon. Got bout six moh head a me."

"Golly!" Al said. "How come?"

"Ah done a fool thing . . ."

"Say which?"

"—Ah done a fool thing. The ornery sherf what rested me made me mad. Aftah he had done ketched me he taken me inta his office an slapped me side the head thout me sayin nothin. Then he ast me whur ah stole em—they was some dresses mah wife was needin, she had done taken sick an ah coulden git ary bita work—an when ah diden ansuh him right off he hit me again. Ah jus coulden stan hit. I went an taken a Coc-Cola bottle ofen his desk an popped him. Lak'd ta haf killed him. Then three moh fellahs come in an whaled tar outen me. Ah knowed better, but ah's proud ah done hit."

"Bet ya diden ebm git way wid de dresses."

"Yeah ah did—two of em. Wuth nine-ty eight cent apiece."

"Das good."

Al was still talking when Sugar fell asleep. Most of the night he lay awake on his cot, listening to the snores rumbling down the corridor. He wondered how many nights he would be there before Tinnie got him out.

At six o'clock in the morning he was shoveling crushed oyster shell onto the road approaching the Farm. Across the fields he could see the negro women working in groups of four. Three of them were harnessed with leather straps around the waist to ploughs guided by the fourth.

"Huh!" he grunted. "Jus lak mules . . ."

By mid-afternoon he was exhausted, yet the rest of the gang worked steadily. "Mus spect me ta work hard as dese othah niggahs, an me jus got heah . . ."

That night he gulped down his supper, and reaching his cell was the first asleep. Next morning he ached so badly he could hardly walk to the fields, but by noon was feeling better. Working hard until Sunday finally came. He at last wrote to his wife Tinnie. He told her where he was, how he got there, and asked her to please hurry and get him out. Another week he worked and worried, but no answer came from Tinnie . . . Another week, and still no letter . . .

"Boss," he asked every day, "ain ah got no lettah fum Tinnie yet?"

By the end of the third week the boss got mad. "Niggah," he said, "I reckons as how you thinks we's runnin a corspondance club—well, we *ain't!* Bout one moh word outa you, an I puts ya on ice!"

A fourth week Al brooded and grumbled. Sunday he talked to Sugar: "Ah gotta fine out whas wrong wid Tinnie. Sumpum done happen ta her, else she'd a wrote by now. Nobudy else but me what'll take keer a her—ah got ta try ta git way . . ."

"Felah tried hit week foh you got heah," warned Sugar. "Boss tore his head off with buck-shot."

"Ah know. But *five* moh munts—ah gotta do sumpum—ah jus gotta! . . ."

Sugar-Hill was a trusty. He had privileges, like watching the gang while the Boss went to lunch. It was about two o'clock Monday afternoon when he called the Boss' attention to the fact that one of the gang was missing. The Superintendent took charge of the manhunt and locked up all the gang except Sugar—he needed Sugar to handle the bloodhounds. The Bosses got their .30-.30 riot guns and all went out to the fields together.

It was the hound "Man-Eater" that found Al's trail, and the pack took it up and disappeared bellowing into the hammock that surrounds Rice Creek. Deep in the hammock Al was running. With a low crouch he sped through the creeks and shallow pools. He stumbled knee-deep into thick, clinging black mud. "Shoulden a tried ta git way so soon aftah de rain.

Heaps easier foh dem dawgs ta fine mah scent . . . *Oh Jesus! Ah heahs em*—das Man-Eater! Now ah ketches hit . . ."

The hammock was dark because the sun was almost down; tall cypress trees shut out all but a few rays of light, leaving the ground smelling damp and mouldy. For a while it was quiet, except for the faint baying of the hounds and the drip of cold rain from the branches. The breeze was laden with heavy and chilling fog.

Suddenly Al whirled and looked back. A tremulous moan, like a woman in pain, drifted down from a cypress . . . "Oh-mah Gawd! Screech owl is a sign of *death*—could choke him ifen ah had time to turn mah shoes upsides down . . ." All through the cold moonless night he twisted and plunged like a ghost through the hammock, the steady baying of the hounds at his back, and the echo of the screech owl in the shadows overhead.

"Ah done run a mighty fur piece—kaint go on much longah," he panted. "Gotta git rid a dese stripes."

Breaking out on the edge of the hammock, he forced his way slowly through heavy palmetto thickets, cutting his arms and legs. Down by the river he could see smoke rising from the settlement of the hands at Griss Mill. The hounds seemed closer. He crept down to the nearest shack and whistled. A girl came out, stared a moment, and darted back inside. Soon she was back with dungarees and blue shirt.

"Ya can change deah in de outhouse," she whispered, "an den *git!* Ah'll burn dem stripes soon's you've gone."

Al changed and dashed down to the river. Wading in the shallow water along shore he splashed back toward the hammock. "Lissen at ole Man-Eater beller! Heah he comes, full tilt! Ah gotta swim—river mus be two mile wide—*Good Gawd-amighty!* Wahtah's cold!"

In mid-stream he heard the baying change from its roll to a frenzied clamor—short, and ardent. "Guess ah got shed of em at las. Look at em race up and down de bank—busy as a cat on a tin roof. *Christ! Man-Eater's swimin out!* Two moh gon follow! Gotta swim now . . . golly ah's tired . . . tired . . . when is ah gon touch bottom? Ifen ah doan soon, ah drowns sho. Musn let dis water scare me. Howm ah gon do no runnin aftah ah gits ovah?—ifen ah gits ovah . . . *Praise Gawd!* Heah's bottom."

He crawled up the bank and fell exhausted, feet hanging in the water.

On the other side of the river the hounds were still baying. Man-Eater and the other two were almost across, but were having a hard time; their front paws struck out feebly as they fought to keep from going under. At last they touched bottom and waddled ashore. Al drew up his feet, clenched his fists . . . "Ah kill dem fool dawgs! *Damn em!* Ah kaint run no moh . . ."

The hounds flopped down on the leaves, heads resting between their paws, too tired to even shake off the water. Al stretched out his hand—scratched Man-Eater's ear . . . "*Glory be!*" he choked, and lost consciousness.

꒣   ꒣

The next day, Deputy Charlie stopped at the Commissary in Spring Junction for a drink. "Yep Chahlie," said Alvery Pickett, proprietor, "got me some fine dogs—bought em offen a niggah what was by hyear yestiddy evenin. Said they was the bes coon an vahmint dogs in this hyear county! Come out an have a look."

He had Man-Eater and the other two Blue Jay hounds tied to his back fence.

They found Al sobbing on the floor of his shack in Garnet. It was empty except for a picture of Joe Louis and a little framed card that Al had given Tinnie on her last birthday:

> "*Best wishes I send you,*
> *Good fortune attend you,*
> *Prosperity fair be ever*
> *Beside you.*
> *And nothing betide you*
> *Save happiness rare.*"

Al's black shoulders shook because he was sobbing and saying, "Tinnie—Tinnie—how come ya done lef me?"

He went quietly back to the Blue Jay Farm, and after they finished beating him they put him on ice. The ice-box was cold and damp because it was made of concrete and only had one small window near the roof. It wasn't large enough for him to sit down, so he stood up.

"Please doan put me on ice, Boss," begged Al. "Ah kaint stan hit . . . ah's sick . . . an ah's hongry—gimme some sumpum ta eat Boss . . ."

They gave him bread and water and soon he forgot all about standing up.

The next day they took him out of the ice-box so he wouldn't die in there. They put him on a cot and told him he had pneumonia. Then they gave him a letter from his wife Tinnie that had been lying on the Superintendent's desk for a month. It was nice of them to let Al read it before he died, because it was the answer he had waited for:

Garnet—Al Honey—

I wus so worried Bout yore Bein missin I was mos crazy Before you writ me I diden Know if you had lef me or not But I Knew you haden Darlin I misses you somethin turbul Al I done the Bes I could But it ain no use You Know all our niuse furnichure what we paid on so long I sold hit an paid a Lawyer to git you out But he couldent an Peoples some of them has been so Hateful my own Colored lady friens even worse than pore white trash I just Kaint stan them goin bout Scandalizin my name I ain never goin Confident nobody no more Honey I Been so happy together But now they ain nothin to do But Brake up House-Keepin an me go home to my People in Gawja

Always your Tinnie

Al Honey I done the Bes I Knowed how

Ernest Lyons

Ernest Lyons (1905–90) was born in Laurel, Mississippi, and moved in 1915 to Stuart, Florida, where, as a school correspondent for the fourth grade, he experienced his first excitement of working on a newspaper. Some of that excitement is in the feelings of the young editor in the following story. He quit high school before receiving his diploma and traveled around the country, working on newspapers like the *Sierra Madre News*, the *Pasadena Post*, and the *Carmelite* (in Carmel, California).

In 1929, he returned to Stuart, where he began working on the *Stuart News* and, during the Depression, as a fisherman and odd jobber. In 1937, he married Ezell Gober, a college English teacher, and they later had two children: Mary Lyons, who became an Atlanta lawyer, and William Lyons, who became a marine biologist. Ernest Lyons became editor of the *Stuart News* in 1945 and held the post for forty-four years, during which time he championed both the expansion of the forestry service and tougher environmental laws.

After writing hundreds of newspaper columns over the years, he collected some of his best in two books: *My Florida* (1969) and *The Last Cracker Barrel* (1975). He also wrote fiction for such magazines as *Esquire* and *Good Housekeeping,* from which the following story is reprinted from the January 1948 issue. As charter president of the Florida Outdoor Writers Association and one of the state's leading outdoor writers and conservationists, he did much to make the public aware both of Florida's natural beauties and of dangers to its resources, for example in the straightening of the Kissimmee River by the Army Corps of Engineers.

The scene of the following story, Pahokee, is a small Florida town on the eastern side of Lake Okeechobee. The story of establishing a newspaper in such small towns at the end of the last century and the beginning of this one was repeated over and over again throughout this state. Frank Stoneman, the father of one of the authors presented in this book, Marjory Stoneman Douglas, once received a flat-bed press in lieu of payment for some legal work he had done in Orlando and took the press to Miami, where he founded the city's first morning paper, the *News-Record*, which later became the *Miami Herald*.

The reference in the story to the 1928 hurricane reminds one how devastating such natural disasters have been to this state. A 1926 hurricane generated a wall of water from Lake Okeechobee that swept over Moore Haven, on the southwestern edge of the lake, killing three hundred people. A hurricane two years later killed some two thousand people and led to the building of canals and dikes around this huge lake to try to control waters during a storm.

A Blade of Grass

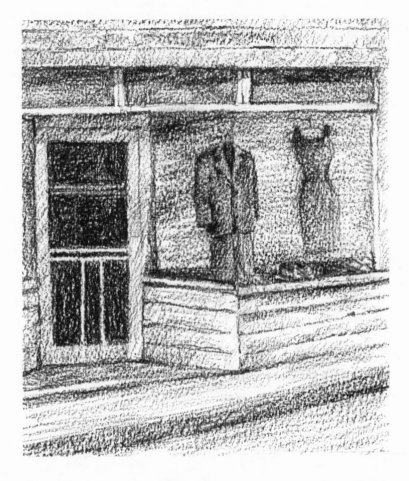

Ernest Lyons

THIS JOLLY dry-goods drummer, N. Margolius, who shared my seat on the packing cases while the tug *Thomas J. Boggs* towed our barge down West Palm Beach Canal through the sea of grass, was a satanic and disillusioned man. That I know today, although back then—and it was long ago—I thought him a merry acquaintance. He flattered me—by the yard.

"'Frederick Lyman Sutton, Editor,'" he read my card aloud, "'of *The Everglades Banner,* Pahokee, Florida.'" He added, of his own invention, "Soon to be the Saw Grass Greeley," and I smiled.

"Young man, I envy you. How wonderful it is," he said, "to be an editor in this new land, bringing the art of Gutenburg to these raw Everglades." He waved a pudgy hand. "Here a people will arise. Your voice will be their voice."

I was so vain. He sounded so sincere. I had just turned twenty-one; and in the wooden cases on the deck was the substance of my dreams: a hand press, the fonts of type and reams of ready-print for the first issue of my newspaper.

Already it was "me, the editor." I loved the sight of my full name on the bright, new cards printed in advance. How bright that day! How beautiful! Every puff of smoke from the tug's stack was like a little shout: "Here he comes!" In the distance the saw grass rippled off, head high, a brown vastness as far as I could see, glistening in the sun, dancing in the wind—for me. For me, the editor.

"Ah, yes," said N. Margolius, following my glance, "the saw grass. Millions upon millions of blades. Stretching for a hundred miles. Magnificent. I always like to watch the wind on it. Reminds me of a dog I used to stroke. A big brown dog—they call them English staghounds, and the ladies like them." He paused, subdued by the shadow of a thought that troubled him, then went on. "But women aren't everything, you know. There's your saw grass sleeping like a giant creature in the sun, and not a woman anywhere about—at least not what *I* would call a woman." He winked satirically. "Just grass, billions upon billions of senseless blades of grass, dying down through the centuries to make an empire richer than the delta of the Nile. And you, my young friend, coming to it, bearing the voice of progress, an emissary of the mind. How I envy you."

I saw no reason he shouldn't.

"Here—" he gave another theatrical wave at the ocean of grass—"the plow will turn the saw grass under. Toil and sweat will build happy homes.

Church bells—" he coughed and made a grimace—"will ring out their message of good will in a prosperous land. Your land. Your people. Your voice. . . . I like the name of your paper. I can see it, *The Banner,* unfurled, recording their births and their deaths, fighting their battles, being their spokesman. 'The Voice of the Empire of the Sun.' Editor Sutton, there's a slogan for you."

I thought the slogan wonderful, back then, and I still do.

ॐ   ॐ

Even today, as I scan the front page this Friday afternoon, read "Uncle Sut Sez," those grandiloquent words are the first things to hit my eye—"Voice of the Empire of the Sun"—spread magnificently all the way below the masthead, just above the obituary of E. J. Creech. It is, I know, a good obituary, as such things go, continued on page two, with poor old Creech's picture in the column alongside. It begins: "A pioneer of the 'Glades has passed," and ends with just a mention of a few odd things he left behind—"the skin of the first cottonmouth he killed in the street of our town, the hide of the first 'coon he traded from the Seminoles, and that intangible asset, the sympathy of a countryside."

Poor old Creech. There is his picture, a human face that dared to look a camera in the eye—how many years ago? The photograph isn't much like him when I saw him last. How people change. A serious, purposeful face, gray-eyed and thin, filled with ambition, straight and hard—and yet, withal, it has a trusting, human look. Could he have wanted to be liked? The picture must have been taken just about the time he started The Big Store, before he married—way back then. How had he ever been weak enough to buy a photograph?

Had I known that day on the barge what I know now—that N. Margolius carried in his battered sample trunk a strange and beautiful object, one of those artfully contrived talismans in the shape of common things that change the lives of men—I would have been justified in seizing the red dress, stamping on it, destroying it then and there. It was an evil thing.

He ladled praise on me all the long way into the Lake—we were the only passengers. He pretended to be proposing toasts, and I couldn't get enough of them. They still echo in my mind.

"To the young editor; may his way be smooth and his venture prosperous. . . . To the Everglades, God bless them as a land of plenty." But the one he seemed to relish most was this: "To the women—to the beautiful women in this world, and to what helps enshrine their loveliness. To diamonds and sapphire bracelets, to terrapin and dinner music, to the happiest times I can remember," and he sighed. "You'll have them, too. Good times. Wonderful times. Special concessions to the press—suppers and champagne on the house; they won't let you pay for anything. But I must say—" he surveyed me critically—"you aren't quite dressed for it. Take a tip from Margolius: always wear your best. You'll be called in frequently to consult with the Mayor about policy. And your advertisers—first impressions count; always dress your best for them. There might even be—" he poked me—"who can tell?—a good-looking girl or two out there for the young editor."

He was so old; I was so young—I almost laughed. Let me give you a better picture of this N. Margolius. I see him more clearly now that the years have passed. There I was, dressed very plainly, a skinny young man with a big Adam's apple, my wrists protruding from my shirt sleeves, and a couple of inches of ankles showing below my trouser cuffs—gawky was the word for me. And Margolius, suave and jolly, in a well-tailored, slightly soiled Palm Beach suit, with a flashy necktie below his full and florid face. Above his whisky nose and baggy eyes a dirty Panama sat rakishly. He was dressed in what I would have called "classy style" back then, and had been handsome once—I could see that. Altogether, he was a man of the world to me. I admired him, although of course I couldn't help but pity him for being old. Just this side of fifty, I assumed.

"I *have* a girl in West Palm Beach," I said.

"Then *you* know where *she* is," he laughed, "and what *she* don't know won't hurt her. Send her a few baubles now and then. It pays to treat the ladies right. They like to be remembered. Say, by George!" He patted the pockets of his suit. "Now, isn't that surprising. Of all fool things! Left my wallet in West Palm Beach. I can get all I need, of course, from the stores in the 'Glades—" he turned to me with the easy familiarity of one gentleman to another—"but in the meantime, would you mind letting me have fifty until tomorrow night?"

My face turned red. Embarrassment is awful for the young. "Mister

Margolius, besides this printing equipment and the clothes on my back, I have just two further assets, a one-dollar bill and a receipt for thirty days' rent from a man named Creech at Pahokee."

At the mention of the name, Margolius stiffened. The blood vessels on his face showed up. He bristled. "Not E. J. Creech?" he asked loudly. "Did I hear you rightly? Creech? At The Big Store?"

I nodded. "He's the reason for my coming out here. He kept writing my employer on the *Tropical Sun*," I said lamely, under Margolius' accusing eye, "that the 'Glades are growing and they need a newspaper and—"

"Don't finish! No need to tell me." Margolius held up his hand. "I knew it when I saw you. You're only a printer. I could tell by your hands. Saved your money, didn't you," he said scathingly, as though it were a crime. "Put your savings into that stuff—" he pointed at the packing cases— "and you're coming here on the word of E. J. Creech—" he laughed a bitter laugh—"to this hellhole, to this most damnable jumping-off spot on the face of the earth, to bring out a one-lunged weekly for that rascal. I'll bet he's even offered to assist you."

"I was given to understand he would be helpful," I replied stiffly. "He's a leader in the community and wants to see it grow."

"Boy," said N. Margolius, "I give you exactly thirty days before Creech has a mortgage on the machinery. In sixty days he'll own it, and he'll own you, too, body and soul. You'll be working for *him*, mark my words. Look here, now, if you're smart, you'll turn around at Canal Point and skedaddle back. Don't let him get his claws on you."

"You're prejudiced."

"Boy, I love your innocence, but that's mild for it," said Margolius. "I hate E. J. Creech." His humor was restored. "I'm not the only one. Some hate him with a nice, quiet, sociable hate. Others hate him with a slow-burning, long-nursed hate. I hate him with a particular, contemptuous hate. You'll come to hate him, too. I'm sorry for you." He looked at me pityingly. "Don't let him get you. Don't. Remember, all the people can't be wrong, not all the time. Lincoln said it.

"There are a hundred reasons why he is detested by the fine folk of this region. Good reasons. Every one of them would hold in court. I'll bank on it. My particular grievance," he started to explain, "but wait. For some strange reason the truth begins to appeal to me.

"First, let me tell you what is meant by hell on earth. It is to have a job like mine, selling dry goods and notions for the B.L. Kahn Company of St. Louis, 'Specialists in Women's Wear.' A minute, now. Look in this trunk." He opened it. "Panties and hankies and slips—" he ruffled through the stuff—"guaranteed part-silk no-run stockings, and top-quality, fast-color 'Lucy Allen' gingham frocks at eighteen eighty the dozen.

"These atrocities—" he indicated the trunk's contents ferociously— "go on the legs, the backs and bodies of slovenly women to make them more slovenly. I am reduced," said N. Margolius, "to selling the worth-less to the worthless to be worn by the utterly unnecessary. Me. N. Margolius. My life is like something lifted bodily from a Greek tragedy.

"And the worst of it—the very worst of it," he continued savagely, "is that these barbarians prosper while I go from bad to worse. I detest the B.L. Kahn Company. I wish that it and St. Louis were evaporated off the map. If I could rub my two hands together and do it, like this—" he demonstrated—"I would. I hate my job," he said with venom, "and I hate the 'little merchants' from whom I must wheedle orders for this loath-some stuff.

"Their prospering irks me almost as much as their slogans, and their slogans fly like bats through my mind. 'We Clothe the Multitude.' 'The Family Store.' 'Emporium of Economy.' But the worst of the lot, the most galling of them all, is the motto of The Big Store: 'Where Quality Reigns Supreme.'" He said it again, as if to test the full savor.

"And *he* prospers. He gets rich. He owns half the town—before he's through, he'll own it all. They all prosper, those despicable 'self-made' men who raise themselves by their own boot straps to say, 'Why don't you save your money, Margolius? Leave the ladies be,'" he mimicked. "By God, boy, they remind me of the corpses of human beings, so hon-est, so righteous, so ignorant—and so successful. Quality!" snorted N. Margolius. "What do the living dead know of quality? Here's quality." He reached into the open trunk, down into a recess at the side, and drew out the red dress, a simple dress, dark red, the color of blood.

"There isn't anywhere in all the Everglades," he said, "a woman fit to wear this dress." The wind rippled the tops of the saw grass as we went on. "Here is a dress that was designed by a genius for a beautiful woman— for love and life and laughter. It's a simple thing, like a beautiful painting or a song. An artist dreamed it; a genius with the scissors cut it out." He motioned again at the saw grass. "God did not make that stuff for a dress like this. He made it for poverty and suffering, for ugliness and tawdriness, for meanness—for poor fools like you to eat your heart out trying. Believe it or not," continued Margolius, fondly holding the dress at arm's length, "*this* is the sort of stuff I used to sell.

"What is it? Just a dress—but for some woman, the particular woman for which it was designed, a glorification of her personality, an awakening of her spirit, a quickening of the fires of her body.

"What is a dress?" he asked in mellow spirit. " Only a woman could tell you the answer to that, boy—but if any man appreciates women, put it down in your book, it's me, N. Margolius. I keep this dress," he said, lovingly folding it, "only as a reminder of happier days, when I would have laughed at the thought of working for the B.L. Kahn Company," he added bitterly, "of St. Louis. This is an original. A genius dreamed its lines. An artist shaped it. Styles come and styles go, but the beauty of this cloth is timeless. In my day I have sold hundreds as distinctive. They were my specialty." He shrugged.

"I gave them away, too," he said quite simply. "Generous to a fault, that was me. I presented them to lovely women of my fancy, which worked very well for a while—and certainly gave me many happy days and nights. I don't regret it. What situations! What explanations! Mine was a silver tongue in those days, boy.

"Eventually—" he came back to earth—"I was caught up with and thoroughly discredited. I am blacklisted," said N. Margolius, "by every couturier of note in Paris, by the London trade, and wherever there is anything fine in the art of creating beautiful things for women to wear. Just for giving a few little dresses away. Simple things like this—" he winked, putting it back in the trunk—"worth only a few hundred dollars apiece. To beautiful women. Ah, and there are beautiful women, somewhere, I suppose, still today. A pity we must all grow old."

Just then our tug nearly ran down a ramshackle skiff in the canal at the saw-grass edge. Our wake piled over the boat's gunwale, swamping it, and a man, woman, and child were thrown into the water. The man swam powerfully, holding the child and brushing aside a few shabby floating household goods as he made for the bank; but the woman beat him ashore. She swam like a wildcat. I still remember her. I never can forget her. Even at that distance as we chugged on, the wet garment clinging to her body as she struggled ashore was patently made of flour sacking. She turned, screamed some outrageous abuse our way, and shook her fist at us.

"Welcome to the Everglades," smiled N. Margolius, and the tug gave three toots for Canal Point. "Don't worry about them." He must have noticed the concern on my face. "If we had drowned them, it might have been a blessing. What lives of poverty! What misery! What uselessness!"

జ్ఞ జ్ఞ

It wasn't easy to start "The Voice of the Empire of the Sun." No brass band welcomed me. How I ever got the equipment from Canal Point to Pahokee and into that corrugated iron warren E. J. Creech called an office building is still a mystery. I know I paid the drayman eventually; a dollar down to start with, the last dollar I had.

Despite the falsity of N. Margolius, it is wonderful and marvelous to be the editor of a town's first newspaper. "Your voice is going to be their voice." He wasn't so far wrong. I don't regret a thing. I love the smell of ink on paper; I love to see my name in print. It gives me a feeling of importance; fulfills a hunger in my soul. You can be flat busted, with a pay roll due, the paper company on your neck, the advertisers frozen out and drowned out, you and the bank both busted—and yet, so long as you can say, "It's me, the editor," you're satisfied.

That was how I felt the first day, after the press was set up and the type stacked away. I remember wiping my hands on a piece of waste and looking at myself in a cracked mirror on the washroom wall. It was me, the guiding light of the *Banner* yet unborn, and yet to be so much—I knew for certain. Behind my green eyeshade, beneath those smudges on my only shirt and on my dirty, ink-stained pants—my only pair—was a greatness that others would appreciate someday, I didn't doubt.

I remember walking to the door and looking out again at Pahokee. My town. Rough it was, and ugly, too; a handful of garish stores and shacks risen in the saw grass, with Okeechobee, the great lake, beyond. It all seemed so romantic then. The sign of Zeke's Fish Market—"Fresh Catfish and Turtles, 'Gator Hides Bought and Sold"—intrigued me. Another nearby read: "Buy a Hunk of Paradise, Thaddeus J. Bailey, Real Estate and Insurance." And directly across the way, larger than all the rest, but as ugly and unpainted, was "The Big Store, Where Quality Reigns Supreme."

I decided that the occasion *did* call for new clothes for the editor, walked over and introduced myself.

"Been waiting for you to show up," said E. J. Creech, taking my hand in both of his. "I'd of come over myself, but I got a rule never to bother a man while he's workin'." He looked me up and down approvingly. "Work makes success. Never be ashamed of work, young man. Married? Don't put it off. Foundation of the nation." He led me into the store. "Want you to meet Mrs. Creech. She's my helpmate. The Lord sure was good to me," he said, "when He give me her. Laura, here's the new editor. He's *our* kind of folks. A workin'man."

Mrs. Creech came over timidly. She was colorless, dressed primly in a high-necked something of a shade that didn't register then and doesn't yet—a plain, drab woman, I thought, doomed never to be assertive, fated to be dominated by a host of little fears. She started to shake hands with me, but Creech frowned.

"Mrs. Creech here," he said rather loudly, to cover her confusion, "takes care of the ladies' side, and I handle the gents' furnishings. This woulda been a all-men's store yet if it weren't for Laura. She's good at it, too," he praised her. "You know, ladies' wear is intimate."

"I'd like to buy a suit."

He looked momentarily surprised, then nodded acquiescence, dismissing his wife with the reminder: "Laura, you be sure to fix up a item for Mr. Sutton here about the Women's Mission meeting." He turned briskly back to me. "You'll need something for Sunday wear and Bible Class. Now, here's our best number at nineteen ninety-eight," he said, holding a shoddy gray ready-made against my body. "You'll want the best for church wear, and this won't need altering at all. Quality, too. We don't handle nothin' but the highest-quality merchandise at The Big Store. This here now is something that will last you, and you can tell everybody you meet that you got it 'Where Quality Reigns Supreme.'"

"No need to do that," I said cordially. "You'll be advertising regularly in the *Banner,* and we'll make that slogan known wherever people read the printed word. Now, if you will just please charge this—and a few other little things—to my account, I'll be in to see you about copy later in the day."

Creech carefully brushed the suit and put it back. He went to the cash register and returned with two dollars. "For a subscription," he said bluntly, "although it's against my rule generally to buy a pig in a poke. My slogan is well enough known," he said coldly, "although I will advertise with you—to help the paper—if you prove yourself man enough to be worth helping. When it comes to credit, we have another slogan at The Big Store: 'Pay Cash and Stay Friends.' I want to be your friend. Come back when you've got the money."

꙳ ꙳

You never really see a man until you thoroughly dislike him. That is why today, with twenty years gone by, I can still remember a mole on the left side of E. J. Creech's chin. I can feel exactly the brisk dampness of his handshake, and his quality of being perpetually on guard. I can even hear him saying as I turned to leave, "Laura, put down two dollars—under contributions."

He brought realism to my dream. I guess he shocked me into seeing that the Everglades were not just a romantic budding empire being carved out of a sea of grass—for me. He made me understand why he was so disliked from the trapping camps of Hungry Land to the newest board shack on the saw-grass edge.

How the people hated him back then! They said he was the hardest, tightest, meanest man from Bare Beach to Big Mound. Wherever the saw grass stretched, from Moore Haven to the Hole-in-the-Wall, his name was a byword for sharp dealing.

Folks admired him, yes. They later spread the legend, with a touch of pride, that he had been the first white man to cross Big Saw Grass Swamp. They admitted proudly that he had broken the first ground, started the first store, been the first to push the progress of the 'Glades, and their sympathy poured out to him in the end; but when I went there, they hated him with a double-distilled, communal venom inspired by long years of association in a country of tragic ups and downs with a man who never did business for anything but cash.

I didn't like him either. He hurt my pride.

Today the *Banner* has sixteen pages every Friday, full of local news and advertising, and there are other papers doing right well, too, at Canal Point, Belle Glade, and Clewiston. It isn't "only me" today. There's a girl in the front office, and two men in the shop, Miss Medley helping with the news and ads, and the competition's hot, but it hasn't caught us yet. We're still "The Voice of the Empire of the Sun," although Old Man Creech is dead and gone. How it would have pleased me the first morning to have told him, "The *Banner* will be here when you are laid away." Hate is a peculiar thing.

Yes, the paper is a property today. We own our own building, and I did it all on a shoestring, borrowing and paying back, accepting potatoes, cabbages, and beans for subscriptions—even 'gator hides—trading them for groceries. It seems miraculous.

"Young man—" I can still hear Creech repeating his sententious maxims—"hard work is the secret of success—and moral rectitude. Always do business for cash. It pays to save. But if you ever *really* need help, see me. I want to be your friend."

Disillusion? Who can measure what it does to you? I felt mighty much alone, standing on the steps of The Big Store, looking out at the shabby world I was to conquer—the naked frontier-type frame buildings with Western-style false fronts, a mangy dog lying in the powdery muck of the road, the scattering of frowzy shacks beyond the business district, and beyond all that the saw grass stretching into nothingness.

Up walked N. Margolius. His Palm Beach suit was badly soiled, his Panama was crushed, the gay tie was gone; but still he affected an air of jauntiness. "The dray will be bringing my trunk along directly," he remarked. "Would you mind taking care of the charge for me? You know my temporary condition." Then, quite desperately, he asked, "Did Creech offer you assistance? I really could use that fifty."

"He just wants to be my friend," I said, and walked off. That was the day I rolled my sleeves up, went to work, and really started the *Banner*. E. J. Creech made me mad.

The last time I saw Margolius was a few minutes afterward. That worn-out roué of a traveling salesman reminds me of the Devil in distress, forced to share the ill of mortality. Paris? London? Women of surpassing beauty? Maybe in his dreams. He put each foot carefully before the other as he walked across the street from The Big Store. His face was gray when he came into the printing office and sat down on a stool. Drained. Empty. A stubble of whiskers showed.

I remember thinking, "He's at the bottom of his life; I'm at the start of mine."

"Boy, have you got a drink?" he asked, looking at the floor. "No? Then go get me one. I need it."

I took Creech's subscription money and came back with half a pint.

He drank hastily and then said, "He's snitching on me, boy—to the B.L. Kahn Company—and he's seized my trunk. Just a little matter of a little money he paid me last year for merchandise. I spent it, sure. E. J. Creech's money or B.L. Kahn's money—what difference does it make? I'll pay it back. I always do. I had a little party on it. Money. What's it for? There's always more where it comes from. They print it, don't they, boy?" He stared at the old press as if it held some hope, then said, "Everybody has to juggle money."

"You look sick," I told him. "Better lie down."

"Down?" said N. Margolius wryly. "What do you do, boy, when you're blacklisted by 'Specialists in Knickknacks for Dressy Women'? There's a slogan. B.L. Kahn ought to snatch that one. I suppose he'll send notices to the trade: 'We regret that N. Margolius is not reliable.' Night-clerking in third-rate hotels would not do for me. I have my pride," he said with dignity.

"Now, boy, let's you and me stop and think about it. He's a moral and an upright man. I could handle him all right if I hadn't already kited every store on the circuit. Not checks. Nothing to get me in bad with the police. Just advance orders. Cash in advance. Damn it, what a practice! Why don't they keep their money?" He weighed the problem carefully, but it was far too heavy for him. I can see now he was too tired to care any longer. "Oh, to hell with them," he said finally, staggering to his feet. "I detest the shabby and the cheap. These moral merchants!" He went lurching out of the office.

"Keep the trunk, you miserable skinflint," he yelled from the middle of the street, his face a fiery red. "Steal it from the B.L. Kahn Company. What's in it that's worth anything?" His hat fell off. "There's not a blasted article in the whole trunk that belongs to me—I wouldn't own the stuff—except the dress, and I'm coming back for that. You and your sixty-nine dollars and ninety-five cents! I've spent that much in an hour! I'd like to cram it down that pursy mouth of yours, small change and all! Go ahead. Write the company. I dare you!"

Silence answered from The Big Store. The mangy dog got up and slunk away.

"Remember, that red dress is mine!" he shouted. I've often wondered where he got a dress like that. It *was* unusual. Striking. "I'll ruin you if you dispose of it," he yelled, and some buzzards that had been roosting on a roof flew off. "It's quality. You hear me, Creech? *Quality*. Oh, what the devil," he charged in utter hopelessness, "would you or Mrs. Creech know about the word?"

That was his final challenge to the world of practicality, a defiant last crow at the miserable monsters he detested so. They cramped his style. I can see that now. What a lot they had to answer for, filling his life with evasions and excuses, hasty borrowings and substitutions, embarrassments that called for boldness and quick action—but ended in exposure always.

He fell dead.

Not many days afterward, the trunk with all its shoddy samples, addressed most scrupulously and honestly in the cramped hand of E. J. Creech, went to the B.L. Kahn Company. A few days later the red dress appeared in the show window of The Big Store.

On its right were cheap things of calico, gingham dresses with stiffly penciled price tags, bargains at two ninety-eight, and on its left were part-wool suits as shoddy as the part-wool blankets stacked at the entrance to the store; but the red dress was a thing apart. In its new setting of overalls and work shoes, imitation-silk stockings, cotton socks, and bean-pickers' overalls, this object, so startlingly different from the usual stuff he sold, alone stood in Creech's window without a price tag.

Thus it could have stood, I believe, in a window by itself, anywhere. For there was about it a vibrant personality. Stylishly cut and low, without an ornament, the red dress seemed to say, "Where in all the Everglades is there a woman fit to wear me? I am Palm Beach and Cannes and

Newport, life and love and laughter. Margolius? He said that first? And who was he?"

E. J. Creech joked about the red dress at first. "I guess I got hooked," he said. "I'll never get my money out of it. Sixty-nine ninety-five. Why, I wouldn't even put a price tag on a dress as expensive as that. It's ridiculous. Maybe," he laughed, "I'll have to give it to Mrs. Creech," and she smiled at his humor, but when he turned his back, I thought she gave him a cool look.

The women admired it, though. We used to joke about it in the printing office, I and the boy I finally got to help me. It was worth a chuckle any day to watch a stout farm wife walk past Creech's store—that is, just almost past—and hesitate, and turn, and stop to look at the red dress.

༺   ༻

Despite Margolius' prediction, E. J. Creech did not own my paper at the end of thirty days. By the grace of Providence, I kept the *Banner* going, paid the rent on the dot, and even saw a dollar of my own occasionally. I got a million-dollar education at first hand.

"Frederick Lyman Sutton" was "Freddie" for a while and then plain "Fred L. Sutton" before I dropped the "L.," and darned if I'm not "Uncle Sut" today, "The Saw Grass Sage." They learned me.

Fancy English? I can use it, but what difference does it make if you get the sense across? The big papers have their rules, but I try to make my stories real. I write them in the language the people understand. Little stories about little people. That's all I've ever had. I told who hit it rich, who broke a leg, who got frozen out, who came to town on Saturday.

"They will be your people, and you will be their voice," N. Margolius had said.

He wasn't so far wrong. I remember the faces of the multitude that was erased: the high and the low, the rich and the poor, the gamblers and fast women. I can still see the chattering Saturday-night crowds swinging down the streets, interlacing, pausing, talking, flowing two ways at once: the high-booted farmers, the quiet farm wives, the 'gator hunters, the catfish fishermen, and the Negroes who toiled in the fields. Faces, stolid and contented, pale and frightened, set and purposeful: have you ever looked at the faces of a crowd?

Call it a slice of humanity, if you will; I can't. From a distance there is no more distinguishing them than one blade of grass from another; yet each is set apart, alone. That's one thing I learned in the Everglades: A human face is like a person's name; in all the world there's only one soul looks at it and says, "It's me."

Names made news in the *Banner*. I saw to that. Lord, how I worked. Even E. J. Creech was proud of me. There wasn't an issue appeared in print without three or four hundred names in it—the names of people. That's what makes country newspapers great. I put in print the names of men who couldn't read, and they were my friends for life. I put in the names of women, poor, drab women like Mrs. Creech, with their little "socials." Innocuous? Well, hardly. Every name was a face to me; I knew them all. They got to like the *Banner*.

Those crowds are gone, and I mean gone forever, whoosh, with the finality of death. The wind howled down and picked them up and scattered them, the waters covered them, the saw grass swallowed them—but the *Banner* never forgot. We carry in our left ear—that's the little box alongside the paper's name on the front page—two words: "Remember 1928."

✽   ✽

The red dress became more than just a thirty-day wonder in the window of The Big Store. When Mr. Creech opened his store in the mornings, he would say, "Maybe we will sell the dress today. Only way I'll ever get my money from Margolius."

Mrs. Creech took charge of the dress. She saw that it was moved back out of the sun in the heat of the day and covered with a cloth after hours at night.

The crowds used to circulate down the street, looking in all the windows. When they got to Creech's, the women had eyes only for the red dress. I guess just about every woman in the 'Glades looked at it, but those who knew Creech were suspicious of the absence of a price tag; and anyway, it patently was not for them. They looked, and walked away, resigned. It got to be a speculation in the settlement: who, if anyone ever, was going to buy the dress?

Some made fun of it. I heard Mrs. Cornelius—she was the butcher's wife—remark, "I wouldn't have it. The skeeters would eat your arms alive in that there thing without sleeves." But personally I thought that Creech was smart. It was good advertising.

One Saturday night I was startled to recognize the woman I had seen for just a moment that day our tug foundered the skiff in West Palm Beach Canal.

She had her little girl with her, the towheaded kid, and the two of them just stood looking at the dress in the window of The Big Store. The child kept fidgeting around, but the woman was rooted to the street, hungrily staring through the glass. Both were barefoot, and they both looked wild—I don't mean it in the common sense—especially the woman, like a wild creature that had wandered into town from the swamp and was fascinated by an object strange and new.

How can I describe her so that you will understand just exactly what I mean? I can tell you what I know now: that she was the wife of Ed Trott, an alligator hunter; that they lived—if you can call it living—in a palmetto shack on a canal bank near the edge of Big Saw Grass Swamp; that she was about sixteen going on seventeen—and fated to be what the Crackers down our way call "a good breeder."

There used to be a thousand women like her from St. Johns Marsh to Fish Eating Creek; women who bloom like moonflowers that fade overnight. I suppose they have hope at the start that life will be something other than a succession of pasty infants who miraculously always live and thrive; that home will be something better than a palm-thatched roof, a canvas fly, maybe a strip of old sheet metal for one wall; that their men will settle down, instead of spending in the juke joints everything they make.

But it is beyond me to conceive that such a woman as Della Pearl Trott ever had the faintest hope that her husband Ed could ever be a moral and upright man like E. J. Creech, a leading citizen in an ordered community, instead of something just one degree removed from a wild Indian. That never happens. Well, hardly ever.

Della Pearl was still looking in the window at the dress, oblivious of the crowd passing by, when I strolled over at closing time to meet E. J. Creech and walk to his Bible Class with him. Of course I went—in a suit for which I had paid cash—and I remember that he gave a rousing good talk that night on the Ten Commandments, especially the one about not coveting thy neighbor's wife.

All through the Bible talk I kept thinking about the woman. She was rather small—I guess she hadn't stopped growing yet—with yellow hair and big blue eyes. She wore a dress made of harsh cotton print with small flowers on it—not plain flour sacks, like the first time I saw her, but decorated sacking, the kind some of the mills in the South use to sack grain, chicken feed, and flour. It gives their brands an extra buying appeal in hard times. You can make dresses out of it practically free.

᠅ ᠅

I never did get married myself—old bachelor "Uncle Sut," that's me—because I guess I didn't have the gall to bring my girl out here, raw as it was then. A funny thing. She did come out, and she took one look—and left. I never found another suited me. What difference does it make? I ran the *Banner*. I was the editor. I even got E. J. to advertise. He saw I wasn't going under and gave in, in tribute to the fact that I had what it took. I even got to like the rascal—in a way.

"Frederick," he would say, "the right girl will come along someday. A real helpmate like mine. A steady woman you can trust. The Lord picks 'em out; not us."

He had some shining stars that guided him. They twinkled in his little soul. I see them now. One was hard work, the hardest sort of work, "root-hog-or-die." He worshiped it. Another was his love of what he called merchandising.

"At first," he told me once, "I had a hard time getting Laura to understand just what real merchandising is. She's sentimental underneath. You wouldn't think it, wouldja? People and feelin's—even friendship, Frederick—don't enter in a business deal. Not if you're going to get ahead. I learned that from the Indians. They'd lay a 'gator skin or 'coon hide down in front of me," he said, "and I'd put a quarter on it. Silver money. Cash. They'd walk on off, and come on back, and finally they'd take it. Argue, yes. Pretend they didn't like me, sure. But folks will always meet your price if you hold out. Remember that.

"Why, before I married Mrs. Creech," he said, "and built our home, I was already a success. Saved my money. You'd be surprised how many shiftless folks try to borrow from me. Even now. They say they hate me, but they don't. Don't you believe it. It's envy, Frederick. That's what it is. Jealousy.

"Laura and I often talk about it. How it pays to be careful and saving. We've got security. Happiness, too. Ours is the first real home in the 'Glades—not a shack, a home. We don't have no children—the Lord hasn't seen fit to bless us so far—but we've got The Big Store and our church work and each other.

"Laura—" he lowered his voice to a confidential whisper—"is plain, but smart." We were working over an ad in his office, a cubbyhole on the balcony at the rear of The Big Store. "If I keep trying long enough, some-day I'll teach her how to merchandise."

I was jotting down a monotonous list of "Specials for This Weekend" when we heard the voice of Mrs. Creech below. It was a cool, calm voice, yet somehow strangely patronizing, unlike Mrs. Creech. "Nice of you to ask about it, but really it is not for sale."

"Laura," said E. J. Creech, before he got up to look, "there isn't a dratted thing in The Big Store that we won't sell. You know that. What in Tophet ails you? Want me to come on down and do the merchandising?"

Silence answered. Of course it was Della Pearl Trott, inquiring about the red dress. I knew it would be, when E. J. pushed the ad aside and he and I went to the balcony to look.

He saw the humor of it right away and nudged me. An air of hidden mirth pervaded The Big Store when Mrs. Creech got the red dress out of the window and slowly handed it to Della Pearl. Della Pearl's little kid sat quietly on a chair.

While the woman took the dress and went to put it on, Creech and I stood expectantly above.

Never so long as I live will I forget the sight of Della Pearl Trott in the red dress. She had gone into the ladies' dressing room a tawdry grub, and she emerged a creature in a blood-red gown, with poise and charm and grace. The two were made for each other. Margolius was right: "This dress was made for one woman to wear." In another way, Margolius was wrong: "There isn't anywhere in all the Everglades a woman fit to wear this dress."

Her hopelessness was gone—if one could be hopeless at her age. "It fits," she said, eying herself in the mirror on the wall. "I like it," said the woman—or should I call her child?—and anyone could see that her spirit poured out in gratitude to the image in the mirror. No one will ever know, of course, but I like to think that she was saying to herself, "It's me! Oh, thank the Lord, it's me, so lovely and so beautiful."

E. J. had his chin on the balcony railing, with his hands under it. I never saw a man quite so absorbed. You might say that he was all eyes, didn't hear a word. He was like a creature in a spell, charmed, fascinated, enthralled by the vision spun by Margolius' red dress.

"I'll take it," said Della Pearl. "It suits me to a T."

Mrs. Creech's voice was low and clear. "That will be sixty-nine ninety-five," I heard her say.

"Did you say six ninety-five?" The girl was reaching for her purse.

"Oh, no," said Mrs. Creech, and there was malice in her voice. "This is a quality dress, what they call an original."

"That's quite a lot of money, really more than I have with me." Della Pearl hesitated, looking around like a trapped creature, desperate but gracious still, as though the gown had made a lady of her. "Couldn't you possibly let me pay something down and—"

"I'm very sorry," said Mrs. Creech in the most patronizing tone. She had perfect control of herself. Her voice was firm. I got the impression that this was really Laura Creech herself who spoke, undominated, free. "You'll have to take the dress off and come again when you have the money. Save it up, you know. Mr. Creech never breaks his rule: 'Pay Cash and Stay Friends.'"

"Of course. I understand," said Della Pearl. Her face was white. The red dress hung dejectedly on her now. The radiance was gone. She went into the dressing room and came back wearing her own dress.

And E. J. Creech chose just that moment to laugh, as though he had awakened suddenly from an unbelievable dream.

Not much of a laugh, and he quickly sobered when the woman turned and looked up at him. She gave him a long, cold, heartless look—I'd hate to tell you just how cold it was; it froze my blood—and walked out, taking her child with her.

E. J. was flustered. He said, "My goodness, that wasn't right. I didn't mean it that-a-way," and went hopping down the stairs. I suppose he meant to tell her that he had laughed at something else, or even was going to break the rule and offer her the dress on time, but she was gone, and he soon came up again.

"That was a mistake, me laughin' like that," he said morosely. "I mighta hurt her feelin's, and it ain't good business ever to lose a customer. Maybe she won't ever come back—" he looked out at the store again, but there was only Mrs. Creech calmly putting the dress back in the window— "and if she don't, it's my fault, not my wife's. My wife done right. It was the wrong thing to do, though, for me to of laughed out loud. Not good taste."

He brooded—I thought altogether too weightily—and I tried to bring his mind back to the ad, but he would have nothing of it.

"Let's skip the ad this week. I always do the wrong thing when I want to the least. I never intended to keep the dress more than a few days, but then he died. I wish I could give it back," he finished, as though he had a presentiment of the evil power of the red dress and sensed the great storm that was on its way.

や や

After that embarrassing incident, it seemed to me that E. J. deliberately put himself out to make amends. The Trotts stayed around—'gator hunting was pretty good in Big Saw Grass—and E. J. never lost a chance to give them a friendly wave when the little family passed his store. I was in there once when they were buying shoes for Lura Mae—that was the little girl—and an odd thing happened. He sold a pair under price.

Mrs. Creech reminded him about it afterward. "Those baby Oxfords, size three," she said, "generally sell for one ninety-eight. You must have made a mistake. The register says one eighteen. Shall I call them back?"

"Forget it," said E. J. "It's only eighty cents."

You might say the Trott family chose the neighborhood of The Big Store as a sort of hangout on Saturdays. There was hardly a Saturday night, at least, but what one or the other was around. Once just before closing time I noticed Della Pearl standing again outside the show window. She had a hand on her hip and was swaying ever so slightly to the music of a juke box down the street blaring *Rattlesnakin' Daddy, Don't You Two-Time Me,* as if a little of the music of the red dress had entered her soul.

When I was walking home with Mr. Creech from Bible Class to my quarters in the office—it must have been about eleven thirty that night, and the street was dark—we encountered all three of them headed back toward Big Saw Grass Swamp.

The street was just about deserted, and Ed was staggering along, trailing a sack of flour in one hand and holding the child by the other, coming from the juke-joint district. Those buzzards, I bet, had picked him clean.

E. J. looked at him. "It would be a real Christian act to help that man," he said.

Behind them walked Della Pearl. She was talking to herself. "Their rotten town, I'd like to see it blown off the map."

I heard her. So did Creech. Ed lurched against the side of The Big Store so hard he made the window rattle in the night.

"Yes, sir, that man needs help," said E. J.

ॐ ॐ

This Ed Trott—at least the one I knew back then—was really rugged. I don't suppose he had ever seen a comb or a toothbrush. He was heavy-built, born over around Immokalee, I later learned, not much different from an Indian, except his hair was bushier and he had thick black stubble along his brown jaws. Black eyebrows, too.

I ran a little item about him: "Edward Trott of Big Saw Grass is bringing his trade to Pahokee, The Empire City. He came in with twenty-six prime 'gator bellies last week, including one twelve-footer."

He dropped by the *Banner* office next Saturday to buy a copy. He had had several drinks, but was in a jovial mood. I suppose somebody down at one of the bars had told him his name was in the paper, because he asked me to point out just where it was and he had me underline the letters.

E. J. Creech sort of cottoned up to him. "Ed," I heard him say once, "you oughta get out of 'gator huntin' into something with a future in it, if for no more than that woman of yours. You got you a cute little trick there. Better treat her right. She might run off."

None of us was particularly surprised when E. J. appeared one Saturday night at Bible Class dragging along an embarrassed Ed Trott.

"Mr. Trott here," he said excitedly, "has made up his mind to join us. He has won a great victory. Fellows, I want you to welcome him."

Which we did, although Ed never lost his awkwardness. He was, I always thought, like an Indian in the church, wanting to burst out through the wooden walls. That first night E. J. took the floor and gave a rousing good talk on the story of Cain and Abel.

Every Saturday night after that they came to Bible meeting together, except of course those times when Mr. Creech had to go back to get his books straight, and even then he was always considerate enough to bring Ed over and stay a while, if no more than to see that he was at ease with us.

శ్ర   శ్ర

You've heard about the hurricane of 1928. It blew Lake Okeechobee right out of its bed, the way a giant would blow coffee from a saucer. It smashed every ramshackle shack in the 'Glades from hell to breakfast, poured a wall of water over our town and all the rest, and drowned—how many? Who knows? Two thousand? Three? What difference is there if disaster strikes a thousand or just one?

Sure I'm philosophic. You would be, too. "Uncle Sut, the Saw Grass Sage," that's me. I never wrote a ponderous editorial. Nobody ever ohed and ahed at me. But I hung all night to a water tower while the great wind raged and a town was destroyed, a people decimated. A lot of little things humbled me.

The day the big storm first began to be felt, E. J. was gone all day, looking out for his property interests over at Okeechobee City, we supposed. It's funny how a little place keeps track of everyone. He got back that night just in time to see the front of The Big Store going up in the holocaust.

How the fire occurred we didn't know; it all seems part of a dream today. The wind that morning came in puffs, and the storm warnings had us all on edge. When night fell, we knew for certain that the hurricane was on us. I remember the mixture of calmness and confusion, the frantic sound of hammers boarding up the shacks and store fronts, the little, futile efforts that we made to get the women and children to safe places. The fire had practically enveloped The Big Store when it was first discovered, eating away at the great mass of dry goods and notions, dresses and slips, rayon and calico. How, I thought, N. Margolius would have enjoyed this! We fought it for a little while, racing in and out. Someone, I remember, came bursting out with the old cash register and dumped it on its face. One man plunged in and then came out again with an armful of gingham frocks and tossed them in the mud, where they were trampled on by the crowd.

The old building flared. Its timbers were of pitch pine, and the wind roared at it like the bellows of a furnace.

E. J. showed up just at the end. I didn't see his car. He grabbed an ax, busted the show window, and wanted to jump in. The flames were there already. I remember now that the red dress was gone, as though the ghost of old Margolius had come to claim it.

"It ain't no use, E. J.," I yelled at him, above the roaring of the wind and flames. "You better go see about Mrs. Creech. They're evacuating everyone. The Lake may spill its banks."

He didn't nod; he just walked off—while the wind ripped at his clothes, and buffeted him, and pushed him on.

Don't ever low-rate a puff of wind, a drop of water, or a blade of grass. Don't you ever. That's "Uncle Sut" talking, and I know.

We never found the half of them.

Ed Trott and his little girl were saved, although he had a bad wound in his left shoulder. It would have killed an ordinary man. One of those freak things that happen in all hurricanes—people get their heads lopped off by flying sheets of roofing. A stick or something had gone through him like a bullet. Searchers found him tied in the crotch of a cypress some distance from his camp two days after the water went down; they marveled how he'd got there, and they marveled that he lived, but he did. It's hard to kill a man. The little girl, she showed up afoot, like a swamp rabbit, at the edge of town. She was unharmed. It passed here for a miracle. I made a big play about it in the *Banner*.

No one ever found a trace of Della Pearl. Mrs. Creech was missing, too.

Hundreds just disappeared. The saw grass was so vast; often we couldn't even reach the bodies when the buzzards circled. It was a terrible thing, a shocking thing, with absolute finality about it. Where some homes had been there was absolutely nothing. Even the best of them, like Creech's, were blown away, with never a board or a nail of them seen again.

Creech showed up the morning after, poor man, draggled and wet, beat and bruised, his face drained dry. You could tell he had been through a horrible experience; but so had just about everyone else, and what with rescue work and recovering the bodies, no one had time to sympathize. Someone did hear him say, "The Lord has taken away," and somehow, as often happens in the hysteria of tragedy, the story got spread around that Mrs. Creech had been torn from his hands by the hurricane.

He worked like a crazy man, helping to locate the bodies. There wasn't any spot in the saw grass, it looked like, too dense for him to penetrate—even after we got the amazing news that Mrs. Creech was alive. She had gotten out on the last truck to leave the 'Glades. The news didn't seem to change him much. He kept going long after all the rest of us had quit. It took a week, you know, to make even a halfway job of it, and the buzzards were still circling when we stopped.

♪   ♪

There weren't any real funeral rites. Just the Pentecostal preacher from our church. I doubt he was ordained. We piled the bodies on trucks and carted them to Big Mound for burning and for burial in one great, yawning, faceless grave. How he did it I don't know, but E. J. seemed to manage to be everywhere at once. He never missed a truckload, and he was there when the final load came in.

"She isn't here," he said.

Then we knew that the storm had affected him.

"Your wife's all right. She's back in Pahokee right now," some friendly soul reminded him. It was right pitiful. "Snap out of it, man. You're lucky. She's saved."

E. J. just stood there with tears in his eyes. Two big drops coursed down his cheeks. "It's a terrible loss," he said. Then he dug his hands in his pockets, felt all through them, sorted out the junk, and handed me a water-soaked hundred dollar bill. It was almost illegible. Today I don't know whether it would pass. What a story it could tell!

"Fred—" he forced it in my pocket—"I want you to take this and keep it until the day I die, like these—" he motioned at the grave—"and when

I do, I want you to write my obituary. Not now," he said, waving me away. "I'll send for you."

And so he did.

ᔛ ᔛ

Just the day before yesterday someone brought word that E. J. Creech was dying. So I got my pencil and my pad, felt in my pocket to see if I still had the hundred-dollar bill after twenty years, and started over.

Driving along, I thought, "What a difference a few years can make."

Today one of the outstanding men in Pahokee is Edward P. Trott, "Tractors and Diesel Engines, Disc Harrowing a Specialty." He's one of my best advertisers. Many a thousand acres of saw grass he's plowed up. Folks say his wife—well, we all call her his wife—made a man out of him; taught him to read and write, helped him get ahead. He's president of the Civitans this year; and his daughter, that little towheaded kid saved from the storm by Providence, has three half-brothers and two half-sisters. The *Banner*— it seems just a year or two ago—announced her graduation from high school, "most popular girl in the Senior Class."

They are a real American family, and I like to think of somebody like Ed Trott coming up from the swamps to turn into a successful businessman. It shows there's opportunity in the 'Glades.

The 'Glades have spawned enough characters. E. J. Creech turned into one. Folks said that the loss of his store, and then the terrible illusion that he had lost his wife, wrecked his mind. He built a little palmetto shack for himself over near the edge of Big Saw Grass, where his car was found after the storm, and sometimes he would be gone from it for days, scrounging around in the saw grass, the 'gator hunters said. One of their jokes was that it was a wonder he had any hair left on him, he spent so much time prowling through the knife-edged grass.

Laura Creech stayed on in Pahokee. She was a heartless and shameless woman, we all thought then; but anybody who knows Laura Trott today has to admit she's different. What a personality. She's the president of the Women's Club, rouges up her face, paints her lips, and dresses in the loudest stuff you ever saw. If she could get royal purple, I think she would wear it, and her hats always have loads of flowers and doodads on them.

Public indignation almost ran her out of town when she first tried to get her divorce from poor old crazy E. J. The county judge gave her a good, stern dressing-down for her heartlessness; but she didn't seem to care. She went "Phooey!" at every known convention, took up with Edward Trott and, take it from me, she runs the women's side of our town now just like Ed does the men's. I wouldn't want to cross her.

Which reminds me about the argument we had about the memorial at Big Mound. The *Banner* started it. I tried to return E. J.'s hundred dollars half a dozen times, but he sent it back each time; so finally I got the idea: why not make it the basis of a monument for the people who had perished in the storm? We started a campaign and had two thousand dollars raised when the controversy rose about what words were to go on the monument.

"The Civitan Club," said Edward Trott, "has picked 'To Our Heroic Dead.'"

"What's heroic about them, Ed?" I asked. "They were just poor, luckless humans caught in a trap of wind and water."

"I'm not here to argue," he replied, biggity as all get-out. "I'm here to tell you what the Civitans want on that there monument. And it either goes on it or we withdraw our contribution."

The Women's Club selected: "Their Memory Will Never Be Forgotten—They Gave Their Lives That We Might Live." It was a pretty sentiment, but Laura Trott laughed it down; it wasn't true. "Half of them are long forgot already. I know," she said. "That storm took; nobody gave. Why don't you call the whole thing off," she suggested, "and start a hospital-fund drive with the money?"

I did, although I held out E. J.'s hundred bucks. The *Banner* got the credit, the 'Glades got a hospital, and Laura did the work. She's no slouch, that gal. A natural leader.

When you're running a newspaper, it pays to act for the living and let the dead wait. I remember back right after the storm, when folks were saying that the disaster proved the Everglades never would be fit for human beings to live in, how we campaigned for the federal government to build the giant levee around the Lake. I can hear myself talking at that town meeting, making them see hope again. "This here's going to be a land of homes and farms—safe homes and farms," I told them. It sounded like the false voice of Margolius: "With the fear of the shadow of disaster forever taken away."

Yes, today I will admit that for a while at least the *Banner* did live up to that vainglorious slogan, "Voice of the Empire of the Sun." We spurred delegations to Washington; jumped on Congressmen; we never let an issue hit the streets that didn't yell in banner type for the big levee—and there it stands today, fifty miles of breastworks, eighteen million dollars' worth of sand and rock, bulwarking a people. The rich farms and the fields stretch off from it. Our people struggle, yes; they gamble, and they win or lose; storms destroy their crops, floods cover their fields, sometimes the frost reaches down and withers everything; they're rich tonight and poor by morning; but Okeechobee is tied down, Big Saw Grass Swamp is licked; we've got schools and churches, and they're safe—at least until another red dress comes along.

჻ ჻

I found him alone in his shack near Big Bend, where we had found his car wrecked after the blow. He was half sitting up in an iron cot.

"Make yourself at home, Fred. You know why I want to see you. I'm dying. On my way."

"Pshaw, E. J.," I said, "there's nothing wrong with you. Here—" I reached into my pocketbook and took out the hundred-dollar bill—"all you need to do is, take this and go on a toot."

He waved it off. "Keep it. Give it away," he said. "What's money? That hundred dollars was just to make sure you'd come. Freddie, I wanted somebody to listen to me when I got ready to talk. About what happened. I knew you'd come if you thought you owed it. Too bad you've got a conscience, Fred. Throw it away. I got insurance. And it won't cost nothin' to bury me, nohow. I want to be planted in the mass grave at Big Mound, just like they were.

"When was I born? Put your dratted pencil and pad away. I didn't start to live until I met that woman. I been lonesome all my life, Fred. You know what lonesome is? You against the world? I always bragged about how I set out from home to make my way. You know what really happened? They run me off because I ate so much.

"Forget the obituary. Just put it in the paper: 'E. J. Creech, 1888–1947.' That's all. I was a proud man, Freddie. That N. Margolius didn't half know what pride was. Him," he scoffed. "Being hurt? I didn't have nobody I cared a hoot for," he said, "till that day I seen Della Pearl in the red dress.

"I took five thousand dollars in cash, every cent I could lay my hands on, and give it to her to keep while I went into the swamp with her husband Ed," he said grimly, "to kill him—but I didn't have the guts to finish what I started.

"Laura knows. She ain't had a midgeon of use for me since the night of the big storm. I left her alone," he said, "while I went back to Big Saw Grass.

"Della Pearl stood there in the clearing when Ed and I walked into the swamp," said E. J. Creech, "holding the kid in her arms like a child holding a doll. She waved at us; she meant that wave for me. She knew right well Ed wasn't coming back."

He was silent for a while. "Big Saw Grass Swamp," he resumed, "swallowed us up. It gulped us down. There ain't no other words for it. You never been in the big saw grass, have you, where the blades are six feet tall? That's where we went, me following him. I shot him through the back, and saw him fall. I can still see the little wisp of smoke rising up from the gunshot.

"Me and Della Pearl," he continued calmly, "had planned it out. I cousined up to him for quite a while before I got him to invite me 'gator hunting. Even got him to come to the Bible Class. You remember that?"

I nodded.

"Me and her," said Old Man Creech, "were going to run away together afterward. It would be weeks before the body would be found. A couple of things went wrong. We planned it out so good, too. Every detail. I kept putting away money that wouldn't be missed until I had five thousand dollars, but the books didn't show it. Mrs. Creech couldn't find it. A smart man," he said, and I thought of N. Margolius, "has to juggle things.

"All the long way into the swamp," he continued, "I kept thinking how pretty Della Pearl looked in that red dress. You know, a funny thing about it, I tried to give it to her—on time, of course—a few weeks after that happened in the store; but she refused it. Then I tried to give it to her outright after she hugged and kissed me, when Ed was at Bible Class. Don't mind it—I ain't got no shame so far as she's concerned. But she said, 'All good things come in due time; you wait, and I'll get the dress.'

"First it was the saw grass balled me up, and then the storm," said E. J. Creech. "You know how the clouds scudded in that day, gray and low; there wasn't any sun. Directly after I shot Ed, I got lost. Me. I couldn't find my way out of Big Saw Grass Swamp.

"I hate the saw grass," he said impassionately. "It's like something without any feelings, yet hostile. I remember pushing my way through it until I knew I was lost, and my conscience said to me, 'E. J. Creech, you just killed a man because a woman wanted a new dress.' You know, Freddie, my conscience didn't bother me at all. What bothered me was the thought of Della Pearl waiting there with the five thousand dollars.

"I wanted out the worst way, Freddie, but that grass wouldn't let me go. It was taller than my head, denser than a field of wheat, sharper than a thousand swords. I remember taking out my watch and looking at it long after I should have come out of the grass into the clearing, and I was still down in the middle of it somewhere, lost. I fought it, Freddie, while it slashed at my face and hands and the muck grabbed at my feet, slowing me down. You know what it made me feel like? Like the saw grass and the muck was getting revenge on me for being 'the pioneer of the 'Glades.'

"Don't never think that a blade of grass is weak. Put ten million blades of grass together, and they make a power, a mighty power," said E. J. Creech. "Get lost among ten times ten million blades of grass, like I did— They brought me back to him. I'm sure of that. I'd try to go this-a-way, and the saw grass would be a brown wall I couldn't force, but that-a-way it'd open up. There ain't never been anything in my life I wanted to do so much as get back to her. She meant the world to me.

"The saw grass wouldn't let me out, that was all. An hour went by while I walked and pushed and fought, and then I came back to where Ed ought to have been lying dead; but he was sitting up, holding onto a red patch on his shoulder.

"Freddie, I never knew I could be so hard. For just a second I thought of shooting him again, but then I figured, 'Maybe *he* can get me out.' So far as the life of the man went, or his soul, or anything you might put a value on, he wasn't no more important to me than a blade of grass. I started to lie that it had all been an accident and I had lost my nerve and run away.

"'You don't need to explain nothing, Mr. Creech,' he said—that's what got me, Freddie. 'You had every reason to shoot me. The Lord will pardon you. I was just on the point of shootin' *you*.'"

Then he went on: "I got him up, and he knew the way. All the long way back, with my left arm around him and his good arm and shoulder over mine, he kept telling me how *he* had planned to kill *me*. Him and Della Pearl, he said; imagine that! It wasn't true. She didn't have no use for him. It didn't make no more impression on me than rain on the roof, not even when he said, 'But every time I'd get it in my mind, Mr. Creech, I'd see you in the Bible Class a-tellin' the story of Cain and Abel. "Am I my brother's keeper?"'"

"It was how slow we had to go that made me feel so small, Freddie. Dragging him was like dragging chains. He was so grateful. Swore he'd never breathe a word. Freddie, I didn't do right. I should have killed him then or just run off and left him when I got the way clear in my mind. I wasn't man enough.

"When we come out into the clearing, she was gone. That little kid of hers was squalling, all alone. And the wind was really starting in to blow.

"You all thought I was busted up when The Big Store burned. Why, it didn't mean no more to me than saw grass burning. Just a lot of wood and clothes and furnishing—gents' and ladies' wear.

"I just knowed she had gone there to get that red dress," he continued. "I run all the way from Ed's camp to town, and when I saw the store burning, I wasn't a bit surprised. I didn't even care, except when I found the red dress was missing from the show window, I knowed she'd been and gone, and I knowed I had missed her.

"That storm you were all so bothered about, the hurricane—" E. J. dismissed quickly the greatest disaster that had ever hit the 'Glades—"all I could think about was Della Pearl. You know a woman will always come back to a child," he said seriously. "There ain't no woman so hardhearted she won't do that. That's why I figure Della Pearl got drowned.

"I never went to my own home that night; I walked all the way back through the wind and the water to Ed's camp, figgerin' she'd be bound to show up there. She never did. I was the one who tied him in the cypress tree, so he wouldn't be blowed away. I held her little girl all that night, with ropes tied around us, while the wind howled and the water licked away below us. Every once in a while Ed would come to and thank me, Freddie. He never even mentioned her, not once. She could have been blown away clean out of the Everglades to China, for all he seemed to care. I could have strangled him. I wanted to.

"Next morning, when the water began to go down, as soon as it was low enough to wade, I left him there. A pity that they ever found him," said E. J. Creech. "I hoisted Della Pearl's daughter on my shoulder and dropped her at the edge of town. That was your miracle. It was me.

"It just don't seem like justice, though," he said, "that I had to save the man's life twice. He's no good, no good at all; he had no faith in her. The way he acted, you'da thought he believed she run away. That woulda been a cheap and dirty thing to do. That wasn't in her. Not Della Pearl. Big Saw Grass got her. She's still out there somewhere yet."

꒰ ꒱

I was with E. J. Creech when he died. The woman? I know no more than E. J. Creech; she simply vanished, that was all, the way N. Margolius had wanted to rub St. Louis off the map.

The hundred-dollar bill? I've sent it off for a tombstone. Plain granite. Simple. With nobody's name on it. Sentimental? Sure, that's me, "Uncle Sut." I'm going to have it put up at Big Mound, off to one side, not over anybody. Maybe that will end the squabble over the sort of memorial we ought to have for those who are buried there. I've ordered four words cut on it; and I don't give a whoop whether anybody understands what they mean; but to me they are sort of going to stand for those who died in the hurricane and those who were the victims of a different sort of storm.

Just four words, not for all of them in a faceless mass, but for each of them, the faces that I knew, even Margolius—from me, the editor—saying nothing much, only this: "A Blade of Grass."

Kirk Munroe

Kirk Munroe (1850–1930) was a popular writer of adventure stories, in the form of both short stories and novels. Unlike many writers of such fiction set in Florida, Munroe actually lived in the state, making his home in Coconut Grove on Biscayne Bay for forty years. Born in Indian territory in Wisconsin, educated in Massachusetts, and given a taste of dangerous adventure in this country's Southwest, Munroe developed a wanderlust that would take him to exotic places like Alaska, Hudson Bay, the Far East, and the Pacific islands. He sailed, hunted, fished, and camped in remote outposts, many of which he wrote about for the youth of the nation in the numerous magazines that featured short, adventurous fiction.

In the late nineteenth century, Florida attracted him with its canoeing and sailing facilities. After an 1881 visit to Harriet Beecher Stowe in Mandarin near Jacksonville, he embarked on a sixteen-hundred-mile cruise in Florida waters before settling down at Lake Worth with his bride; in 1886 they moved south to Coconut Grove. Like so many writers, he traipsed the world in search of adventures and then returned home to write about them in pleasant, temperate surroundings. He wrote thirty-five book-length stories, including the following about Florida: *Wakulla: A Story of Adventure in Florida* (1885), *The Flamingo Feather* (1887), *The Coral Ship: A Story of the Florida Reef* (1893), and *Through Swamp and Glade: A Tale of the Seminole War* (1896).

The following story, which appeared in *Harper's Young People* (October 25, 1892), takes place east of the Gulf Stream, the river of water that flows north along Florida's east coast. The story deals with one of a sailor's worst nightmares: fire at sea, especially when the vessel has explosives on board.

Several terms in the story may be unclear to landlubbers. A *gig* is a long, light boat that has oars and a sail and is usually reserved for the commanding officer. The *painter of the gig* is the rope, usually at the bow of a ship, that fastens the light boat to the larger vessel. A ship's *davits* are the curved uprights that project over the sides of a ship and are used for suspending, lifting, or lowering a small boat by pulley. *Cat's-paws* refers to ruffles on the water that indicate a wind during a calm; one superstitious practice among some sailors who saw such a ruffle would be to whistle and rub the ship's rigging the way they would fondle a cat in hopes of convincing the wind to come up. A *bobstay* is a heavy wire, rope, or chain rigging that runs near the bow; its purpose is to keep the vessel's bowsprit down and therefore counteract the upward strain of the stays. The *scuttle-butt* on a ship is a drinking fountain.

Cap'n I's Closest Call: A Tale of the Sea

Kirk Munroe

ONE WARM moonlit evening, not many months ago, I stood on the bridge of a great south-bound steamship. We were somewhere off the Florida coast, but far from it, and well to the eastward of the Gulf Stream. Consequently, though the season was winter, the air was as balmy as that of a northern June. The sea was perfectly smooth, and a school of porpoises, darting close to our bows through the phosphorescent waters, gleamed like flashes of liquid silver. The first officer, who was on watch, stood at one end of the bridge, and I leaned on its railing near Captain Ira Carey— or "Cap'n I," as he was always called by his intimates—at the other. My companion was as fine a specimen of a Yankee seaman as ever trod a deck, and had been on the water, boy and man, for nearly forty years. No one of us had spoken for many minutes, when the silence was at length broken by "Cap'n I," who, straightening up and speaking half aloud, as though continuing a train of thought, said,

"Yes, it must have been just about here."

"What?" I asked, anxiously, thinking he had spoken to me.

The Captain regarded me in silence for some seconds before he answered: "The closest call of my life. And though I've sailed these same waters a hundred times or more since, I always look for the place, and never leave the deck until I feel certain that we have passed it. Now I am quite sure that we have; so let's go below for a smoke."

A minute later we were seated in the Captain's spacious and handsomely furnished room, where the warm breeze softly rustled the curtains and wafted the fragrance of our cigars through the open doorways.

"Now for it, Captain," I said.

"For what?"

"Your yarn"

"What yarn?"

"Why, the yarn of your closest call, of course."

"Oh, that! It isn't much of a yarn, and I don't know as I can remember the facts very well, anyhow, it all happened so long ago. But if you must have it, here goes:

"It was more than thirty years ago, and I was only a youngster, in spite of being first mate of the good brig *Rover*, of and from New York, with a general cargo for Mobile. After we'd taken in the bulk of our freight, among which was a lot of what in those days we called 'straw goods,' or carriages knocked down and wrapped in straw, we dropped down to

Bedlows Island, and took aboard five tons of powder. It was in canisters, packed in white pine boxes, and I stowed it directly under the main hatch, where it could be easily got at in case of accident. With this our lading was completed, and having nothing more to detain us, we towed down to the Hook and put to sea. We stood well to the eastward of south until we were clear of the Gulf, and then laid a course for the Hole in the Wall, down here in the Bahamas.

"For a week nothing of incident occurred, except that we got blown farther to the eastward than we liked, and pretty well out of the usual track of vessels passing through the Hole in the Wall. At length the last day that any of us ever spent aboard the old brig came on, bright and hot, with a fair but light breeze that allowed us to set everything alow and aloft, and even to put 'stun sails' on her. When night fell we were not far from where this ship was a couple of hours ago, or about two hundred miles from the northern end of the Bahamas.

"That evening was very much such a one as this, and found us slipping along as smooth as silk, leaving a phosphorescent wake like silver ribbons behind us. The 'old man' and I both turned in at eight bells, leaving the second mate on deck. It seemed uncommon hot and close down below, even for these latitudes; but leaving our doors open for the sake of what air did circulate, the Captain and I kept up the talk we had begun on deck. We occupied the two starboard state-rooms, he the after one, and I the one nearest the bulkhead that separated the cabin from the hold. In this bulkhead was a door.

"Getting started on an old sea-yarn, the Captain kept me awake for more than an hour; but I was getting drowsy at last, and hardly knew what he was saying, when suddenly he sung out, 'Hello, Iry! Don't you smell smoke?' I was wide awake in an instant, and I should say I did smell smoke. It was what had been putting me to sleep, though I had not realized it until that moment. I sprang out of my bunk and into the cabin. There was no fire there, but as I opened the door in the bulkhead such a burst of red flames greeted me that I closed it again in a hurry. Then I made one bound up the companionway, yelling to the Captain as I went that we'd no time to lose in getting out of there.

"As I gained the deck the second mate was taking a turn along the weather-side as cool and unconcerned as you please, without a suspicion that anything was going wrong. He stared at me as though he thought I was a lunatic when I shouted to him that the brig was on fire, and to lower away the gig that hung from the stern davits if he valued his life. At the same time I ran forward to call all hands. The tone of my voice must have frightened them, for I never saw a more scared set of men than those that came aft at my summons.

"A couple of them helped me uncover and lift the main hatch. I thought if the fire hadn't yet got to the powder, we might find time to throw it overboard, and then have a chance of saving the ship. But bless you! the flames were not only *near* the powder, they were all around it, and it is a great wonder we hadn't been blown to eternity long before. As I caught sight of their red tongues licking those pine boxes, I got the hatch back into place in a hurry, and ordered the men into the boat, which by this time was towing astern. All this had happened so quickly that the crew were tumbling over the stern by the time the Captain put his head out of the companionway. There he stood staring about him like one who is dazed. He had stopped to slip into some clothes, and had a medicine chest under his arm in place of the chronometer he thought he was saving.

"With all the calmness I could command I reported to him that our powder was liable to explode at any instant, and begged him to drop into the gig, from which the men were already shouting that they were about to cut her adrift. The 'old man' glanced at the boat, and seeing that it was crowded, ordered me to cut away the starboard-quarter boat, which also hung from davits.

"At this I hesitated. It seemed like deliberate suicide to remain on that brig's deck a moment longer, and I didn't feel any more ready to die then than I do now. At the same time I never had disobeyed an order from a superior officer, and I wasn't inclined to do so for no better cause than cowardice. So I did as I was told; but while hacking at those falls beside that smouldering volcano my heart was so high in my throat that it came nigh choking me. When the boat fell clear, and drifted astern with the Captain, who had jumped into her as she touched the water, yelling to me to follow him, I hadn't the strength to do it. My knees weakened so that I couldn't have lifted my feet to save me. On my hands and knees I crawled aft, and rolled overboard just as the men cut the painter of the gig.

"The instant I touched the water I was all right again, and inside of another minute I had swum to the gig, and was standing in its bows watching the brig. She was slipping away from us very quietly, but more swiftly than I had supposed her to be moving, and her towering pyramid of canvas, bleached to a snowy whiteness or barred with black shadows by the moonlight, formed as perfect a picture of marine life as ever a sailor would care to look upon. At that moment I fairly loved the old brig, and wished that I could regain her deck so as to make one effort to save her. There were no flames to be seen, nor even a trace of smoke, and I heard one of the men behind me mutter that he didn't see why we had left her in such a hurry anyway.

"The words had hardly left his mouth before there came the most blinding glare and deafening crash that mortals ever saw and heard and yet lived to tell of. I was hurled, stunned and blinded, backward into the boat; and before I could in any degree recover my senses, the place where I had stood was crushed into a shapeless mass of splinters by the brig's foreyard that the explosion had sent crashing down on us. A moment later the boat sank, and left us eight souls, dazed, bruised, and bleeding from many wounds, instinctively clinging to the great spar that had so nearly destroyed us.

"That, I say, was the closest call of my life. I hadn't left the brig's deck more than a minute before the explosion took place, and the falling yard would have crushed me to jelly had I been sitting instead of standing in the bows of the boat. Indeed, to go back further, if the 'old man' hadn't taken the notion to spin one of his long-winded yarns, and so kept us both awake for some time after we had turned in, every soul on that brig would have been ushered into eternity without a moment's warning, and her unknown fate would have been recorded as one more of the unexplained mysteries of the sea."

"It was indeed a close call," I said, as the Captain paused to relight his cigar, "and about the very narrowest escape from sudden death that I ever heard of. But how did the brig catch fire? and how were you finally rescued?"

"As to how she caught fire," replied the Captain, "none of us ever knew; but I have always believed that it was through the spontaneous combustion of a lot of oil-skins that formed part of her cargo. As to our rescue, we were taken from the yards by the Captain in the quarter boat, which had escaped without injury from the shower of heavy debris that fell all around it immediately after the explosion. And that reminds me of another feature of my 'closest call'; for if my instinct of obedience had not been strong enough to force me to cut loose that boat at the Captain's bidding, we should probably have drifted helplessly on that yard until we perished from thirst, or could cling to it no longer.

"We had no sail in the boat, and it leaked so badly that one man was kept constantly bailing. Of course we had saved nothing, not even a drop of fresh water or a biscuit. I was in my shirt and drawers, while some of the men had even less clothing. At first we were helplessly bewildered by the suddenness and frightful character of the disaster that had befallen us. It had all happened within a few minutes, and more than once I rubbed my eyes to see if I were not dreaming. While we were in this state, a mass of the floating wreckage, that was burning or smoking in every direction about us, surged against our little craft with such force that she was nearly stove. The hint was sufficient, and taking to the oars, we soon pulled clear of this danger. Then the Captain said that as our nearest land was the Bahamas, less than two hundred miles away, the best thing we could do was to pull in that direction, with a slim chance of making one of the islands and a better one of falling in with some vessel. As all hands agreed that we could do no better, the 'old man' laid a star course that he thought would fetch us to one of the Abacos, and we set out.

"I was thirsty before we started, and the knowledge that we hadn't a drop of anything to drink made me doubly so. Of course I took my turn at the oars with the rest, and this so increased my thirst that by morning I was well-nigh crazy with the terrible longing for water. I recalled all the cool springs and rippling brooks I had ever known; and with closed eyes I could see the old well at home, with its mossy stones, its tall sweep, and its shadowy depths, as plainly as I can see you now. I tell you what, there is nothing equal to a raging thirst for stimulating the imagination.

"At length the long night came to an end, and the sun rose, red and hot, from a sea unruffled by a breath. With this our sufferings were increased, until finally one of the men threw down his oar and declared he would rather die where he was than pull another stroke. Two others followed his example, and for an hour or so we lay idly drifting up the slopes of the glassy swells and into the hollows beyond.

"All at once the Captain, who was standing up, called out that he saw a sail; and as our boat rose on the next swell, we all saw it. An electric shock could not have dispelled our listlessness more completely. The men bent to their oars with such new life that our craft sprang forward as though she were engaged in a race. An hour showed the strange sail to be a schooner, and brought her hull in sight. At the end of another, we were within half a mile of her. Then a breeze came—only in cat's-paws, to be sure, but enough to move her, and in the wrong direction. She sailed away from us at such a rate that while we could hold our own with her, we couldn't gain an inch. For a few minutes we rowed like madmen. Then, as we saw that it was of no use, we began to yell. Singly and all together we shouted until only hoarse whispers came from our blistered throats. The schooner might have been manned by the dead for all the notice her people took of us. Finally we gave up the hopeless struggle, and flung ourselves down in the bottom of our boat, where some of the men cried, while others swore, and still others lay like logs. No one would even look after the retreating schooner, except the Captain, who never took his eyes off her. Suddenly he shouted: 'The breeze has died out again, and her sails are flapping. Now for one more try, men! Remember it's for your lives!' With this he motioned me to the tiller, and took my oar. This time we made it, and I think I was never so grateful for anything in my life, nor so happy, as when we ranged alongside of that little schooner, and made fast to her bobstay. Up to this time we had not seen a human being nor a sign of life aboard her. We clambered up over her bows, and made a mad rush aft for the scuttle-butt. As we did so I saw a man near the wheel rubbing his eyes and staring at us wildly, as though he had just waked. Then we heard him yell: 'Pirates! All hands on deck! We're boarded by pirates!' With that the crew came tumbling up from below, where they had been taking advantage of the calm to indulge in a late morning nap.

"The craft was the schooner *Diamond* from Baracoa, with cocoanuts for Boston. She was only about the size of a Gloucester fisherman, but she answered our purpose as well as though she had been a Cunarder. We could have kissed every plank of her deck in our joy at treading them, and at that moment I for one would not have exchanged her scuttle-butt for all the wells in Christendom.

"No one could be kinder than were the *Diamond*'s people, when they learned of our misfortune. They furnished us with clothing, with food, and with drink to the full extent of their means. Then the schooner was headed for the scene of the explosion, which we reached a few hours later. The sea for miles was covered with the charred wreckage of the brig; but we recovered nothing of value except a few cases of patent-medicines, and the ship's cat, which, with half her hair singed off, we found floating about on a straw-wrapped carriage-wheel. A week later we were in Boston, with our recent sufferings wellnigh forgotten, and ready to ship for another voyage. They are very vividly recalled to me, though, by the knowledge that I am in the very waters where they were endured, and by passing the place of my 'closest call,' as we did this evening."

Padgett Powell

Padgett Powell (1952–) was born John Padgett Powell, Jr., in Gainesville, Florida. He grew up in north Florida and earned a B.A. in chemistry from the College of Charleston (1975) and an M.A. in English from the University of Houston (1982). His grandmother, Rubylea Hall, also featured in this collection of stories, dedicated her novel about Osceola, *Flamingo Prince*, to him: "For my grandson, John (Padgett) Powell, who bears (through coincidence) the name the Flamingo Prince was known by [Powell] until he chose his warrior name, Assi Yohola."

While working as a roofer in Houston, Powell studied under Donald Barthelme and wrote his first novel, *Edisto* (1984). That work, which received very favorable reviews and was excerpted in the *New Yorker*, is about twelve-year-old Simons Manigault growing up along the South Carolina coast. Reviewers made special note of Powell's skillful use of language, his infectious humor, and his accurate portrayal of the modern South. The book has been translated into Finnish, French, German, Hebrew, Italian, Japanese, Norwegian, Portuguese, Spanish, and Swedish.

His second novel, *A Woman Named Drown* (1987), from which the following short story is taken—with slight alterations by Powell—was about a young man's journey from Tennessee through Florida, on to his family's home in Louisiana and back to Tennessee. He meets eccentrics along the way as he travels with an aging actress, and they discover a Florida seldom seen by motorists speeding along the superhighways. The small country towns, rundown motels, and off-the-road attractions remind one of Powell's fellow University of Florida writer, Harry Crews. The main characters in this short story, the traveling young man and Wallace the camp owner, share some beers and darts while they watch Bonaparte spend the day bailing sunken rowboats. Powell has become well known for tight writing and realistic dialogue; one can also see in this story his humorous touches and his identification with those out of the mainstream.

In 1987, Powell spent a year in Rome on the American Academy and Institute of Arts and Letters Rome Fellowship. During that year he and his family traveled to Turkey and liked it so much they spent the 1989–90 academic year on a Fulbright Teaching Lectureship in Istanbul.

Bonaparte's

Padgett Powell

A BUS CAME along and let a load of tourists have at the key-lime pie stand, and I got on. Heading west, through what I think was once Everglades, we passed a HELP WANTED sign and I got off. I walked down a white graded road to a fish camp.

The building was small and low, suggesting an enclosed trailer. It had plywood floors and a plywood ceiling, about head high. Down the longest reach of the joint a woman was throwing darts. She was not throwing them at a dart board and she was not throwing them with the deft, wristy, English toss. She was letting them go like Bob Feller, lead leg higher than her head. On the wall forty feet away was a target painted in crude circles. The bull's-eye alone was big as a bowling ball.

When she finished up the set, I said, "Is there a job here?"

"Ho!" she said, plucking the darts loose. She went behind the bar. She got a beer and slid it to me and took one herself. She broke her pop top without opening the beer, and holding a dart dagger-style, she neatly collapsed the tab with one punch.

"These things changed my world," she said. She flicked the ring off the bar to the floor.

I nodded. I looked out the door, to the water. There was a fallen dock, and tied to it some wooden rowboats sunk to gunwales. They looked like alligators.

"So," she said. "Drink all you want, eat if you want to, don't give any customers a hard time."

"That's it?"

She didn't answer, except to wipe the bar with a ribbed towel which she flopped around like leavening bread. Certain parallels—equivalences were I in a lab instead of a fish camp, in a true reaction series rather than life's—were stunning. Instead of a pool shark, before me stood kind of major-league dart pitcher. Where there had been gin, there was beer. And it looked as though the same no-questions, no-lies ambiance was going to operate.

I suddenly saw that Mary had truly acted according to the constants and coefficients and activities and affinities of the whole series of reactions around me defining this odd interlude. She "left me" with no more wrongful or sorrowful moment than an atom leaves another, than blood becomes iron and oxygen. And I was the evolving product, now in a fish-camp retort with a new reagent not unlike—in fact, startlingly similar to—the last. Who governed these combinations? How could it all be a random walk?

Down near the water was a large kid. He got in one of the sunken boats and started bailing with a cut-out Clorox-bottle scoop tied to his wrist.

"Do we rent those boats to customers?"

She had arranged the darts into a neat parallel arsenal on the bar and lit a cigarette and sat up close on the other side on a stool. She put her beer on a cardboard coaster and passed me one.

"If somebody ever wants a boat, mister, you take their money and drive to Sears and make the down payment on a jonboat. Then, if somebody *else* wants one, we'll rent a boat." She took a giant drag on her cigarette, blowing smoke to the ceiling, in a spreading roil.

At the boats, the kid was bailing away.

"Or let Bonaparte go to Sears," she said. "That kid can *drive*." She leaned a bit to one side and got a look of concentration on her face. I thought she was straining to see Bonaparte. I heard an odd, small, mewing noise. "Hope you don't mind gas," she said.

"It's two things he does. Drive and bail. It would be *Christmas* if he got to drive *and* get a dry boat."

Bonaparte was sitting almost chest deep, scooping the water near him and pouring it out at arm's length.

"Bonaparte," I said.

"That might be cruel," she said. "That might be cruel." She threw the ribbed rag at a big sink behind the bar.

"They told me he had a bone apart in his head to explain his condition. That's how they said it, too. Well, we weren't too excited about it. We weren't too excited about it and got drunk, and next thing we're calling him Bonaparte. Is that cruel?"

"I don't know," I said.

"You ready?"

Before I could gesture, another beer slid to within an inch of the one I was on. Bonaparte, steadily working, seemed to pause and listen to something between pours of his scoop. He was not more than a head and an arm bailing in a blinding disk of sun on water.

"He gives me the *vim* to go on," she said. I noticed him again pause as if listening to distant signals.

"So, where'd you leave your clubs, Arnie?" She laughed at herself. I was wearing my yellow banlon golf outfit.

"Let's get you some khakis and tell all the customers you're the fish guide. Can you see the expression on their face when you wade into one of them wrecks with a Lorance under your arm?" She started wheezing with laughter. Recovering, she said, "That *is* some suit."

We drank, looking at Bonaparte bail.

"You wasn't . . . *golfing,* was you?"

"No," I said.

"You a darts man?"

"Might be."

She marched over, lined up, wound up, and delivered—the dart went a half inch into the wall with a gratifying *thuuung.* On my turn, I missed the whole target, but I hit the wall and I hit it very hard, and she watched me like a spring-training scout, arms folded. "You catch on fast," she said.

We played a game. In the late going—innings, I guess—she'd actually paw the floor as if grooving the mound, and *grunt* when she released. I had never seen better form. Not a customer came.

౫   ౫

Her name was Wallace ("That's cruel, too. Don't call me Wally"). For the regional fishing weekly, *The Glade Wader,* she'd create accounts of boatloads of fish brought in at our nameless camp (in the paper she called us Bonaparte's) and phone this apocrypha in to the editor, when we had not even made the down payment on the jonboat and Bonaparte was flailing away harder than ever.

We would clean the place—it never got messed up, really, but we soaked it down in Pine-Sol in the mornings anyway, because the cats carried crabs and fish under it and we were in effect disinfecting the ground as well as the floors. We poured gallons of pine-smelling ammonia out and swabbed ourselves into sweats by ten in the morning and split a six-pack and looked out of the easy gloom of the bar into the head-achy light, and there, committed as a saint, full of belief, bailing the entire Gulf of Mexico, was Bonaparte. He took to blowing a whistle periodically, perhaps designating invisible progress.

"*Vim,*" Wallace would say, both of us squinting at Bonaparte, both of us nodding, happy to be inside, in the cool gloom, dizzy on fumes and cold carbonation. A man came in one afternoon, sized the place up, had a beer, listened to Bonaparte bail and whistle, said, "Sounds like a disco out there," and left.

A couple came in one morning and watched him bail for a while before suddenly going into a disquisition on hippies. "We saw a van," the man said. "Purple."

"With *butterflies* on it," the woman added.

"All *over* it," the man said.

Wallace served them. We were just finishing the Pine-Sol detail. The woman opened both their beers and poured them into glasses which she inspected in the light before filling, squinting her nose at the ammonia. We could hear Bonaparte working as steadily in the glare coming from outside as a pump in an oilfield. The light came in whole and hot and salty, and reflected off the damp board floor in broken, mirrory planes. The customers were shading their eyes.

"I wish all I had to do was drive around in a dope van all day," the man said.

"With *butterflies* on it," added the woman.

"That would be *the life.*" He motioned to Wallace for beer number two. It was 10:30.

"Hippies," the woman said.

"What's he *doing* out there?" the man asked, with an emphasis that somehow seemed to link Bonaparte with the hippies.

"He's bailing, you sonofabitch," Wallace said, and she walked to the dart wall and planted a foot up on it and yanked out a dart. She wound up and fired one, and the sonofabitch and his wife left.

"See what I mean about you not offending customers?" she asked me. "I can do it, and I can do *enough* of it."

She fired three darts. "Sonofabitch thinks he can drink beer at ten o'clock and some kid can't drive a purple truck." A three-legged cat walked in with a large live crab in its mouth. "Get outside, honey," she said to it, and the cat backed easily out, the crab waving claws to us, as if for help.

After the demonstration of Wallace's diplomacy with customers, I assumed a new demeanor around the few that straggled in. I was a kind of personal valet, the ambassador of good will at Bonaparte's. My job, as I saw it, was to prevent customers from talking, lest they draw Wallace's wrath. I usually took their beer orders with the gravity of a funeral-home operator, giving a long, soulful look directly at them, then the slightest, tenderest nod I could manage toward Bonaparte out at the docks, then another kind of nod toward Wallace. This Wallace nod was in the thumb-jerk category, but was very subdued, and I followed it with a shrug, as if to say, *Given the kid out there, the lady is disturbed, and likely to go off, you understand.* Most did—in fact, some customers, provided this one-two of tactful apprising, gave an exaggerated and solemn nod of their own, clammed up altogether, and would *point* to their brand of beer rather than call it. These folk I had where I wanted—I felt like a matador with the bull quieted and sword ready. Wallace would interrupt the moment of their reverential silence with a great, sudden *thuuung* of dart that would make them spill beer.

Much of the beer consumed was consumed by Wallace and me. We got into a game of drinking certain kinds to correspond with brand deliveries, turning off all the beer clocks and signs except those representing the day's brand. We looked like seven individual low-budget beer commercials. I got inordinately fond of the first beers in the morning that we used to slake through the Pine-Sol, which felt like it was in our throats and *was* in our heads. The clear, cold bubbles of the beer washed in, *stinging* through the piney, gaggy, cottonlike ammoniac air of the freshly mopped bar, and after a good hard mopping that made you sweat and a couple of good cold cold ones to clear the eyes, we'd struggle to the wide, bright door and look out at pure air and heat and Bonaparte bailing and the headachy convection currents already coming off his toiling form and feel, somehow—I did, and I think Wallace did, too—as if the day was wonderful, the place fine, the weather clear, the salt tonic, the world good.

Across this happy-face moment would then waft a small cloud of the real, and we'd step back abruptly and get another beer and realize we were broke, Bonaparte was hopeless, and the sole rescue was hundreds of customers who wanted boats we did not have, fish no one could show them to, hospitality we were fundamentally opposed to granting. Then we'd have a fourth beer, and then it was, well before noon, altogether too bright to look at Bonaparte for any longer than you'd look directly at the sun itself if someone told you it was in lunar eclipse.

It was in all a wonderful time that I knew even during the nose-pinching smallness of it I would remember as fondly as you remember certain mean periods of your life and come to love them for the meanness. Wallace I respected as a soldier—a person who would have gone to West Point and been a rogue general who, despite a career of insubordination, *won;* or a middling prizefighter who won on indomitability alone. Instead, she had a bone-apart child and a fishless fish camp and bottomless boats and won by strategic, stubborn refusal to accede to . . . to what? I did not know: I do not know. She refused to ask for any *relief*—it was as if what she wanted was not a break but one more trial: one more dart in the plywood of her ordeal. And that dart she wanted implanted, solidly, stuck into the heart of the whole losing proposition.

I could not even figure, while I ate it, where the bologna we had for lunch came from. The meat may have been in the chest freezer that Bonaparte froze his crabs in. I never looked in it, because the one time I thought to, it was slept upon by a placid cat with one dusty eyeball goggling out, actually touching the rusty top of the freezer. I saw no cause to wake him. You don't disturb a cat like that to see bologna.

Performing my silent duties as valet to the nearly hypothetical customer, I got to feeling that while Wallace might be set up for the next dart of oppression, I was not, and I hardly saw how my not scaring a couple of couples before they had two beers each could possibly equal my consuming nearly as much bologna as Bonaparte—he was *voracious*—and I decided to get out before the next dark dart struck. In fact, it occurred to me that *I had been it*—the next dart—when I arrived. And now we all awaited the next profitless windfall. These were the events that Bonaparte tracked, perhaps, with his head cockings and whistlings and St. Vitusing out under the broken green-shaded light at the end of the dock.

"Wallace, write me a check for fifteen hundred dollars and I'll give you one for two thousand and you can get him a boat. I'm going." That's my tax philosophy; never write *one* check.

She turned to me, sucking the finger she burned turning the rising mounds of bologna. Bonaparte did not like punctures. "What?"

"Sambo rumbles."

"Kiss my ass."

She turned back to the stove. I got my grocery bag of duds and left, passing Bonaparte in the marsh checking his crab traps.

At the end of the white, graded road where I'd gotten off the bus, nothing had changed, which somehow surprised me. I expected to see even the same bus come barreling down on me from the same direction I had ridden it. I was stunned to be standing where I had stood, and exactly *as* I had stood before, except for the passage of time at the camp, as if I were a boat sunk to my nose and bailing myself out with all the efficacy of Bonaparte up to his chin. You can feel odd standing in a sudden swarm of deerflies—having just thrown darts for a month with a woman you've left with her retarded kid—rippling sawgrass as far as the eye can see, razory salty wheat.

Air brakes caught me dreaming. Before me *was* the same bus, the same driver. I got on. He smiled at me as if I were a traveling salesman returning from a joke. I offered a hundred-dollar bill for the fare and took the smirk off his face.

"Napoleon musta got one dry," he said, expecting me to share with him the lunacy of my days at the camp. I did not. I heard a faint, shrill whistle from behind the bus as we were getting going. Wallace was nailing up the HELP WANTED sign and Bonaparte was whistling and listening vigorously. Then, from too far to tell for sure, I swear he dropped trou and mooned the bus. The driver was looking in his side mirror, but his expression gave no clue.

In Naples I got heroic. I paid for Sears' top-of-the-line jonboat and had it delivered. And I got it in my head to go home.

Jack Rudloe

In the small north Florida town of Panacea lives a man dedicated to preserving the environment, especially its sea creatures, from the pollution of mankind. Whether as a scientist, lecturer, or writer, Jack Rudloe has a persistence, a determination to do his part in saving our world, or at least his little part of it in Florida's Panhandle. Like much of the habitat he studies and writes about, Rudloe is full of paradoxes. A college dropout, he is married to a woman with a Ph.D. in marine biology. Although living near and making a living from the sea, he named his sons after other elements: Sky and Cypress. While he is a serious collector of sea creatures for research, he titled a collector's textbook *The Erotic Ocean*.

In reading the following story, surely the most dramatic of this collection, one must either question the man's sanity or admire his love for his dog. Rudloe, born in 1943, has lived in Florida near the Gulf of Mexico since 1958, when he moved there from Brooklyn, New York. What immediately intrigued this city-born Yankee was the diversity of wildlife in Florida's woods and tide pools. Six years later he started the Gulf Specimen Company and began sending out sea creatures and plants to scientists around the world who used the barnacles, worms, horseshoe crabs, and sea squirts for research into cancer, eye dysfunctions, and radiation.

He also began writing about the wonders he was discovering: *The Sea Brings Forth* (1989), about a scientific expedition he joined in Madagascar; *The Wilderness Coast* (1988), about alligators and giant sea roaches; *The Erotic Ocean* (1984), about collecting sea specimens; *The Living Dock at Panacea* (1977), about life near the Gulf of Mexico; *Time of the Turtle* (1979), about the migration of turtles; and *Search for the Great Turtle Mother* (1995), about the mythology of the sea turtle.

The following story is true. First published in the July 1982 issue of *Audubon* and then reprinted in *Reader's Digest* and included in *The Wilderness Coast*, it tells about a remarkable and deadly encounter with one of the many alligators that live in Florida's lakes and streams. One cannot imagine how fast a gator can move until one sees it dash in water or even on land after nearby prey. As one who has swum with Rudloe in the Wakulla River and seen alligators eyeing us warily (and hungrily?), I can testify not only to Rudloe's courage but also to his knowledge and empathy with such creatures of the wild.

Master of My Lake

Jack Rudloe

My screams burst through the still morning air in desperation and disbelief.

An enormous alligator had rounded the curve of the lakeshore and was bearing down on my Airedale. The cold, yellowish eyes, gliding just above the opaque water of Otter Lake, were fixed on Megan, my companion, my friend for the past three years.

Never had I seen a living creature move so fast, with such overtly grim determination. As the beast sped into the shallows, I could see the ugly white spikes of teeth protruding from its crooked, wavy jaws.

Megan was almost out of the water, swimming to me with a bewildered expression, unaware of the danger closing from behind her in the lake where she swam almost every morning after a three-mile run with me.

Megan's feet hit the bottom.

She's going to escape.

I felt hope, joy. But the black, plated head put on a horrible burst of speed. More and more of the knobby, black body emerged from the eighteen inches of tannin brown water. There seemed to be no end to it.

"No! No! No!" I screamed and rushed forward, somehow hoping to frighten it away, but the reptile couldn't care less. Its attention was fixed on Megan with cold intensity. With an explosion of water, it lunged upward, rearing above my dog almost as tall as a man, its front webbed claws spread menacingly apart. Time seemed to freeze—it was as if *Tyrannosaurus rex* had come to life.

Megan's confusion was transformed to terror. From somewhere inside the reptile came a hissing like a super-heated steam boiler. The hissing became a thunderous, unearthly roar as the alligator struck, clamping its tooth-studded jaws on my pet. Crashing back into the water, it twisted and rolled, driving her down into the mud and weeds.

It's killing Megan . . . My dog . . . My friend!

Something snapped in my brain. I have to *do* something—*make* it let go, intimidate the thing into forgetting its prey. Adrenalin surged through me. With a cry of rage, of fear, of instinct, I found myself running and leaping through the air onto the back of the thing attacking my dog.

Megan and I had been swimming at the lake for two years and had never been bothered by alligators. They were there sometimes, I knew. I had seen them—shy, wild alligators that sank out of sight when approached by humans.

Where this one had come from, or why it attacked, I didn't know. Perhaps it had been hanging around the boat ramp and picnic area on the far end of the lake where weekenders fed it fish heads until it became "tame" and lost all fear of man. But the water had been low, fishing was bad in the scorching July doldrums, and people stopped coming. The handouts dried up.

There was no telling how long the alligator had waited at the landing, a mile from its normal haunt. How many days had it watched us, its bulbous eyes raised just above the dark amber waters, not causing a ripple, measuring each of us against its growing hunger?

Otter Lake was one of my favorite places. Hidden away in north Florida's wilderness, it was a retreat from technology, telephones, doorbells, and monthly bills. When I got tired of sitting at the typewriter in the broiling hot summer, the cool waters of the two-hundred-acre lake always welcomed me and my dog. Towering cypresses with gnarled roots and fat buttresses rose high above the water, their tops lacy with green needles in summer, vivid orange after the first frost, and barren, skeletal, and silver-gray in winter. When it was too cold to swim, I came just to look at the great water oaks with their Spanish-moss-draped branches and green resurrection ferns.

But now the dark water exploded and cascaded as the alligator slapped its tail. I slid over its plates and bumps, groping for a hold on its huge back. I felt numbing pain in my chest as my chin jammed into the ridged back.

My God! What a colossal beast! You're actually on the back of an enormous alligator! It must be ten, twelve feet long.

It was alien, bony to the touch, almost dry, not slimy. There wasn't an inch of give in that rigid, armored back. As I struggled with every bit of my muscle to throw it off Megan, it swelled with air, making the hard-plated scales that normally lay flat rise upward. The thing was suddenly bristling with bony spikes.

Ignoring me, the alligator surged forward and got an even better grip on Megan, who all but disappeared inside the horrid maw. My hands groped the soft underside of the monster's throat and felt the beaded leather and scales that are made into belts and purses. It was almost flabby.

The tail slapped again. Water exploded.

Keep clear of the tail, it can break your leg!

I was a puny, hairless ape trying barehandedly to take on an armored, scaly dinosaur. Every inch of the brute was designed for survival and battle; the only weapon I possessed was a mouthful of ineffectual little teeth. No wonder our species invented sharpened stones!

I hung on, desperately clinging, and tried with all my strength to turn the murderous animal, to keep it from plunging into the sunless, deep waters.

I've got to force it up on land.

My hands groped along its back, and up to its mouth, right where its toothy smile hinged. At least here was a handle of sorts. But it was no more than a skull covered with leather. There was no flesh, no give.

I got a good grip, dug my knees into the sand and yanked upward. The steel-trap jaws wouldn't yield. I sensed them shutting down harder, squeezing life and breath out of my Megan. I saw a flowing trail of bubbles.

If only I had a weapon. A knife!

She's drowning—I'm running out of time!

Again and again I dug in and pulled up on its upper jaw, but nothing I could do distracted it from its single awesome purpose. Fortunately for me, the saurian's only intent was to drag its prey down into the lake and drown it. Its small reptilian brain was able to focus on that and that alone. I was only a hindrance, not an alternative.

I felt my knees dragging through the weeds on the sandy bottom as the alligator pushed inexorably back into the water. I cursed myself for being out of shape from all the hours spent at the typewriter.

With all my might, I slammed my fist down between its eyes, again and again. The only result was pain in my hands. It was like pounding a fencepost. Time, depth, and distance worked against me as the alligator dragged Megan further out into the water. I was losing the territorial battle of terra firma versus the watery world.

The alligator is going to win. It's going to carry Megan into the depths and eat her. It's too strong, I'm going to lose. I won't lose!

Desperately I threw my one hundred seventy pounds into manhandling it, trying to turn it back into my world. For a second, hope returned. I succeeded. The beast did turn. But just for a moment. Then it lifted me up, swung around, and continued on its course.

The eyes . . . go for the eyes.

My fingers worked their way over the unyielding leather-clad skull. I found its eyes, but the two sets of eyelids, one membranous and the other a thick leathery cover, closed, automatically sealing off the alligator's only vulnerable spot. Tightly closed, they weren't soft and yielding. They felt like mechanical ball joints on a car. With all my might I jammed my thumbs down, but it was futile, as if I were jamming my thumbs against hard-rubber handballs.

All my eye-gouging succeeded in doing was making the alligator swim faster. Black water closed over my head; the bottom was now sloping off quickly, and the beast had water beneath it. Any advantage I had was gone. Now it was rapidly entering its own world, and for me it was no longer a battle of land versus water; it was one of oxygen versus the abyss.

I managed to force the alligator up and get my head up for one hard gulp of air before being pulled back down. Again I drove my thumbs into the brute's eyes. By now I knew that my efforts to save Megan were futile. Even if by some miracle I could free her, and she weren't already dead, how could she survive having had her bones crushed and lungs punctured by eighty inch-long spiked teeth?

But I couldn't make myself let go. Again I tried to angle the alligator upward, directing its movement, using its own momentum the way you do when riding a sea turtle. But the water was too deep. And an alligator isn't a sea turtle. Its long tail swept back and forth, sculling it forward. I was towed rapidly out into the middle of the lake.

Once more I got the alligator to the surface long enough to grab another breath; and then we were going down again. Down into the lightless swamp water. I was exhausted, my lungs were bursting. No longer could I see any sign of Megan. My vision was limited to less than a foot—just enough to make out the alligator's coat of mail.

As the light disappeared I felt new fear. I would soon be out in the middle of the lake in twenty or thirty feet of water. The monster might slap me with its tail, drop Megan, and turn on me. The very fury of this primitive battle, the splashing, might draw and excite other hungry alligators. The fear closed over me—fear for myself.

I couldn't hold on any longer. Despairingly I let go and watched its plated trunk churning beneath me into the gloom. It went on and on and on, like a freight train. I saw the rear webbed feet, churning one after the other, and then the narrow, undulating tail with its pale underside flashing. I could not see Megan; I would never see her again.

I boiled up to the surface, erupted into the daylight, filling my lungs with air. When I could breathe again I let out the mindless despairing cry of a wounded animal. My arms and legs thrashed through the water as I headed toward the cypresses and beautiful oaks with their long twisted branches. Finally, hard sand grated beneath my knees; I scrabbled up on the shoreline, crying and yelling incoherently.

In horror, I turned and looked at the empty lake. It had swallowed up all signs of disturbance. Its calm waters mirrored blue sky, stacks of white puffy clouds, and moss-draped oaks. An osprey winged its way across the sky, calling its high-pitched chirp. It was as if nothing had happened.

I fled to my car, wanting to get out of there quickly, to leave it all behind me. I felt betrayed, assaulted, robbed. I sped over the sandy jeep trail, through the palmetto, bouncing over ruts and dips, scratching paint on scrub oak branches, until I spun out onto the highway and raced toward home, still screaming.

Why are you screaming? There's nothing you can do. Control yourself.

꒰   ꒱

FOR DAYS I REMAINED shaken and depressed. I had fought with everything I had and lost. I missed Megan terribly. I kept seeing her golden shaggy face looking at me in bewilderment as I urged her out of the lake. Over and over again, in my mind's eye, that big black head closed in on her. Slowly, from the bruises and scratches and pains in my body, I reconstructed what had happened. The long linear scrapes on my chest had to have come from the alligator's dorsal bumps, the bruises on my ribs and belly were from its thrashing back and forth. The aches in my thighs were from straddling it with a scissor's grip.

"You sure loved your dog all right," my neighbor said incredulously, "but you didn't give a damn about old Jack! People have been hand-feeding that gator all summer until he about crawled up the boat ramp begging food. That's not the first dog he ate. Someone ought to call the game commission and have him shot before he grabs some young 'un."

I was glad to be alive. Jogging along the sandy roads alone, in the following days, I thought a lot about alligators. Fifteen years ago they were nowhere to be seen, hunted to the brink of extinction. Poachers roamed the swamps in small boats, catching those eerie red eyes in their light beam and blasting or clubbing away. Warehouses from Perry, Florida, and Waycross, Georgia, to Newark, New Jersey, were overflowing with illegally taken hides.

Then, in 1970, the U.S. Endangered Species Act banned the international sale of hides and alligator products. Florida passed a similar law, and the market dried up. Large-scale poaching stopped, and the alligator began to recover.

While alligators were increasing their numbers, the human population also swelled in Florida. As dredges sucked up the swamps and turned them into shopping centers and canals, the alligators were driven from their sawgrass and river-swamp homes. But they adapted, taking up residence in golf course ponds, marina basins, and canals. The Florida Game and Fresh Water Fish Commission has found gator nests in people's backyards and chased ten-footers out of carports. In the past ten years there have been three fatal attacks on humans and twenty-two maulings.

In 1978, Florida instituted the Nuisance Alligator Control Program. When someone complains that an aggressive alligator has moved into a backyard, canal, or lake, the state investigates.

If the reptile is deemed a threat, a licensed alligator hunter will be sent to kill it. The game commission auctions off the hides. The hunter, often an ex-poacher, is given 70 percent of the proceeds and is free to sell the tail meat—which tastes something like veal—to restaurants.

Not surprisingly, the game commission now regards alligators as a renewable resource, according to wildlife resources chief Thomas Goodwin.

In 1981, it again became legal to sell alligator products such as purses, belts, and shoes in Florida. State officials claim they can control the market by a complex system of tagging hides and packaging the meat, but the number of poaching violations has more than doubled since 1978.

Archie Carr of the University of Florida strenuously objects to the commercialization of alligators: "Once you open the marketplace and build up the demand for hides, you're dooming alligators and other rarer species of crocodiles to extinction. Overseas the demand for hides is insatiable. This just encourages the worldwide sale of other crocodilian species, most of which are nearly extinct." Then he added, "Aggressive alligators should be shot or carted off but not offered for sale. The state is using the few attacks on humans and the attacks on dogs as ammunition to open up wholesale commercial exploitation. We're going back to the 1940s when you could drive the whole Tamiami Trail and never see an alligator."

The problems of alligator protection are both complex and confusing, and I found myself torn. I couldn't stand the idea of seeing a reptile that has survived unchanged for the past sixty million years exterminated. They are the last of the dinosaurs. Paleontologists have unearthed six-foot-long skulls with six-inch teeth from crocodilians that may have measured forty-five feet long.

But the lake would never be the same for me. I shuddered when I thought that in the very spot where Megan was attacked we had taken our ten-month-old baby swimming.

Again and again I dreamed of the fight, only this time I had a sharp knife. I could stab it over and over into the alligator's corpulent belly and its throat. I could hurt it, make it feel pain. Ex-alligator poachers had told me about the spot in the back of its head where a single stab would kill it instantly, cutting through the spinal column. In my dreams I had a chance.

But those dreams were inconsistent with everything I had worked for. I had been involved in environmental causes for the past twenty years, trying to save blue herons, turtles, and alligators from man's technology, and perhaps in so doing to save ourselves. I knew the importance of these ancient beasts. Without them there would be an overabundance of less desirable fish, like garfish and bowfin, that feed on bass, crappie, and sunfish. Most important, during summer droughts, when swamps are parched and dry, gator holes often become the only source of water for everything from deer to wading birds. Without them the swamp would be a poorer place.

It was three weeks before I returned to Otter Lake and looked out over its placid waters. There was no sign of the alligator, so my wife and I launched our canoe. I wanted to see the alligator again, to begin healing the mental wound it had inflicted, to banish the nightmares. If possible I wanted to restore it to its proper place as a living, flesh-and-blood animal.

We were still close to the landing when suddenly there was an explosive splash; a swirl of water, and there it was—aggressive and brazen. It didn't sink out of sight as we approached but surged ahead away from our canoe, throwing a wake as it crossed our bow. For a moment the hatred and fear returned. I wanted nothing more than revenge—to blast that thing forever to kingdom come.

Before I rode that terrifying beast out into Otter Lake, as it clutched my dog in its jaws, I would have been able to view the whole thing objectively. But now I had been affected personally. Whether I would ever swim in that lake again I couldn't say.

Sitting in the canoe, I watched the new master of my lake move out into the middle and then slowly sink down into the depths. I was hot; the August sun burned down into my back. I wanted to swim in the cool water, but somehow I couldn't bring myself to do it.

The alligator surfaced again and looked at us boldly. It was just a matter of time. He was too bold. If not this year, then next year he would be destroyed as the nuisance alligator he had become. And when that happened—even though he had dragged me through hell and killed the dog I loved—it would be a tragedy.

Harriet Beecher Stowe

When Harriet Beecher Stowe (1811–96) moved to the pleasant town of Mandarin on the St. Johns River near Jacksonville, she had already achieved great fame as the author of the acclaimed novel *Uncle Tom's Cabin* (1851). She came to Florida to help her ailing husband regain his health and remained for eighteen winters, from 1867 to 1884. Although her home at 12447 Mandarin Road no longer exists, one can see in the Episcopal Church of Our Saviour a replica of the church that she and her husband helped establish.

Her original plan for her investment in north Florida was to rent a ten-thousand-acre plantation to provide freed slaves a chance to earn a living, but that project did not succeed to her expectations. She and her family eventually bought a riverfront home in Mandarin, and there she wrote the sketches and short stories that make up her *Palmetto-leaves,* from which the following short story is taken. Originally published in 1873 and republished by the University of Florida Press in 1968, the book described her delight in the many pleasures she found in north Florida, as well as the disagreeable aspects of life in this southern state. Her great enthusiasm for her newly adopted home was so infectious that many more northerners headed south to experience for themselves the pleasures of mild winters and a slower pace of life.

She wrote the following about her new home: "For ourselves, we are getting reconciled to a sort of tumble-down, wild, picnicky kind of life,— this general happy-go-luckiness which Florida inculcates." And again: "The great charm, after all, of this life, is its outdoorness. To be able to spend your winter out of doors, even though some days be cold; to be able to sit with windows open; to hear birds daily; to eat fruit from trees, and pick flowers from hedges, all winter long,—is about the whole of the story. This you can do; and this is why Florida is life and health to the invalid."

The following story is about one of the African Americans she and her husband, the "Professor" in the story, met in their stay in Mandarin. Like many northerners after the Civil War, Mrs. Stowe was appalled at the mistreatment such African Americans received at the hands of unscrupulous land developers who preyed on the innocence and gullibility of the former slaves.

Mrs. Stowe was well aware how rich the land she (and the protagonist in this story) cultivated. She had an orange grove behind her house, and from there crates full of oranges would head north after the harvest with big letters proclaiming the source of the fruit: "Oranges from HARRIET BEECHER STOWE, MANDARIN, FLA."

Old Cudjo and the Angel

Harriet Beecher Stowe

THE LITTLE WHARF at Mandarin is a tiny abutment into the great blue sea of the St. John's waters, five miles in width. The opposite shores gleam out blue in the vanishing distance; and the small wharf is built so far out, that one feels there as in a boat at sea. Here, trundled down on the truck along a descending tram-way, come the goods which at this point await shipment on some of the many steamboats which ply back and forth upon the river; and here are landed by almost every steamer goods and chattels for the many families which are hidden in the shadows of the forests that clothe the river's shore. In sight are scarce a dozen houses, all told; but far back, for a radius of ten or fifteen miles, are scattered farmhouses whence come tributes of produce to this point. Hundreds of barrels of oranges, boxes of tomatoes and early vegetables, grapes, peaches, and pomegranates, here pause on their way to the Jacksonville market.

One morning, as the Professor and I were enjoying our morning stroll on the little wharf, an unusual sight met our eye,—a bale of cotton, long and large, pressed hard and solid as iron, and done up and sewed in a wholly workmanlike manner, that excited our surprise. It was the first time since we had been in Mandarin—a space of some four or five years—that we had ever seen a bale of cotton on that wharf. Yet the whole soil of East Florida is especially adapted not only to the raising of cotton, but of the peculiar, long staple cotton which commands the very highest market-price. But for two or three years past the annual ravages of the cotton-worm had been so discouraging, that the culture of cotton had been abandoned in despair.

Whence, then, had come that most artistic bale of cotton, so well pressed, so trim and tidy, and got up altogether in so superior a style?

Standing by it on the wharf was an aged negro, misshapen, and almost deformed. He was thin and bony, and his head and beard were grizzled with age. He was black as night itself; and but for a glittering, intellectual eye, he might have been taken for a big baboon,—the missing link of Darwin. To him spoke the Professor, giving a punch with his cane upon the well-packed, solid bale:—

"Why, this is splendid cotton! Where did it come from? Who raised it?"

"*We* raise it, sah,—me 'n dis yer boy," pointing to a middle-aged black man beside him: "we raise it."

"Where?"

"Oh! out he'yr a piece."

A lounging white man, never wanting on a wharf, here interposed:—
"Oh! this is old Cudjo. He lives up Julington. He's an honest old fellow."

Now, we had heard of this settlement up Julington some two or three years before. A party of negroes from South Carolina and Georgia had been induced to come into Florida, and take up a tract of government land. Some white man in whom they all put confidence had undertaken for them the task of getting their respective allotments surveyed and entered for them, so that they should have a solid basis of land to work upon. Here, then, they settled down; and finding, accidentally, that a small central lot was not enclosed in any of the allotments, they took it as an indication that *there* was to be their church, and accordingly erected there a prayer-booth, where they could hold those weekly prayer-meetings which often seem with the negroes to take the place of all other recreations. The neighboring farmers were not particularly well disposed towards the little colony. The native Floridian farmer is a quiet, peaceable being, not at all disposed to infringe the rights of others, and mainly anxious for peace and quietness. But they supposed that a stampede of negroes from Georgia and Carolina meant trouble for them, meant depredations upon their cattle and poultry, and regarded it with no friendly eye; yet, nevertheless, they made no demonstration against it. Under these circumstances, the new colony had gone to work with untiring industry. They had built log-cabins and barns; they had split rails, and fenced in their land; they had planted orange-trees; they had cleared acres of the scrub-palmetto: and any one that ever has seen what it is to clear up an acre of scrub-palmetto will best appreciate the meaning of that toil. Only those black men, with sinews of steel and nerve of wire,—men who grow stronger and more vigorous under those burning suns that wither the white men,—are competent to the task.

But old Cudjo had at last brought his land from the wild embrace of the snaky scrub-palmetto to the point of bearing a bale of cotton like the one on the wharf. He had subdued the savage earth, brought her under, and made her tributary to his will, and demonstrated what the soil of East Florida might, could and would do, the cotton-worm to the contrary notwithstanding.

And yet this morning he stood by his cotton, drooping and dispossessed. The white man that had engaged to take up land for these colonists had done his work in such a slovenly, imperfect manner, that another settler, a foreigner, had taken up a tract which passed right through old Cudjo's farm, and taken the land on which he had spent four years of hard work,—taken his log-cabin and barn and young trees, and the very piece that he had just brought to bearing that bale of cotton. And there he stood by it, mournful and patient. It was only a continuation of what he had always experienced,—always oppressed, always robbed and cheated. Old Cudjo was making the best of it in trying to ship his bale of cotton, which was all that was left of four years' toil.

"What!" said the Professor to him, "are you the old man that has been turned out by that foreigner?"

"Yes, sah!" he said, his little black eyes kindling, and quivering from head to foot with excitement. "He take ebry t'ing, ebry t'ing,—my house I built myself, my fences, and more'n t'ree t'ousand rails I split myself: he take 'em all!"

There is always some bitter spot in a great loss that is sorer than the rest. Those rails evidently cut Cudjo to the heart. The "t'ree t'ousand rails" kept coming in in his narrative as the utter and unbearable aggravation of injustice.

"I split 'em myself, sah; *ebry one*, t'ree t'ousand rails! and he take 'em all!"

"And won't he allow you any thing?"

"No, sah: he won't 'low me not'ing. He say, 'Get along wid you! don't know not'ing 'bout *you*! dis yer land mine.' I tell him, '*You* don't know old Cudjo; but de Lord know him: an by'm by, when de angel Gabriel come and put one foot on de sea, and t'odder on de land, and blow de trumpet, he blow once for old Cudjo! You mind now!'"

This was not merely spoken, but acted. The old black kindled, and stepped off in pantomime. He put, as it were, one foot on the sea and the other on the land; he raised his cane trumpet-wise to his mouth. It was all as vivid as reality to him.

None of the images of the Bible are more frequent, favorite, and operative among the black race than this. You hear it over and over in every prayer-meeting. It is sung in wild chorus in many a "spiritual." The great angel Gabriel, the trumpet, the mighty pomp of a last judgment, has been the appeal of thousands of wronged, crushed, despairing hearts through ages of oppression. Faith in God's justice, faith in a final triumph of right over wrong,—a practical faith,—such had been the attainment of this poor, old, deformed black. That and his bale of cotton were all he had to show for a life's labor. He had learned two things in his world-lesson,—work and faith. He had learned the power of practical industry in things possible to man: he had learned the sublimer power of faith in God for things impossible.

⌁   ⌁

Well, of course we were indignant enough about poor old Cudjo: but we feared that the distant appeal of the angel, and the last trump, was all that remained to him; and, to our lesser faith, that seemed a long way to look for justice.

But redress was nearer than we imagined. Old Cudjo's patient industry and honest work had wrought favor among his white neighbors. He had lived down the prejudice with which the settlement had first been regarded; for among quiet, honest people like the Floridians, it is quite possible to live down prejudice. A neighboring justice of the peace happened to have an acquaintance in Washington from this very district, acquainted with all the land and land-titles. He wrote to this man an account of the case; and he interested himself for old Cudjo. He went to the land-office to investigate the matter. He found, that, in both cases, certain formalities necessary to constitute a legal entrance had been omitted; and he fulfilled for old Cudjo these formalities, thus settling his title; and, moreover, he sent legal papers by which the sheriff of the county was enabled to do him justice: and so old Cudjo was re-instated in his rights.

The Professor met him, sparkling and jubilant, on the wharf once more.

"Well, Cudjo, 'de angel' blew for you quicker than you expected."

He laughed all over. "Ye', haw, haw! Yes, massa." Then, with his usual histrionic vigor, he acted over the scene. "De sheriff, he come down dere. He tell dat man, 'You go right off he'yr. Don't you touch none dem rails. Don't you take one chip,—not one chip. Don't you take'—Haw, haw, haw!" Then he added,—"He come to me, sah, 'Cudjo, what you take for your land?' He say he gib me two hunder dollars. I tell him, 'Dat too cheap; dat all too cheap.' He say, 'Cudjo, what will you take?' I say, 'I take ten t'ousand million dollars! dat's what I take.' Haw, haw, haw!"

John W. B. Thompson

The Key Biscayne area is one of the oldest sites explored by Europeans, having been visited by John Cabot in 1497 and Juan Ponce de León in 1513. Today's Bill Baggs Cape Florida State Recreation Area was the site of the 1836 Indian attack related in the following true story. Four years after the United States acquired Florida from Spain in 1821, workers built Cape Florida Lighthouse; but relatively few people settled in the Key Biscayne area, partly because the threat of Indian attacks, the lack of good roads, and the area's desolation made living there quite difficult.

This sixty-five-foot lighthouse, which still stands today, guided mariners past the dangerous Florida Reef or into safe anchorage in Cape Florida Channel. Sailors had been using the area for decades as both a source of fresh water supplies and a place to careen their vessels of barnacles and other parasites. For the decade after the building of the lighthouse, its keepers and their families lived a quiet, isolated life interrupted by an occasional trip to Key West for supplies and a taste of civilization.

When the Second Seminole War started in the mid-1830s, the Indians of Florida tried to drive out the settlers and soldiers who were attempting to move in and make the land part of the United States. When the Indians massacred a family on the north side of New River, other families moved out, some to the safe port of Key West. A number of families gathered near Cape Florida Lighthouse, from which they eventually sailed to Key West, after obtaining the necessary sailing vessels. Two men stayed behind to maintain the lighthouse: a white man named John Thompson, who wrote the following account of the attack in a letter to *Niles' Weekly Registery* (November 19, 1836), and an African American named Henry.

Although the tower withstood the gunpowder explosion described by Thompson, a subsequent investigation revealed that the contractor who had originally built the structure had made the walls of the tower hollow from the base upward, instead of solid as he had agreed to in his contract. Congress appropriated money to repair the tower, but delays and the threat of renewed Indian attack put off completion of the work until 1846. Ships of deeper draft required the raising of the tower to ninety-five feet, which was done in 1855. The light was put out of service during the Civil War, but resumed its service in 1867. The completion of the Fowey Rocks Lighthouse made the continued operation of the Cape Florida Lighthouse unnecessary in 1878, and it was darkened. The Coast Guard reinstalled a light on top of the tower in 1978 to serve as a navigational aid. It stands tall today in a 406-acre park that honors in its name a newspaper editor, Bill Baggs, who did much to promote the area as a state park.

Cape Florida Light House

John W. B. Thompson

ON THE 23D July last, about 4 P.M., as I was going from the kitchen to the dwelling house, I discovered a large body of Indians within 20 yards of me back of the kitchen. I ran for the light house and called out to the old negro man that was with me to run, for the Indians are here. At that moment they discharged a volley of rifle balls, which cut my clothes and hat and perforated the door in many places. We got in, and as I was turning the key the savages had hold of the door. I stationed the negro at the door with orders to let me know if they attempted to break in; I then took my three muskets, which were loaded with ball and buck shot, and went to the second window. Seeing a large body of them opposite the dwelling house, I discharged my muskets in succession amongst them, which put them in some confusion; they then, for the second time, began their horrid yells, and in a minute no sash or glass was left at that window, for they vented all their rage at that spot. I fired at them from some of the other windows and from the top of the house; in fact, I fired whenever I could get an Indian for a mark. I kept them from the house until dark. They then poured in a heavy fire at all the windows and lantern; that was the time that they set fire to the door and window even with the ground. The window was boarded up with plank and filled up with stones inside, but the flames spread fast, being fed with yellow pine wood. Their balls had perforated the tin tanks of oil, consisting of 225 gallons. My bedding, clothing, and in fact everything I had was soaked in oil. I stopped at the door until driven away by the flames.

I then took a keg of gunpowder, my balls and one musket to the top of the house, then went below and began to cut away the stairs about halfway up from the bottom. I had great difficulty in getting the old negro man up the space I had already cut; but the flames now drove me from my labor, and I retreated to the top of the house. I covered over the skuttle that leads to the lantern, which kept the fire from me for some time. At last the awful moment arrived; the cracking flames burst around me.

The savages at the same time began their hellish yells. My poor old negro looked up to me with tears in his eyes, but he could not speak. We went out of the lantern and lay down on the edge of the platform, two feet wide. The lantern was now full of flames, the lamps and glasses bursting and flying in all directions, my clothes on fire, and to move from the place where I was would be instant death from their rifles. My flesh was roasting, and, to put an end to my horrible suffering, I got up, threw the keg of gunpowder down the skuttle—instantly it exploded and shook the tower from the top to the bottom. It had not the desired effect of blowing me to eternity, but it threw down the stairs and all the wooden work near the top of the house; it damped the fire for a moment, but soon blazed as fierce as ever. The negro man said he was wounded, which was the last word he ever spoke. By this time I had received some wounds myself; and finding no chance for my life, for I was roasting alive, I took the determination to jump off. I got up, went inside the iron railing, recommending my soul to God, and was on the point of going head foremost on the rocks below, when something dictated to me to return and lie down again. I did so, and in two minutes the fire fell to the bottom of the house. It is a remarkable circumstance that not one ball struck me when I stood up outside the railing although they were flying all around me like hail stones. I found the old negro man dead, being shot in seven places and literally roasted. A few minutes after the fire fell, a stiff breeze sprung up from the southward, which was a great blessing to me. I had to lie where I was, for I could not walk, having received six rifle balls, three in each foot.

The Indians, thinking me dead, left the light house and set fire to the dwelling house, kitchen and other out houses, and began to carry their plunder to the beach. They took all the empty barrels, the drawers of the bureaus, and in fact everything that would act as a vessel to hold any thing. My provisions were in the light house, except a barrel of flour, which they took off. The next morning they hauled out of the light house by means of a pole, the tin that composed the oil tanks, no doubt to make graters to manufacture the coonty root into what we call arrow root. After loading my little sloop, about ten or twelve went into her; the rest took to the beach to meet at the other end of the island. This happened, as I judge, about 10 A.M. My eyes, being much affected, prevented me from knowing their actual force, but I judge there were from forty to fifty, perhaps more. I was now almost as bad off as before; a burning fever on me, my feet shot to pieces, no clothes to cover me, nothing to eat or drink, a hot sun over my head, a dead man by my side, no friend near or any to expect, and placed between seventy and eighty feet from the earth and no chance of getting down. My situation was truly horrible.

About 12 o'clock I thought I could perceive a vessel not far off. I took a piece of the old negro's trousers that had escaped the flames by being wet with blood and made a signal. Sometime in the afternoon I saw two boats with my sloop in tow coming to the landing. I had no doubt but they were the Indians having seen my signal; but it proved to be boats of the United States schooner Motto, captain Armstrong, with a detachment of seamen and marines under the command of Lieutenant Lloyd, of the sloop-of-war Concord. They had retaken my sloop after the Indians had stripped her of her sails and rigging and every thing of consequence belonging to her.

They informed me they heard my explosion twelve miles off and ran down to my assistance, but did not expect to find me alive. Those gentlemen did all in their power to relieve me, but, night coming on, they returned on board the Motto after assuring me of their assistance in the morning. Next morning, Monday, July 5th, three boats landed, amongst them captain Cole, of the schooner Pee Dee, from New York. They had made a kite during the night to get a line to me, but without effect—they then fired twine from their muskets made fast to a ramrod, which I received, and hauled up a tail block and made fast round an iron stanchion, rove the twine through the block, and they below, by that means, rove a two-inch rope and hoisted up two men, who soon landed me on terra firma.

I must state here that the Indians had made a ladder by lashing pieces of wood across the lightning rod, near forty feet from the ground, as if to have my scalp, nolens volens. This happened on the 4th. After I got on board the Motto, every man from the captain to the cook tried to alleviate my sufferings. On the 7th I was received in the military hospital through the politeness of lieutenant Alvord of the 4th regiment of United States infantry. He has done every thing to make my situation as comfortable as possible.

I must not omit here to return my thanks to the citizens of Key West generally, for their sympathy and kind offers of any thing I would wish, that was in their power to bestow. Before I left Key West, two balls were extracted, and one remains in my right leg; but since I am under the care of Dr. Ramsey, who has paid every attention to me, he will know best whether to extract it or not.

These lines were written to let my friends know that I am still in the land of the living, and am now in Charleston, S.C., where every attention is paid me. Although a cripple, I can eat my allowance and walk without the use of a cane.

Constance Fenimore Woolson

Constance Fenimore Woolson (1840–94) was born in New Hampshire and spent much of her life in that state, as well as in Cleveland and New York, living in Italy toward the end of her life. In 1873 she made the first of several long trips to the South, spending the next five winters in Florida, usually St. Augustine, with her mother. Although she complained that St. Augustine was too expensive and too fashionable for her simple tastes, she later wrote from Europe: "I hardly appreciated myself, until I was separated from it, how much I loved that warm hazy peninsula where I spent five long happy winters with my dear Mother." Her niece established the Constance Fenimore Woolson Memorial House at Rollins College in Winter Park, Florida; there one can see memorabilia associated with Woolson, the great-niece of American novelist James Fenimore Cooper.

From her experience in Florida and the South, Woolson wrote about southerners coping after the Civil War and how southern women had unique problems. Her Florida stories—especially "Felipa," "Sister St. Luke," "Miss Elisabetha," *East Angels* (1886), and *Horace Chase* (1894)—showed what a difficult time southerners had changing their ways of living in the late nineteenth century; her novel *East Angels* dealt with what effects exotic St. Augustine could have on the human personality, a theme she would touch in "The South Devil," reprinted here.

First published in the *Atlantic* in 1880, "The South Devil" was included in her *Rodman the Keeper: Southern Sketches* (1880). Although ostensibly about two brothers living near San Miguel, a fictional version of St. Augustine, the nearby swamp plays a large role in shaping the lives of the characters, especially the musician Carl. He is like Frederick Delius (1862–1934), the European composer who lived on the St. Johns River near Mandarin, Florida, and was inspired by the music he heard along the river. Just as Carl tried "'to write out the beautiful music of the South Devil,'" Delius tried to imbue his music with the Florida ambience in his *Florida Suite* and in the opera *Koanga*.

Two references in the story need clarification. The name of the old African American, Scipio, whom one of the men nicknamed "Africanus" after Scipio Africanus (236–184/3 B.C.), refers to a Roman commander who defeated Hannibal in Africa. The King's Road is the thoroughfare that the British built in 1765 from New Smyrna, Florida, through St. Augustine to the Georgia line. This thoroughfare enabled the British colonies in Florida to keep in touch by land. The story also touches on old beliefs about miasma, or swamp gas, a poisonous atmosphere that people once thought came from swamps and caused malaria and yellow fever. This Poe-like story has descriptions of a vast swamp that could describe parts of today's Okefenokee Swamp, the Panhandle, or the Everglades.

The South Devil

Constance Fenimore Woolson

The trees that lean'd in their love unto trees,
That lock'd in their loves, and were made so strong,
Stronger than armies; ay, stronger than seas
That rush from their caves in a storm of song.

The cockatoo swung in the vines below,
And muttering hung on a golden thread,
Or moved on the moss'd bough to and fro,
In plumes of gold and array'd in red.

The serpent that hung from the sycamore bough,
And sway'd his head in a crescent above,
Had folded his head to the white limb now,
And fondled it close like a great black love.

JOAQUIN MILLER

ON THE AFTERNOON of the 23d of December, the thermometer marked eighty-six degrees in the shade on the outside wall of Mark Deal's house. Mark Deal's brother, lying on the white sand, his head within the line of shadow cast by a live-oak, but all the remainder of his body full in the hot sunshine, basked like a chameleon, and enjoyed the heat. Mark Deal's brother spent much of his time basking. He always took the live-oak for a head-protector; but gave himself variety by trying new radiations around the tree, his crossed legs and feet stretching from it in a slightly different direction each day, as the spokes of a wheel radiate from the hub. The live-oak was a symmetrical old tree, standing by itself; having always had sufficient space, its great arms were straight, stretching out evenly all around, densely covered with the small, dark, leathery leaves, unnotched and uncut, which are as unlike the Northern oak-leaf as the leaf of the willow is unlike that of the sycamore. Behind the live-oak, two tall, ruined chimneys and a heap of white stones marked where the mansion-house had been. The old tree had watched its foundations laid; had shaded its blank, white front and little hanging balcony above; had witnessed its destruction, fifty years before, by the Indians; and had mounted guard over its remains ever since, alone as far as man was concerned, until this year, when a tenant had arrived, Mark Deal, and, somewhat later, Mark Deal's brother.

The ancient tree was Spanish to the core; it would have resented the sacrilege to the tips of its small acorns, if the new-comer had laid hands upon the dignified old ruin it guarded. The new-comer, however, entertained no such intention; a small out-building, roofless, but otherwise in good condition, on the opposite side of the circular space, attracted his attention, and became mentally his residence, as soon as his eyes fell upon it, he meanwhile standing with his hands in his pockets, surveying the place critically. It was the old Monteano plantation, and he had taken it for a year.

The venerable little out-building was now firmly roofed with new, green boards; its square windows, destitute of sash or glass, possessed new wooden shutters hung by strips of deer's hide; new steps led up to its two rooms, elevated four feet above the ground. But for a door it had only a red cotton curtain, now drawn forward and thrown carelessly over a peg on the outside wall, a spot of vivid color on its white. Underneath the windows hung flimsy strips of bark covered with brightly-hued flowers.

"They won't live," said Mark Deal.

"Oh, I shall put in fresh ones every day or two," answered his brother. It was he who had wanted the red curtain.

As he basked, motionless, in the sunshine, it could be noted that this brother was a slender youth, with long, pale-yellow hair—hair fine, thin, and dry, the kind that crackles if the comb is passed rapidly through it. His face in sleep was pale and wizened, with deep purple shadows under the closed eyes; his long hands were stretched out on the white, hot sand in the blaze of the sunshine, which, however, could not alter their look of blue-white cold. The sunken chest and blanched temples told of illness; but, if cure were possible, it would be gained from this soft, balmy, fragrant air, now soothing his sore lungs. He slept on in peace; and an old green chameleon came down from the tree, climbed up on the sleeve of his brown sack-coat, occupied himself for a moment in changing his own miniature hide to match the cloth, swelled out his scarlet throat, caught a fly or two, and then, pleasantly established, went to sleep also in company. Butterflies, in troops of twenty or thirty, danced in the golden air; there was no sound. Everything was hot and soft and brightly colored. Winter? Who knew of winter here? Labor? What was labor? This was the land and the sky and the air of never-ending rest.

Yet one man was working there, and working hard, namely, Mark Deal. His little central plaza, embracing perhaps an acre, was surrounded when he first arrived by a wall of green, twenty feet high. The sweet orange-trees, crape-myrtles, oleanders, guavas, and limes planted by the Spaniards had been, during the fifty years, conquered and partially enslaved by a wilder growth—andromedas, dahoons, bayberries, and the old field loblollies, the whole bound together by the tangled vines of the jessamine and armed smilax, with bear-grass and the dwarf palmetto below. Climbing the central live-oak, Deal had found, as he expected, traces of the six paths which had once led from this little plaza to the various fields and the sugar plantation, their course still marked by the tops of the bitter-sweet orange-trees, which showed themselves glossily, in regular lines, amid the duller foliage around them. He took their bearings and cut them out slowly, one by one. Now the low-arched aisles, eighty feet in length, were clear, with the thick leaves interlacing overhead, and the daylight shining through at their far ends, golden against the green. Here, where the north path terminated, Deal was now working.

He was a man slightly below middle height, broad-shouldered, and muscular, with the outlines which are called thickset. He appeared forty-five, and was not quite thirty-five. Although weather-beaten and bronzed, there was yet a pinched look in his face, which was peculiar. He was working in an old field, preparing it for sweet potatoes—those omnipresent, monotonous vegetables of Florida which will grow anywhere, and which at last, with their ugly, gray-mottled skins, are regarded with absolute aversion by the Northern visitor.

The furrows of half a century before were still visible in the field. No frost had disturbed the winterless earth; no atom had changed its place, save where the gopher had burrowed beneath, or the snake left its waving trail above in the sand which constitutes the strange, white, desolate soil, wherever there is what may be called by comparison solid ground, in the lake-dotted, sieve-like land. There are many such traces of former cultivation in Florida: we come suddenly upon old tracks, furrows, and drains in what we thought primeval forest; rose-bushes run wild, and distorted old fig-trees meet us in a jungle where we supposed no white man's foot had ever before penetrated; the ruins of a chimney gleam whitely through a waste of thorny *chaparral*. It is all natural enough, if one stops to remember that fifty years before the first settlement was made in Virginia, and sixty-three before the Mayflower touched the shores of the New World, there were flourishing Spanish plantations on this Southern coast—more flourishing, apparently, than any the indolent peninsula has since known. But one does not stop to remember it; the belief is imbedded in all our Northern hearts that, because the narrow, sun-bathed State is far away and wild and empty, it is also new and virgin, like the lands of the West; whereas it is old—the only gray-haired corner our country holds.

Mark Deal worked hard. Perspiration beaded his forehead and cheeks, and rolled from his short, thick, red-brown hair. He worked in this way every day from daylight until dusk, and was probably the only white man in the State who did. When his task was finished, he made a circuit around the belt of thicket through which the six paths ran to his orange-grove on the opposite side. On the way he skirted an edge of the sugar-plantation, now a wide, empty waste, with the old elevated causeway still running across it. On its far edge loomed the great cypresses of South Devil, a swamp forty miles long; there was a sister, West Devil, not far away, equally beautiful, dark, and deadly. Beyond the sugar waste were the indigo-fields, still fenced by their old ditches. Then came the orange-grove; luxuriant, shady word—the orange-grove!

It was a space of level white sand, sixty feet square, fertilized a century before with pounded oyster-shells, in the Spanish fashion. Planted in even rows across it, tied to stakes, were slips of green stem, each with three leaves—forlorn little plants, five or six inches in height. But the stakes were new and square and strong, and rose to Deal's shoulder; they were excellent stakes, and made quite a grove of themselves, firm, if somewhat bare.

Deal worked in his grove until sunset; then he shouldered his tools and went homeward through one of the arched aisles to the little plaza within, where stood his two-roomed house with its red cotton door. His brother was still sleeping on the sand, at least, his eyes were closed. Deal put his tools in a rack behind the house, and then crossed to where he lay.

"You should not sleep here after sunset, Carl," he said, somewhat roughly. "You know better; why do you do it?"

"I'm not asleep," answered the other, sitting up, and then slowly getting on his feet. "Heigh-ho! What are you going to have for dinner?"

"You are tired, Carl; and I see the reason. You have been in the swamp." Deal's eyes as he spoke were fixed upon the younger man's shoes, where traces of the ink-black soil of South Devil were plainly visible.

Carl laughed. "Can't keep anything from your Yankee eyes, can I, Mark?" he said. "But I only went a little way."

"It isn't the distance, it's the folly," said Mark, shortly, going toward the house.

"I never pretended to be wise," answered Carl, slouching along behind him, with his hands wrapped in his blue cotton handkerchief, arranged like a muff.

Although Deal worked hard in his fields all day, he did not cook. In a third out-building lived a gray-headed old negro with one eye, who cooked for the new tenant—and cooked well. His name was Scipio, but Carl called him Africanus; he said it was equally appropriate, and sounded more impressive. Scip's kitchen was out-of-doors—simply an old Spanish chimney. His kettle and few dishes, when not in use, hung on the sides of this chimney, which now, all alone in the white sand, like an obelisk, cooked solemnly the old negro's messes, as half a century before it had cooked the more dignified repasts of the dead hidalgos. The brothers ate in the open air also, sitting at a rough board table which Mark had made behind the house. They had breakfast soon after daylight, and at sunset dinner; in the middle of the day they took only fruit and bread.

"Day after to-morrow will be Christmas," said Carl, leaving the table and lighting his long pipe. "What are you going to do?"

"I had not thought of doing anything in particular."

"Well, at least don't work on Christmas day."

"What would you have me do?"

Carl took his pipe from his mouth, and gazed at his brother in silence for a moment. "Go into the swamp with me," he urged, with sudden vehemence. "Come—for the whole day!"

Deal was smoking, too, a short clay pipe, very different from the huge, fantastic, carved bowl with long stem which weighed down Carl's thin mouth. "I don't know what to do with you, boy. You are mad about the swamp," he said, smoking on calmly.

They were sitting in front of the house now, in two chairs tilted back against its wall. The dark, odorous earth looked up to the myriad stars, but was not lighted by them; a soft, languorous gloom lay over the land. Carl brushed away the ashes from his pipe impatiently.

"It's because you can't understand," he said. "The swamp haunts me. I *must* see it once; you will be wise to let me see it once. We might go through in a canoe together by the branch; the branch goes through."

"The water goes, no doubt, but a canoe couldn't."

"Yes, it could, with an axe. It has been done. They used to go up to San Miguel that way sometimes from here; it shortens the distance more than half."

"Who told you all this—Scip? What does he know about it?"

"Oh, Africanus has seen several centuries; the Spaniards were living here only fifty years ago, you know, and that's nothing to him. He remembers the Indian attack."

"Ponce de Leon, too, I suppose; or, to go back to the old country, Cleopatra. But you must give up the swamp, Carl. I positively forbid it. The air inside is thick and deadly, to say nothing of the other dangers. How do you suppose it gained its name?"

"Diabolus is common enough as a title among Spaniards and Italians; it don't mean anything. The prince of darkness never lives in the places called by his name; he likes baptized cities better."

"Death lives there, however; and I brought you down here to cure you."

"I'm all right. See how much stronger I am! I shall soon be quite well again, old man," answered Carl, with the strange, sanguine faith of the consumptive.

The next day Deal worked very hard. He had a curious, inflexible, possibly narrow kind of conscience, which required him to do double duty to-day in order to make up for the holiday granted to Carl to-morrow. There was no task-master over him; even the seasons were not task-masters here. But so immovable were his own rules for himself that nothing could have induced him to abate one jot of the task he had laid out in his own mind when he started afield at dawn.

When he returned home at sunset, somewhat later than usual, Carl was absent. Old Scipio could give no information; he had not seen "young marse" since early morning. Deal put up his tools, ate something, and then, with a flask in his pocket, a fagot of light-wood torches bound on his back, and one of these brilliant, natural flambeaux in his hand, he started away on his search, going down one of the orange-aisles, the light gleaming back through the arch till he reached the far end, when it disappeared. He crossed an old indigo-field, and pushed his way through its hedge of Spanish-bayonets, while the cacti sown along the hedge—small, flat green plates with white spines, like hideous tufted insects—fastened themselves viciously on the strong leather of his high boots. Then, reaching the sugar waste, he advanced a short distance on the old causeway, knelt down, and in the light of the torch examined its narrow, sandy level. Yes, there were the footprints he had feared to find. Carl had gone again into the poisonous swamp—the beautiful, deadly South Devil. And this time he had not come back.

The elder brother rose, and with the torch held downward slowly traced the footmarks. There was a path, or rather trail, leading in a short distance. The footprints followed it as far as it went, and the brother followed the footprints, the red glare of the torch foreshortening each swollen, gray-white cypress-trunk, and giving to the dark, hidden pools below bright gleamings which they never had by day. He soon came to the end of the trail; here he stopped and shouted loudly several times, with pauses between for answer. No answer came.

"But I know the trick of this thick air," he said to himself. "One can't hear anything in a cypress-swamp."

He was now obliged to search closely for the footprints, pausing at each one, having no idea in which direction the next would tend. The soil did not hold the impressions well; it was not mud or mire, but wet, spongy, fibrous, black earth, thinly spread over the hard roots of trees, which protruded in distorted shapes in every direction. He traced what seemed footmarks across an open space, and then lost them on the brink of a dark pool. If Carl had kept on, he must have crossed this pool; but how? On the sharp cypress-knees standing sullenly in the claret-colored water? He went all around the open space again, seeking for footmarks elsewhere; but no, they ended at the edge of the pool. Cutting a long stick, he made his way across by its aid, stepping from knee-point to knee-point. On the other side he renewed his search for the trail, and after some labor found it, and went on again.

He toiled forward slowly in this way a long time, his course changing often; Carl's advance seemed to have been aimless. Then, suddenly, the footprints ceased. There was not another one visible anywhere, though he searched in all directions again and again. He looked at his watch; it was midnight. He hallooed; no reply. What could have become of the lad? He now began to feel his own fatigue; after the long day of toil in the hot sun, these hours of laboring over the ground in a bent position, examining it inch by inch, brought on pains in his shoulders and back. Planting the torch he was carrying in the soft soil of a little knoll, he placed another one near it, and sat down between the two flames to rest for a minute or two, pouring out for himself a little brandy in the bottom of the cup belonging to his flask. He kept strict watch as he did this. Venomous things, large and small, filled the vines above, and might drop at any moment upon him. But he had quick eyes and ears, and no intention of dying in the South Devil; so, while he watched keenly, he took the time to swallow the brandy. After a moment or two he was startled by a weak human voice saying, with faint decision, "*That's* brandy!"

"I should say it was," called Deal, springing to his feet. "Where are you, then?"

"Here."

The rescuer followed the sound, and, after one or two errors, came upon the body of his brother lying on a dank mat of water-leaves and ground-vines at the edge of a pool. In the red light of the torch he looked as though he was dead; his eyes only were alive.

"Brandy," he said again, faintly, as Deal appeared.

After he had swallowed a small quantity of the stimulant, he revived with unexpected swiftness.

"I have been shouting for you not fifty feet away," said Deal; "how is it that you did not hear?" Then in the same breath, in a soft undertone, he added, "Ah-h-h-h!" and without stirring a hair's breadth from where he stood, or making an unnecessary motion, he slowly drew forth his pistol, took careful aim, and fired. He was behind his brother, who lay with closed eyes, not noticing the action.

"What have you killed?" asked Carl languidly. "I've seen nothing but birds; and the most beautiful ones, too."

"A moccasin, that's all," said Deal, kicking the dead creature into the pool. He did not add that the snake was coiled for a spring. "Let us get back to the little knoll where I was, Carl; it's drier there."

"I don't think I can walk, old man. I fell from the vines up there, and something's the matter with my ankles."

"Well, I can carry you that distance," said Deal. "Put your arms around my neck, and raise yourself as I lift you—so."

The burning flambeau on the knoll served as a guide, and, after one or two pauses, owing to the treacherous footing, the elder brother succeeded in carrying the other thither. He then took off the light woolen coat he had put on before entering the swamp, spread it over the driest part of the little knoll, and laid Carl upon it.

"If you can not walk," he said, "we shall have to wait here until daylight. I could not carry you and the torch also; and the footing is bad—there are twenty pools to cross, or go around. Fortunately, we have lightwood enough to burn all night."

He lit fresh torches and arranged them at the four corners of their little knoll; then he began to pace slowly to and fro, like a picket walking his beat.

"What were you doing up among those vines?" he asked. He knew that it would be better for them both if they could keep themselves awake; those who fell asleep in the night air of South Devil generally awoke the next morning in another world.

"I climbed up a ladder of vines to gather some of the great red blossoms swinging in the air; and, once up, I went along on the mat to see what I could find. It's beautiful there—fairyland. You can't see anything down below, but above the long moss hangs in fine, silvery lines like spray from ever so high up, and mixed with it air-plants, sheafs, and bells of scarlet and cream-colored blossoms. I sat there a long time looking, and I suppose I must have dozed; for I don't know when I fell."

"You did not hear me shout?"

"No. The first consciousness I had was the odor of brandy—"

"The odor reached you, and the sound did not; that is one of the tricks of such air as this! You must have climbed up, I suppose, at the place where I lost the trail. What time did you come in?"

"I don't know," murmured Carl drowsily.

"Look here! You *must* keep awake!"

"I can't," answered the other.

Deal shook him, but could not rouse him even to anger. He only opened his blue eyes and looked reproachfully at his brother, but as though he was a long distance off. Then Deal lifted him up, uncorked the flask, and put it to his lips.

"Drink!" he said, loudly and sternly; and mechanically Carl obeyed. Once or twice his head moved aside, as if refusing more; but Deal again said, "Drink!" and without pity made the sleeper swallow every drop the flask contained. Then he laid him down upon the coat again, and covered his face and head with his own broad-brimmed palmetto hat, Carl's hat having been lost. He had done all he could—changed the lethargy of the South Devil into the sleep of drunkenness, the last named at least a human slumber. He was now left to keep the watch alone.

During the first half hour a dozen red and green things, of the centipede and scorpion kind, stupefied by the glare of the torches, fell from the trees; and he dispatched them. Next, enormous grayish-white spiders, in color exactly like the bark, moved slowly one furred leg into view, and then another, on the trunks of the cypresses near by, gradually coming wholly into the light—creatures covering a circumference as large as that of a plate. At length the cypresses all around the knoll were covered with them; and they all seemed to be watching him. He was not watching the spiders, however; he cared very little for the spiders. His eyes were upon the ground all the time, moving along the borders of his little knoll-fort. It was bounded on two sides by pools, in whose dark depths he knew moccasins were awake, watching the light, too, with whatever of curiosity belongs to a snake's cold brain. His torches aroused them; and yet darkness would have been worse. In the light he could at least see them, if they glided forth and tried to ascend the brilliant knoll. After a while they began to rise to the surface; he could distinguish portions of their bodies in waving lines, moving noiselessly hither and thither, appearing and disappearing suddenly, until the pools around seemed alive with them. There was not a sound; the soaked forest stood motionless. The absolute stillness made the quick gliding motions of the moccasins even more horrible. Yet Deal had no instinctive dread of snakes. The terrible "coach-whip," the deadly and grotesque spread-adder, the rattlesnake of the barrens, and these great moccasins of the pools were endowed with no imaginary horrors in his eyes. He accepted them as nature made them, and not as man's fancy painted them; it was only their poison-fangs he feared.

"If the sea-crab could sting, how hideous we should think him! If the lobster had a deadly venom, how devilish his shape would seem to us!" he said.

But now no imagination was required to make the moccasins terrible. His revolver carried six balls; and he had already used one of them. Four hours must pass before dawn; there could be no unnecessary shooting. The creatures might even come out and move along the edge of his knoll; only when they showed an intention of coming up the slope must their gliding life be ended. The moccasin is not a timorous or quick-nerved snake; in a place like the South Devil, when a human foot or boat approaches, generally he does not stir. His great body, sometimes over six feet in length, and thick and fat in the middle, lies on a log or at the edge of a pool, seemingly too lazy to move. But none the less, when roused, is his coil sudden and his long spring sure; his venom is deadly. After a time one of the creatures did come out and glide along the edge of the knoll. He went back into the water; but a second came out on the other side. During the night Deal killed three; he was an excellent marksman, and picked them off easily as they crossed his dead-line.

"Fortunately they come one by one," he said to himself. "If there was any concert of action among them, I couldn't hold the place a minute."

As the last hour began, the long hour before dawn, he felt the swamp lethargy stealing into his own brain; he saw the trees and torches doubled. He walked to and fro more quickly, and sang to keep himself awake. He knew only a few old-fashioned songs, and the South Devil heard that night, probably for the first time in its tropical life, the ancient Northern strains of "Gayly the Troubadour touched his Guitar." Deal was no troubadour, and he had no guitar. But he sang on bravely, touching that stringed instrument, vocally at least, and bringing himself "home from the war" over and over again, until at last faint dawn penetrated from above down to the knoll where the four torches were burning. They were the last torches, and Deal was going through his sixtieth rehearsal of the "Troubadour"; but, instead of "Lady-love, lady-lo-o-o-ve," whom he apostrophized, a large moccasin rose from the pool, as if in answer. She might have been the queen of the moccasins, and beautiful—to moccasin eyes; but to Deal she was simply the largest and most hideous of all the snake-visions of the night. He gave her his fifth ball, full in her mistaken brain; and, if she had admired him (or the "Troubadour"), she paid for it with her life.

This was the last. Daylight appeared. The watchman put out his torches and roused the sleeper. "Carl! Carl! It's daylight. Let us get out of this confounded crawling hole, and have a breath of fresh air."

Carl stirred, and opened his eyes; they were heavy and dull. His brother lifted him, told him to hold on tightly, and started with his burden toward home. The snakes had disappeared, the gray spiders had vanished; he could see his way now, and he followed his own trail, which he had taken care to make distinct when he came in the night before. But, loaded down as he was, and obliged to rest frequently, and also to go around all the pools, hours passed before he reached the last cypresses and came out on the old causeway across the sugar-waste.

It was Christmas morning; the thermometer stood at eighty-eight.

Carl slept off his enforced drunkenness in his hammock. Mark, having bandaged his brother's strained ankles, threw himself upon his rude couch, and fell into a heavy slumber also. He slept until sunset; then he rose, plunged his head into a tub of the limpid, pure, but never cold water of Florida, drawn from his shallow well, and went out to the chimney to see about dinner. The chimney was doing finely: a fiery plume of sparks waved from its white top, a red bed of coals glowed below. Scip moved about with as much equanimity as though he had a row of kitchen-tables upon which to arrange his pans and dishes, instead of ruined blocks of stone, under the open sky. The dinner was good. Carl, awake at last, was carried out to the table to enjoy it, and then brought back to his chair in front of the house to smoke his evening pipe.

"I must make you a pair of crutches," said Deal.

"One will do; my right ankle is not much hurt, I think."

The fall, the air of the swamp, and the inward drenching of brandy had left Carl looking much as usual; the tenacious disease that held him swallowed the lesser ills. But for the time, at least, his wandering footsteps were staid.

"I suppose there is no use in my asking, Carl, *why* you went in there?" said Deal, after a while.

"No, there isn't. I'm haunted—that's all."

"But what is it that haunts you?"

"Sounds. *You* couldn't understand, though, if I was to talk all night."

"Perhaps I could; perhaps I can understand more than you imagine. I'll tell you a story presently; but first you must explain to me, at least as well as you can, what it is that attracts you in South Devil."

"Oh—well," said Carl, with a long, impatient sigh, closing his eyes wearily. "I am a musician, you know, a musician *manque;* a musician who can't play. Something's the matter; I *hear* music, but can not bring it out. And I know so well what it ought to be, ought to be and isn't, that I've broken my violin in pieces a dozen times in my rages about it. Now, other fellows in orchestras, who *don't* know, get along very well. But I couldn't. I've thought at times that, although I can not sound what I hear with my own hands, perhaps I could *write* it out so that other men could sound it. The idea has never come to anything definite yet—that is, what *you* would call definite; but it haunts me persistently, and *now* it has got into that swamp. The wish," here Carl laid down his great pipe, and pressed his hand eagerly upon his brother's knee—"the wish that haunts me—drives me—is to write out the beautiful music of the South Devil, the sounds one hears in there—"

"But there are no sounds."

"No sounds? You must be deaf! The air fairly reeks with sounds, with harmonies. But there—I told you you couldn't understand." He leaned back against the wall again, and took up the great pipe, which looked as though it must consume whatever small store of strength remained to him.

"Is it what is called an opera you want to write, like—like the 'Creation,' for instance?" asked Deal. The "Creation" was the only long piece of music he had ever heard.

Carl groaned. "Oh, *don't* talk of it!" he said; then added, irritably, "It's a song, that's all—the song of a Southern swamp."

"Call it by its real name, Devil," said the elder brother, grimly.

"I would, if I was rich enough to have a picture painted—the Spirit of the Swamp—a beautiful woman, falsely called a devil by cowards, dark, languorous, mystical, sleeping among the vines I saw up there, with the great red blossoms dropping around her."

"And the great mottled snakes coiling over her?"

"*I* didn't see any snakes."

"Well," said Mark, refilling his pipe, "now I'm going to tell you *my* story. When I met you on that windy pier at Exton, and proposed that you should come down here with me, I was coming myself, in any case, wasn't I? And why? I wanted to get to a place where I could be warm—warm, hot, baked; warm through and through; warm all the time. I wanted to get to a place where the very ground was warm. And *now*—I'll tell you why."

He rose from his seat, laid down his pipe, and, extending his hand, spoke for about fifteen minutes without pause. Then he turned, went back hastily to the old chimney, where red coals still lingered, and sat down close to the glow, leaving Carl wonder-struck in his tilted chair. The elder man leaned over the fire and held his hands close to the coals; Carl watched him. It was nine o'clock, and the thermometer marked eighty.

For nearly a month after Christmas, life on the old plantation went on without event or disaster. Carl, with his crutch and cane, could not walk far; his fancy now was to limp through the east orange-aisle to the place of tombs, and sit there for hours, playing softly, what might be called crooning, on his violin. The place of tombs was a small, circular space surrounded by wild orange-trees in a close, even row, like a hedge; here were four tombs, massive, oblong blocks of the white conglomerate of the coast, too coarse-grained to hold inscription or mark of any kind. Who the old Spaniards were whose bones lay beneath, and what names they bore in the flesh, no one knew; all record was lost. Outside in the wild thicket was a tomb still more ancient, and of different construction: four slabs of stone, uncovered, about three feet high, rudely but firmly placed, as though inclosing a coffin. In the earth between these low walls grew a venerable cedar; but, old as it was, it must have been planted by chance or by hand after the human body beneath had been laid in its place.

"Why do you come here?" said Deal, pausing and looking into the place of tombs, one morning, on his way to the orange-grove. "There are plenty of pleasanter spots about."

"No; I like this better," answered Carl, without stopping the low chant of his violin. "Besides, they like it too."

"Who?"

"The old fellows down below. The chap outside there, who must have been an Aztec, I suppose, and the original proprietor, catches a little of it; but I generally limp over and give him a tune to himself before going home. I have to imagine the Aztec style."

Mark gave a short laugh, and went on to his work. But he knew the real reason for Carl's fancy for the place; between the slim, clean trunks of the orange-trees, the long green line of South Devil bounded the horizon, the flat tops of the cypresses far above against the sky, and the vines and silver moss filling the space below—a luxuriant wall across the broad, thinly-treed expanses of the pine barrens.

One evening in January Deal came homeward as usual at sunset, and found a visitor. Carl introduced him. "My friend Schwartz," he said. Schwartz merited his name; he was dark in complexion, hair, and eyes, and if he had any aims they were dark also. He was full of anecdotes and jests, and Carl laughed heartily; Mark had never heard him laugh in that way before. The elder brother ordered a good supper, and played the host as well as he could; but, in spite of the anecdotes, he did not altogether like friend Schwartz. Early the next morning, while the visitor was still asleep, he called Carl outside, and asked in an undertone who he was.

"Oh, I met him first in Berlin, and afterward I knew him in New York," said Carl. "All the orchestra fellows know Schwartz."

"Is he a musician, then?"

"Not exactly; but he used to be always around, you know."

"How comes he down here?"

"Just chance. He had an offer from a sort of a—a restaurant, up in San Miguel, a new place recently opened. The other day he happened to find out that I was here, and so came down to see me."

"How did he find out?"

"I suppose you gave our names to the agent when you took the place, didn't you?"

"I gave mine; and—yes, I think I mentioned you."

"If you didn't, I mentioned myself. I was at San Miguel, two weeks you remember, while you were making ready down here; and I venture to say almost everybody remembers Carl Brenner."

Mark smiled. Carl's fixed, assured self-conceit in the face of the utter failure he had made of his life did not annoy, but rather amused him; it seemed part of the lad's nature.

"I don't want to grudge you your amusement, Carl," he said; "but I don't much like this Schwartz of yours."

"He won't stay; he has to go back to-day. He came in a cart with a man from San Miguel, who, by some rare chance, had an errand down this forgotten, God-forsaken, dead-alive old road. The man will pass by on his way home this afternoon, and Schwartz is to meet him at the edge of the barren."

"Have an early dinner, then; there are birds and venison, and there is lettuce enough for a salad. Scip can make you some coffee."

But, although he thus proffered his best, none the less did the elder brother take with him the key of the little chest which contained his small store of brandy and the two or three bottles of orange wine which he had brought down with him from San Miguel.

After he had gone, Schwartz and Carl strolled around the plantation in the sunshine. Schwartz did not care to sit down among Carl's tombs; he said they made him feel moldy. Carl argued the point with him in vain, and then gave it up, and took him around to the causeway across the sugar-waste, where they stretched themselves out in the shade cast by the ruined wall of the old mill.

"What brought this brother of yours away down here?" asked the visitor, watching a chameleon on the wall near by. "See that little beggar swelling out his neck!"

"He's catching flies. In a storm they will come and hang themselves by one paw on our windows, and the wind will blow them out like dead leaves, and rattle them about, and they'll never move. But, when the sun shines out, there they are all alive again."

"But about your brother?"

"He isn't my brother."

"What?"

"My mother, a widow, named Brenner, with one son, Carl, married his father, a widower, named Deal, with one son, Mark. There you have the whole."

"He is a great deal older than you. I suppose he has been in the habit of assisting you?"

"Never saw him in my life until this last October, when, one windy day, he found me coughing on the Exton pier; and, soon afterward, he brought me down here."

"Came, then, on your account?"

"By no means; he was coming himself. It's a queer story; I'll tell it to you. It seems he went with the Kenton Arctic expedition—you remember it? Two of the ships were lost; his was one. But I'll have to get up and say it as he did." Here Carl rose, put down his pipe, extended one hand stiffly in a fixed position, and went on speaking, his very voice, by force of the natural powers of mimicry he possessed, sounding like Mark's:

"We were a company of eight when we started away from the frozen hulk, which would never see clear water under her bows again. Once before we had started, thirty-five strong, and had come back thirteen. Five had died in the old ship, and now the last survivors were again starting forth. We drew a sledge behind us, carrying our provisions and the farcical records of the expedition which had ended in death, as they must all end. We soon lose sight of the vessel. It was our only shelter, and we look back; then, at each other. 'Cheer up!' says one. 'Take this extra skin, Mark; I am stronger than you.' It's Proctor's voice that speaks. Ten days go by. There are only five of us now, and we are walking on doggedly across the ice, the numbing ice, the killing ice, the never-ending, gleaming, taunting, devilish ice. We have left the sledge behind. No trouble now for each to carry his share of food, it is so light. Now we walk together for a while; now we separate, sick of seeing one another's pinched faces, but we keep within call. On the eleventh day a wind rises; bergs come sailing into view. One moves down upon us. Its peak shining in the sunshine far above is nothing to the great mass that moves on under the water. Our ice-field breaks into a thousand pieces. We leap from block to block; we cry aloud in our despair; we call to each other, and curse, and pray. But the strips of dark water widen between us; our ice-islands grow smaller; and a current bears us onward. We can no longer keep in motion, and freeze as we stand. Two float near each other as darkness falls; 'Cheer up, Mark, cheer up!' cries one, and throws his flask across the gap between. Again it is Proctor's voice that speaks.

"In the morning only one is left alive. The others are blocks of ice, and float around in the slow eddy, each solemnly staring, one foot advanced, as if still keeping up the poor cramped steps with which he had fought off death. The one who is still alive floats around and around, with these dead men standing stiffly on their islands, all day, sometimes so near them that the air about him is stirred by their icy forms as they pass. At evening his cake drifts away through an opening toward the south, and he sees them no more, save that after him follows his dead friend, Proctor, at some distance behind. As night comes, the figure seems to wave its rigid hand in the distance, and cry from its icy throat, 'Cheer up, Mark, and good-by!'"

Here Carl stopped, rubbed his hands, shivered, and looked to see how his visitor took the narrative.

"It's a pretty cold story," said Schwartz, "even in this broiling sun. So he came down here to get a good, full warm, did he? He's got the cash, I suppose, to pay for his fancies."

"I don't call that a fancy, exactly," said Carl, seating himself on the hot white sand in the sunshine, with his thin hands clasped around his knees. "As to cash—I don't know. He works very hard."

"He works because he likes it," said Schwartz, contemptuously; "he looks like that sort of a man. But, at any rate, he don't make *you* work much!"

"He *is* awfully good to me," admitted Carl.

"It isn't on account of your beauty."

"Oh, I'm good looking enough in my way," replied the youth. "I acknowledge it isn't a common way; like yours, for instance." As he spoke, he passed his hand through his thin light hair, drew the ends of the long locks forward, and examined them admiringly.

"As he never saw you before, it couldn't have been brotherly love," pursued the other. "I suppose it was pity."

"No, it wasn't pity, either, you old blockhead," said Carl, laughing. "He *likes* to have me with him; he *likes* me."

"I see that myself, and that's exactly the point. Why should he? You haven't any inheritance to will to him, have you?"

"My violin, and the clothes on my back. I believe that's all," answered Carl, lightly. He took off his palmetto hat, made a pillow of it, and stretched himself out at full length, closing his eyes.

"Well, give *me* a brother with cash, and I'll go to sleep, too," said Schwartz. When Deal came home at sunset, the dark-skinned visitor was gone.

But he came again; and this time stayed three days. Mark allowed it, for Carl's sake. All he said was, "He can not be of much use in the restaurant up there. What is he? Cook? Or waiter?"

"Oh, Schwartz isn't a servant, old fellow. He helps entertain the guests."

"Sings, I suppose."

Carl did not reply, and Deal set Schwartz down as a lager-beer-hall ballad-singer, borne southward on the tide of winter travel to Florida. One advantage at least was gained—when Schwartz was there, Carl was less tempted by the swamp.

And now, a third time, the guest came. During the first evening of this third visit, he was so good-tempered, so frankly lazy and amusing, that even Deal was disarmed. "He's a good-for-nothing, probably; but there's no active harm in him," he said to himself.

The second evening was a repetition of the first.

When he came home at sunset on the third evening, Carl was lying coiled up close to the wall of the house, his face hidden in his arms.

"What are you doing there?" said Deal, as he passed by, on his way to put up the tools.

No answer. But Carl had all kinds of whims, and Deal was used to them. He went across to Scip's chimney.

"Awful time, cap'en," said the old negro, in a low voice. "Soon's you's gone, dat man make young marse drink, and bot' begin to holler and fight."

"Drink? They had no liquor."

"Yes, dey hab. Mus' hab brought 'em 'long."

"Where is the man?"

"Oh, he gone long ago—gone at noon."

Deal went to his brother. "Carl," he said, "get up. Dinner is ready." But the coiled form did not stir.

"Don't be a fool," continued Deal. "I know you've been drinking; Scip told me. It's a pity. But no reason why you should not eat."

Carl did not move. Deal went off to his dinner, and sent some to Carl. But the food remained untasted. Then Deal passed into the house to get some tobacco for his pipe. Then a loud cry was heard. The hiding-place which his Yankee fingers had skillfully fashioned in the old wall had been rifled; all his money was gone. No one knew the secret of the spot but Carl.

"Did he overpower you and take it?" he asked, kneeling down and lifting Carl by force, so that he could see his face.

"No; I gave it to him," Carl answered, thickly and slowly.

"You *gave* it to him?"

"I lost it—at cards."

"*Cards!*"

Deal had never thought of that. All at once the whole flashed upon him: the gambler who was always "around" with the "orchestra fellows"; the "restaurant" at San Miguel where he helped "entertain" the guests; the probability that business was slack in the ancient little town, unaccustomed to such luxuries; and the treasure-trove of an old acquaintance within a day's journey—an old acquaintance like Carl, who had come also into happy possession of a rich brother. A rich brother!—probably that was what Schwartz called him!

At any rate, rich or poor, Schwartz had it all. With the exception of one hundred dollars which he had left at San Miguel as a deposit, he had now only five dollars in the world; Carl had gambled away his all.

It was a hard blow.

He lifted his brother in his arms and carried him in to his hammock. A few minutes later, staff in hand, he started down the live-oak avenue toward the old road which led northward to San Miguel. The moonlight was brilliant; he walked all night. At dawn he was searching the little city.

Yes, the man was known there. He frequented the Esmeralda Parlors. The Esmeralda Parlors, however, represented by an attendant, a Northern mulatto, with straight features, long, narrow eyes, and pale-golden skin, a bronze piece of insolence, who was also more faultlessly dressed than any one else in San Miguel, suavely replied that Schwartz was no longer one of their "guests"; he had severed his connection with the Parlors several days before. Where was he? The Parlors had no idea.

But the men about the docks knew. Schwartz had been seen the previous evening negotiating passage at the last moment on a coasting schooner bound South—one of those nondescript little craft engaged in smuggling and illegal trading, with which the waters of the West Indies are infested. The schooner had made her way out of the harbor by moonlight. Although ostensibly bound for Key West, no one could say with any certainty that she would touch there; bribed by Schwartz, with all the harbors, inlets, and lagoons of the West Indies open to her, pursuit would be worse than hopeless. Deal realized this. He ate the food he had brought with him, drank a cup of coffee, called for his deposit, and then walked back to the plantation.

When he came into the little plaza, Carl was sitting on the steps of their small house. His head was clear again; he looked pale and wasted.

"It's all right," said Deal. "I've traced him. In the mean time, don't worry, Carl. If I don't mind it, why should you?"

Without saying more, he went inside, changed his shoes, then came out, ordered dinner, talked to Scip, and when the meal was ready called Carl, and took his place at the table as though nothing had happened. Carl scarcely spoke; Deal approved his silence. He felt so intensely for the lad, realized so strongly what he must be feeling—suffering and feeling— that conversation on the subject would have been at that early moment unendurable. But waking during the night, and hearing him stirring, uneasy, and apparently feverish, he went across to the hammock.

"You are worrying about it, Carl, and you are not strong enough to stand worry. Look here—I have forgiven you; I would forgive you twice as much. Have you no idea why I brought you down here with me?"

"Because you're kind-hearted. And perhaps, too, you thought it would be lonely," answered Carl.

"No, I'm not kind-hearted, and I never was lonely in my life. I didn't intend to tell you, but—you *must not* worry. It is your name, Carl, and— and your blue eyes. I was fond of Eliza."

"Fond of Leeza—Leeza Brenner? Then why on earth didn't you marry her?" said Carl, sitting up in his hammock, and trying to see his step-brother's face in the moonlight that came through the chinks in the shutters.

Mark's face was in shadow. "She liked some one else better," he said.
"Who?"

"Never mind. But—yes, I will tell you—Graves."

"John Graves? That dunce? No, she didn't."

"As it happens, I know she did. But we won't talk about it. I only told you to show you why I cared for you."

"*I* wouldn't care about a girl that didn't care for me," said Carl, still peering curiously through the checkered darkness. The wizened young violin-player fancied himself an omnipotent power among women. But Deal had gone to his bed, and would say no more.

Carl had heard something now which deeply astonished him. He had not been much troubled about the lost money; it was not in his nature to be much troubled about money at any time. He was sorry; but what was gone was gone; why waste thought upon it? This he called philosophy. Mark, out of regard for Carl's supposed distress, had forbidden conversation on the subject; but he was not shutting out, as he thought, torrents of shame, remorse, and self-condemnation. Carl kept silence willingly enough; but, even if the bar had been removed, he would have had little to say. During the night his head had ached, and he had had some fever; but it was more the effect of the fiery, rank liquor pressed upon him by Schwartz than of remorse. But *now* he had heard what really interested and aroused him. Mark in love!—hard-working, steady, dull old Mark, whom he had thought endowed with no fancies at all, save perhaps that of being thoroughly warmed after his arctic freezing. Old Mark fond of Leeza—in love with Leeza!

Leeza wasn't much. Carl did not even think his cousin pretty; his fancy was for something large and Oriental. But, pretty or not, she had evidently fascinated Mark Deal, coming, a poor little orphan maid, with her aunt, Carl's mother, to brighten old Abner Deal's farm-house, one mile from the windy Exton pier. Carl's mother could not hope to keep her German son in this new home; but she kept little Leeza, or Eliza, as the neighbors called her. And Mark, a shy, awkward boy, had learned to love the child, who had sweet blue eyes, and thick braids of flaxen hair fastened across the back of her head.

"To care all that for Leeza!" thought Carl, laughing silently in his hammock. "And then to fancy that she liked that Graves! And then to leave her, and come away off down here just on the suspicion!"

But Carl was mistaken. A man, be he never so awkward and silent, will generally make at least one effort to get the woman he loves. Mark had made two, and failed. After his first, he had gone North; after his second, he had come South, bringing Leeza's cousin with him.

In the morning a new life began on the old plantation. First, Scipio was dismissed; then the hunter who had kept the open-air larder supplied with game, an old man of unknown, or rather mixed descent, having probably Spanish, African, and Seminole blood in his veins, was told that his services were required no more.

"But are you going to starve us, then?" asked Carl, with a comical grimace.

"I am a good shot, myself," replied Deal; "and a fair cook, too."

"But *why* do you do it?" pursued the other. He had forgotten all about the money.

The elder man looked at his brother. Could it be possible that he had forgotten? And, if he had, was it not necessary, in their altered circumstances, that the truth should be brought plainly before his careless eyes?

"I am obliged to do it," he answered, gravely. "We must be very saving, Carl. Things will be easier, I hope, when the fields begin to yield."

"Good heavens, you don't mean to say I took all you had!" said Carl, with an intonation showing that the fact that the abstracted sum was "all" was impressing him more than any agency of his own in the matter.

"I told you I did not mind it," answered Mark, going off with his gun and game-bag.

"But *I* do, by Jove!" said Carl to himself, watching him disappear.

Musicians, in this world's knowledge and wisdom, are often fools, or rather they remain always children. The beautiful gift, the divine gift, the gift which is the nearest to heaven, is accompanied by lacks of another sort. Carl Brenner, like a child, could not appreciate poverty unless his dinner was curtailed, his tobacco gone. The petty changes now made in the small routine of each day touched him acutely, and roused him at last to the effort of connected, almost practical thought. Old Mark was troubled—poor. The cook was going, the hunter discharged; the dinners would be good no longer. This was because he, Carl, had taken the money. There was no especial harm in the act *per se;* but, as the sum happened to be all old Mark had, it was unfortunate. Under the circumstances, what could he, Carl, do to help old Mark?

Mark loved that light-headed little Leeza. Mark had brought him down here and taken care of him on Leeza's account. Mark, therefore, should have Leeza. He, Carl, would bring it about. He set to work at once to be special providence in Mark's affairs. He sat down, wrote a long letter, sealed it with a stern air, and then laid it on the table, got up, and surveyed it with decision. There it was—done! Gone! But no; not "gone" yet. And how could it go? He was now confronted by the difficulty of mailing it without Mark's knowledge. San Miguel was the nearest post-office; and San Miguel was miles away. Africanus was half crippled; the old hunter would come no more; he himself could not walk half the distance. Then an idea came to him: Africanus, although dismissed, was not yet gone. He went out to find him.

Mark came home at night with a few birds. "They will last us over one day," he said, throwing down the spoil. "You still here, Scip? I thought I sent you off."

"He's going to-morrow," interposed Carl. Scip sat up all night cooking.

"What in the world has got into him?" said Deal, as the light from the old chimney made their sleeping-room bright.

"He wants to leave us well supplied, I suppose," said Carl, from his hammock. "Things keep better down here when they're cooked, you know." This was true; but it was unusual for Carl to interest himself in such matters.

The next morning Deal started on a hunting expedition, intending to be absent two days. Game was plenty in the high lands farther west. He had good luck, and came back at the end of the second day loaded, having left also several caches behind to be visited on the morrow. But there was no one in the house, or on the plantation; both Scip and Carl were gone.

A slip of paper was pinned to the red cotton door. It contained these words: "It's all right, old fellow. If I'm not back at the end of three days, counting this as one, come into South Devil after me. You'll find a trail."

"Confound the boy!" said Deal, in high vexation. "He's crazy." He took a torch, went to the causeway, and there saw from the foot-prints that two had crossed. "Scip went with him," he thought, somewhat comforted. "The old black rascal used to declare that he knew every inch of the swamp." He went back, cooked his supper, and slept. In the matter of provisions, there was little left save what he kept under lock and key. Scipio had started with a good supply. At dawn he rose, made a fire under the old chimney, cooked some venison, baked some corn-bread, and, placing them in his bag, started into South Devil, a bundle of torches slung on his back as before, his gun in his hand, his revolver and knife in his belt. "They have already been gone two days," he said to himself; "they must be coming toward home, now." He thought Carl was carrying out his cherished design of exploring the swamp. There was a trail—hatchet marks on the trees, and broken boughs. "That's old Scip. Carl would never have been so systematic," he thought.

He went on until noon, and then suddenly found himself on the bank of a sluggish stream. "The Branch," he said—"South Devil Branch. It joins West Devil, and the two make the San Juan Bautista (a queer origin for a saint!) three miles below Miguel. But where does the trail go now?" It went nowhere. He searched and searched, and could not find it. It ended at the Branch. Standing there in perplexity, he happened to raise his eyes. Small attention had he hitherto paid to the tangled vines and blossoms swinging above him. He hated the beauty of South Devil. But now he saw a slip of paper hanging from a vine, and, seizing it, he read as follows: "We take boat here; wait for me if not returned."

Mark stood, the paper in his hand, thinking. There was only one boat in the neighborhood, a canoe belonging to the mongrel old hunter, who occasionally went into the swamp. Carl must have obtained this in some way; probably the mongrel had brought it in by the Branch, or one of its tributaries, and this was the rendezvous. One comfort—the old hunter must then be of the party, too. But why should he, Mark, wait, if Carl had two persons with him? Still, the boy had asked. It ended in his waiting.

He began to prepare for the night. There was a knoll near by, and here he made a camp-fire, spending the time before sunset in gathering the wood by the slow process of climbing the trees and vines, and breaking off dead twigs and branches; everything near the ground was wet and sogged. He planted his four torches, ate his supper, examined his gun and revolver, and then, as darkness fell, having nothing else to do, he made a plot on the ground with twigs and long splinters of light-wood, and played, one hand against the other, a swamp game of fox-and-geese. He played standing (his fox-and-geese were two feet high), so that he could keep a lookout for every sort of creature. There were wild-cats and bears in the interior of South Devil, and in the Branch, alligators. He did not fear the large creatures, however; his especial guard, as before, was against the silent snakes. He lighted the fire and torches early, so that whatever uncanny inhabitants there might be in the near trees could have an opportunity of coming down and seeking night-quarters elsewhere. He played game after game of fox-and-geese; and this time he sang "Sweet Afton." He felt that he had exhausted the "Troubadour" on the previous occasion. He shot five snakes, and saw (or rather it seemed to him that he saw) five thousand others coiling and gliding over the roots of the cypresses all around. He made a rule not to look at them if he could help it, as long as they did not approach. "Otherwise," he thought, "I shall lose my senses, and think the very trees are squirming."

It was a long, long night. The knoll was dented all over with holes made by the long splinters representing his fox-and-geese. Dizziness was creeping over him at intervals. His voice, singing "Sweet Afton," had become hoarse and broken, and his steps uneven, as he moved to and fro, still playing the game dully, when at last dawn came. But, although the flat tops of the great cypresses far above were bathed in the golden sunshine, it was long before the radiance penetrated to the dark glades below. The dank, watery aisles were still in gray shadow, when the watcher heard a sound—a real sound now, not an imaginary one—and at the same moment his glazed eyes saw a boat coming up the Branch. It was a white canoe, and paddled by a wraith; at least, the creature who sat within looked so grayly pale, and its eyes in its still, white face so large and unearthly, that it seemed like a shade returned from the halls of death.

"Why, Carl!" said Mark, in a loud, unsteady voice, breaking through his own lethargy by main force. "It's you, Carl, isn't it?"

He tramped down to the water's edge, each step seeming to him a rod long, and now a valley, and now a hill. The canoe touched the bank, and Carl fell forward; not with violence, but softly, and without strength. What little consciousness he had kept was now gone.

Dawn was coming down from above; the air was slightly stirred. The elder man's head grew more steady, as he lifted his step-brother, gave him brandy, rubbed his temples and chest, and then, as he came slowly back to life again, stood thinking what he should do. They were a half-day's journey from home, and Carl could not walk. If he attempted to carry him, he was fearful that they should not reach pure air outside before darkness fell again, and a second night in the thick air might be death for both of them; but there was the boat. It had come into South

Devil in some way; by that way it should go out again. He laid Carl in one end, putting his own coat under his head for a pillow, and then stepped in himself, took the paddle, and moved off. Of course he must ascend the Branch; as long as there were no tributaries, he could not err. But presently he came to an everglade—a broadening of the stream with apparently twenty different outlets, all equally dark and tangled. He paddled around the border, looking first at one, then at another. The matted water-vines caught at his boat like hundreds of hands; the great lily-leaves slowly sank and let the light bow glide over them. Carl slept; there was no use trying to rouse him; but probably he would remember nothing, even if awake. The elder brother took out his compass, and had decided by it which outlet to take, when his eye rested upon the skin of a moccasin nailed to a cypress on the other side of the pond. It was the mongrel's way of making a guide-post. Without hesitation, although the direction was the exact opposite of the one he had selected, Deal pushed the canoe across and entered the stream thus indicated. At the next pool he found another snake-skin; and so on out of the swamp. Twenty-five snakes had died in the cause. He came to firm land at noon, two miles from the plantation. Carl was awake now, but weak and wandering. Deal lifted him on shore, built a fire, heated some meat, toasted corn-bread, and made him eat. Then, leaning upon his brother's arm, walking slowly, and often pausing to rest, the blue-eyed ghost reached home at sunset— two miles in five hours.

Ten days now passed; the mind of the young violin player did not regain its poise. He rose and dressed himself each morning, and slept in the sunshine as before. He went to the place of tombs, carrying his violin, but forgot to play. Instead, he sat looking dreamily at the swamp. He said little, and that little was disconnected. The only sentence which seemed to have meaning, and to be spoken earnestly, was, "It's all right, old fellow. Just you wait fifteen days—fifteen days!" But, when Mark questioned him, he could get no definite reply, only a repetition of the exhortation to "wait fifteen days."

Deal went over to one of the mongrel's haunts, and, by good luck, found him at home. The mongrel had a number of camps, which he occupied according to convenience. The old man acknowledged that he had lent his canoe, and that he had accompanied Carl and Scip part of the way through South Devil. But only part of the way; then he left them, and struck across to the west. Where were they going? Why, straight to San Miguel; the Branch brought them to the King's Road crossing, and the rest of the way they went on foot. What were they going to do in San Miguel? The mongrel had no idea; he had not many ideas. Scip was to stay up there; Brenner was to return alone in the canoe, they having made a trail all the way.

Deal returned to the plantation. He still thought that Carl's idea had been merely to explore the swamp.

Twelve days had passed, and had grown to fourteen; Carl was no stronger. He was very gentle now, like a sick child. Deal was seized with a fear that this soft quiet was the peace that often comes before the last to the poor racked frame of the consumptive. He gave up all but the necessary work, and stayed with Carl all day. The blue-eyed ghost smiled, but said little; into its clouded mind penetrated but one ray—"Wait fifteen days." Mark had decided that the sentence meant nothing but some wandering fancy. Spring in all her superb luxuriance was now wreathing Florida with flowers; the spring flowers met the old flowers, the spring leaves met the old leaves. The yellow jessamine climbed over miles of thicket; the myriad purple balls of the sensitive-plant starred the ground; the atamasco lilies grew whitely, each one shining all alone, in the wet woods; chocolate-hued orchids nodded, and the rose-colored ones rang their bells, at the edge of the barren. The old causeway across the sugar waste was blue with violets, and Mark carried Carl thither; he would lie there contentedly in the sunshine for hours, his pale fingers toying with the blue blossoms, his eyes lifted to the green line of South Devil across the sapphire sky.

One afternoon he fell asleep there, and Mark left him, to cook their dinner. When he came back, his step-brother's eyes had reason in them once more, or rather remembrance.

"Old fellow," he said, as Mark, surprised and somewhat alarmed at the change, sat down beside him, "you got me out of the swamp, I suppose? I don't remember getting myself out. Now I want to ask something. I'm going to leave this world in a few days, and try it in another; better luck next time, you know. What I want to ask is that you'll take me up and bury me at San Miguel in a little old burying-ground they have there, on a knoll overlooking the ocean. I don't want to lie here with the Dons and the Aztecs; and, besides, I particularly want to be carried through the swamp. Take me through in the canoe, as I went the last time; it's the easiest way, and there's a trail. And I want to go. And do not cover my face, either; I want to see. Promise."

Mark promised, and Carl closed his eyes. Then he roused himself again.

"Inquire at the post-office in San Miguel for a letter," he said drowsily. "Promise." Again Mark promised. He seemed to sleep for some minutes; then he spoke again.

"I heard that music, you know—heard it all out plainly and clearly," he said, looking quietly at his brother. "I know the whole, and have sung it over to myself a thousand times since. I can not write it down *now*. But it will not be lost."

"Music is never lost, I suppose," answered Mark, somewhat at random.

"Certainly not," said Carl, with decision. "My song will be heard some time. I'm sure of that. And it will be much admired."

"I hope so."

"You try to be kind always, don't you, old fellow, whether you comprehend or not?" said the boy, with his old superior smile—the smile of the artist, who, although he be a failure and a pauper, yet always pities the wise. Then he slept again. At dawn, peacefully and with a smile, he died.

It should not have been expected, perhaps, that he could live. But in some way Mark had expected it.

A few hours later a canoe was floating down the Branch through South Devil. One man was paddling at the stern; another was stretched on a couch, with his head on a pillow placed at the bow, where he could see the blossoming network above through his closed eyes. As Carl had said, Scipio had left a trail all the way—a broken branch, a bent reed, or a shred of cloth tied to the lily-leaves. All through the still day they glided on, the canoe moving without a sound on the bosom of the dark stream. They passed under the gray and solemn cypresses, rising without branches to an enormous height, their far foliage hidden by the moss, which hung down thickly in long flakes, diffusing the sunshine and making it silvery like mist; in the silver swung the air-plants, great cream-colored disks, and wands of scarlet, crowded with little buds, blossoms that looked like butterflies, and blossoms that looked like humming-birds, and little dragon-heads with grinning faces. Then they came to the region of the palms; these shot up, slender and graceful, and leaned over the stream, the great aureum-ferns growing on their trunks high in the air. Beneath was a firmer soil than in the domain of the cypresses, and here grew a mat of little flowers, each less than a quarter of an inch wide, close together, pink, blue, scarlet, yellow, purple, but never white, producing a hue singularly rich, owing to the absence of that colorless color which man ever mingles with his floral combinations, and strangely makes sacred alike to the bridal and to death. Great vines ran up the palms, knotted themselves, and came down again, hand over hand, wreathed in little fresh leaves of exquisite green. Birds with plumage of blush-rose pink flew slowly by; also some with scarlet wings, and the jeweled paroquets. The great Savannah cranes stood on the shore, and did not stir as the boat moved by. And, as the spring was now in its prime, the alligators showed their horny heads above water, and climbed awkwardly out on the bank; or else, swimming by the side of the canoe, accompanied it long distances, no doubt moved by dull curiosity concerning its means of locomotion, and its ideas as to choice morsels of food. The air was absolutely still; no breeze reached these blossoming aisles; each leaf hung motionless. The atmosphere was hot, and heavy with perfumes. It was the heart of the swamp, a riot of intoxicating, steaming, swarming, fragrant, beautiful, tropical life, without man to make or mar it. All the world was once so, before man was made.

Did Deal appreciate this beauty? He looked at it, because he could not get over the feeling that Carl was looking at it too; but he did not admire it. The old New England spirit was rising within him again at last, after the crushing palsy of the polar ice, and the icy looks of a certain blue-eyed woman.

He came out of the swamp an hour before sunset, and, landing, lifted his brother in his arms, and started northward toward San Miguel. The little city was near; but the weight of a dead body grown cold is strange and mighty, and it was late evening before he entered the gate, carrying his motionless burden. He crossed the little plaza, and went into the ancient cathedral, laying it down on the chancel-step before the high altar. It was the only place he could think of; and he was not repelled. A hanging lamp of silver burned dimly; in a few moments kind hands came to help him. And thus Carl, who never went to church in life, went there in death, and, with tapers burning at his head and feet, rested all night under the picture of the Madonna, with nuns keeping watch and murmuring their gentle prayers beside him.

The next morning he was buried in the dry little burial-ground on the knoll overlooking the blue Southern ocean.

When all was over, Deal, feeling strangely lonely, remembered his promise, and turned toward the post-office. He expected nothing; it was only one of the poor lad's fancies; still, he would keep his word. There was nothing for him.

He went out. Then an impulse made him turn back and ask if there was a letter for Carl. "For Carl Brenner," he said, and thought how strange it was that there was now no Carl. There was a letter; he put it into his pocket and left the town, going homeward by the King's Road on foot; the South Devil should see *him* no more. He slept part of the night by the roadside, and reached home the next morning; everything was as he had left it. He made a fire and boiled some coffee; then he set the little house in order, loaded his gun, and went out mechanically after game. The routine of daily life had begun again.

"It's a pleasant old place," he said to himself, as he went through one of the orange-aisles and saw the wild oranges dotting the ground with their golden color. "It's a pleasant old place," he repeated, as he went out into the hot, still sunshine beyond. He filled his game-bag, and sat down to rest a while before returning. Then for the first time he remembered the letter, and drew it forth. This was the letter Carl meant; Carl asked him to get it after he was dead; he must have intended, then, that he, Mark, should read it. He opened it, and looked at the small, slanting handwriting without recognizing it. Then from the inside a photograph fell out, and he took it up; it was Leeza. On the margin was written, "For Mark."

She had written; but, womanlike, not, as Carl expected, to Mark. Instead, she had written to Carl, and commissioned *him* to tell Mark— what? Oh, a long story, such as girls tell, but with the point that, after all, she "liked" (liked?) Mark best. Carl's letter had been blunt, worded with unflattering frankness. Leeza was tired of her own coquetries, lonely, and poor; she wrote her foolish little apologizing, confessing letter with tears in her blue eyes—those blue eyes that sober, reticent Mark Deal could not forget.

Carl had gone to San Miguel, then, to mail a letter—a letter which had brought this answer! Mark, with his face in his hands, thanked God that he had not spoken one harsh word to the boy for what had seemed obstinate disobedience, but had tended him gently to the last.

Then he rose, stretched his arms, drew a long breath, and looked around. Everything seemed altered. The sky was brassy, the air an oven. He remembered the uplands where the oats grew, near Exton; and his white sand-furrows seemed a ghastly mockery of fields. He went homeward and drew water from his well to quench his burning thirst; it was tepid, and he threw it away, recalling as he did so the spring under the cool, brown rocks where he drank when a boy. A sudden repugnance came over him when his eyes fell on the wild oranges lying on the ground, over-ripe with rich, pulpy decay; he spurned them aside with his foot, and thought of the firm apples in the old orchard, a fruit cool and reticent, a little hard, too, not giving itself to the first comer. Then there came over him the hue of Northern forests in spring, the late, reluctant spring of Exton; and the changeless olive-green of the pine barrens grew hideous in his eyes. But, most of all, there seized him a horror of the swamp— a horror of its hot steaming air, and its intoxicating perfume, which reached him faintly even where he stood; it seemed to him that if he staid long within their reach his brain would be affected as Carl's had been, and that he should wander within and die. For there would be no one to rescue *him.*

So strong was this new feeling, like a giant full armed, that he started that very night, carrying his gun and Carl's violin, and a knapsack of clothes on his back, and leaving his other possessions behind. Their value was not great, but they made a princely home for the mongrel, who came over after he had departed, looked around stealthily, stole several small articles, and hastened away; came back again after a day or two, and stole a little more; and finally, finding the place deserted, brought back all his spoil and established himself there permanently, knowing full well that it would be long before Monteano's would find another tenant from the North.

As Mark Deal passed across the King's Road Bridge over the Branch (now soon to be sainted), he paused, and looked down into the north border of South Devil. Then he laid aside his gun and the violin, went off that way, and gathered a large bunch of swamp blossoms. Coming into San Miguel, he passed through the town and out to the little burial-ground beyond. Here he found the new-made grave, and laid the flowers upon it.

"He will like them because they come from *there*," was his thought.

Then, with a buoyant step, he started up the long, low, white peninsula, set with its olive-woods in a sapphire sea; and his face was turned northward.

Selected Bibliography

This bibliography lists the major works by each writer represented in this collection and secondary sources that provide information on the authors' lives and works, particularly the short stories included here.

WYATT BLASSINGAME

The Everglades: From Yesterday to Tomorrow. New York: Putnam, 1974.
The First Book of Florida. New York: F. Watts, 1963.
The Golden Geyser. Garden City, N.Y.: Doubleday, 1961.
Halo of Spears. Garden City, N.Y.: Doubleday, 1962.
Jake Gaither: Winning Coach. Champaign, Ill.: Garrard, 1969.
Live from the Devil. Garden City, N.Y.: Doubleday, 1959.
Osceola, Seminole War Chief. Champaign, Ill.: Garrard, 1967.

NED BUNTLINE

Kirk, Cooper. "Edward Zane Carrol Judson, Alias Ned Buntline." *Broward Legacy* (Fort Lauderdale) 3, no. 3–4 (Fall 1979): 16–27.
Monaghan, Jay. *The Great Rascal: The Life and Adventures of Ned Buntline.* Boston: Little, Brown, 1951.

JAMES TRAMMELL COX

"Ford's 'Passion for Provence.'" *ELH* 28 (1961): 383–98.
"Point of View in Troy." *Epoch* 9 (1958): 97ff.
"Stephen Crane as Symbolic Naturalist: An Analysis of 'The Blue Hotel.'" *Modern Fiction Studies* 3 (1957): 147–58.
"The Structure of *The Red Badge of Courage.*" *Modern Fiction Studies* 5 (1959): 209–19.
"This Is Sedlacek Talking." *Perspective* 9 (1957): 143–56.

LAWRENCE DORR

A Slight Momentary Affliction. Baton Rouge: Lousiana State University Press, 1987.
A Slow, Soft River. Grand Rapids, Mich.: Eerdmans, 1973. Republished as *The Immigrant.* Berkhamsted, England: Lion, 1976.

MARJORY STONEMAN DOUGLAS

Alligator Crossing: A Novel. New York: J. Day, 1959.

The Everglades: River of Grass. 1947. Revised edition, Sarasota, Fla.: Pineapple Press, 1988.

Freedom River: Florida, 1845. New York: Scribner's, 1953.

Marjory Stoneman Douglas: Voice of the River, an Autobiography. Sarasota, Fla.: Pineapple Press, 1987.

Road to the Sun. New York: Rinehart, 1951.

McCarthy, Kevin M., ed. *Nine Florida Stories by Marjory Stoneman Douglas.* Gainesville: University Presses of Florida, 1990.

RUBYLEA HALL

Davey. New York: Duell, Sloan, and Pearce, 1951.

Flamingo Prince. New York: Duell, Sloan, and Pearce, 1954.

God Has a Sense of Humor. New York: Duell, Sloan, and Pearce, 1960.

The Great Tide. New York: Duell, Sloan and, Pearce, 1947.

STETSON KENNEDY

After Appomattox: How the South Won the War. Gainesville: University Press of Florida, 1995.

The Klan Unmasked. Gainesville: University Presses of Florida, 1990. Originally published as *I Rode with the Ku Klux Klan.*

Jim Crow Guide to the U.S.A. 1954. Reprint, Gainesville: University Presses of Florida, 1990.

Palmetto Country. 1942, Reprint, Gainesville: University Presses of Florida, 1989.

Southern Exposure. 1946. Reprint, Gainesville: University Presses of Florida, 1991.

ERNEST LYONS

The Last Cracker Barrel. New York: Newspaper Enterprise Association, 1975.

My Florida. 1969. Second edition, Port Salerno, Fla.: Valentine Books, 1977.

KIRK MUNROE

Primary Sources

Big Cypress: The Story of an Everglade Homestead. Boston: W. A. Wilde, 1894.

Canoemates: A Story of the Florida Reef and Everglades. New York: Harper, 1892.

The Coral Ship: A Story of the Florida Reef. New York: Putnam's Sons, 1893.

The Flamingo Feather. New York: Harper, 1887.

Through Swamp and Glade: A Tale of the Seminole War. New York: Charles Scribner's Sons, 1896.

Wakulla: A Story of Adventure in Florida. New York: Harper and Brothers, 1885.

Secondary Source

Leonard, Irving. *The Florida Adventures of Kirk Munroe.* Chuluota, Fla.: Mickler House, 1975.

PADGETT POWELL

Edisto. New York: Farrar, Straus, and Giroux, 1984.

Typical. New York: Farrar, Straus, and Giroux, 1991.

A Woman Named Drown. New York: Farrar, Straus, and Giroux, 1987.

JACK RUDLOE

The Erotic Ocean: A Handbook for Beachcombers and Marine Naturalists. New York: Dutton, 1984.

The Living Dock at Panacea. New York: Knopf, 1977.

The Sea Brings Forth. New York: Dutton, 1989.

Search for the Great Turtle Mother. Sarasota, Fla.: Pineapple Press, 1995.

Time of the Turtle. New York: Knopf, 1979.

The Wilderness Coast: Adventures of a Gulf Coast Naturalist. New York: Dutton, 1988.

HARRIET BEECHER STOWE

Primary Sources

Dred: Tale of the Great Dismal Swamp. Boston: Phillips, Sampson, 1856.

Palmetto-leaves. 1873. Reprint, Gainesville: University of Florida Press, 1968.

Uncle Tom's Cabin. Boston: Jewett, 1851.

Secondary Sources

Ashton, Jean. *Harriet Beecher Stowe: A Reference Guide.* Boston: G. K. Hall, 1977.

Graff, Mary B. *Mandarin on the St. Johns.* Gainesville: University of Florida Press, 1953.

Hedrick, Joan D. *Harriet Beecher Stowe: A Life.* New York: Oxford University Press, 1994.

Hildreth, Margaret Holbrook. *Harriet Beecher Stowe: A Bibliography.* Hamden, Conn.: Archon, 1976.

Johnston, Johanna. *Runaway to Heaven: The Story of Harriet Beecher Stowe.* Garden City, N.Y.: Doubleday, 1963.

JOHN W. B. THOMPSON

Primary Source

"Cape Florida Light House." *Niles' Weekly Register,* November 19, 1836, 181–82.

Secondary Source

McCarthy, Kevin M. "Cape Florida Lighthouse." In his *Florida Lighthouses,* 41–44. Gainesville: University of Florida Press, 1990.

CONSTANCE FENIMORE WOOLSON

Primary Sources

East Angels. New York: Harper and Brothers, 1886.
Horace Chase. 1894. Reprint, Upper Saddle River, N.J.: Literature House, 1970.
Jupiter Lights. New York: Harper and Brothers, 1889.
Rodman the Keeper: Southern Sketches. New York: Appleton, 1880.

Secondary Sources

Kern, John Dwight. *Constance Fenimore Woolson: Literary Pioneer.* Philadelphia: University of Pennsylvania Press, 1934.
Moore, Rayburn S. *Constance Fenimore Woolson.* New York: Twayne, 1963.
Torsney, Cheryl B. *Constance Fenimore Woolson: The Grief of Artistry.* Athens: University of Georgia Press, 1989.